The

To Dianne

The Oak of Weeping

The Story of Rebekah and Deborah

David Martyn

David Martyn

Blue Forge Press

Port Orchard ✿ Washington

The Oak of Weeping: The Story of Rebekah and Deborah
Copyright 2018
by David Martyn

First eBook Edition
November 2018

First Print Edition
November 2018

For information about film, reprint or other subsidiary rights, contact: blueforgegroup@gmail.com

Blue Forge Press
7419 Ebbert Drive Southeast
Port Orchard, Washington 98367
360.550.2071 ph.txt

For
Karen, Katie, Kristin
Addison and Anna:
the strong women in my life.
And for
my son, David.

Acknowledgements

No book is ever truly the work of one person. Creativity, like all of the gifts which come from our Creator, is sharpened in a community. I would like to acknowledge some of the people who helped and supported me in this effort. Very real encouragement and support in reviewing, content editing and listening to my story were provided by my small writer's group in Gig Harbor: Susan Nordman, Linda Olson, Dennis Percy, and Kimmie Cushner. Thanks.

My decision to write comes in a large part from the encouragement and good will of a church home group and Bible study, "The Wilkinson Home Group." Led by Nancy Wilkinson, our host who always kept us on agenda, Jim Wilkinson who led us in worship, Bob Martin who saw that we laughed (always good for the soul), his wife Pam who led us in works of mercy, Ken and Diane Schutz who read my raw works as I wrote, and Kirk and Bonnie Jones who taught us how to live in strong and patient love for family members in crisis. John Grimsley was our prayer warrior, and Pablo Gutierrez buoyed us with his enthusiasm and praise. Praise can be a gift and Pablo was an example. I will always treasure my time with these brothers and sisters.

I must also acknowledge another Bible Study, who showed me how to get down and deep into the Word, men and women who expected some effort in bringing a passage to life. The Burke Officer's Christian Fellowship Bible Study: Mickey Garverick, his wife Ruth; my good friends Don and Frances Allen who read along with me as I wrote and gave me more help than they realize, Frances was especially helpful when I needed a woman's review; Bill and Addie Law; Tom and Diane Carnahan; Sammy and Ruth Ann Barr and Rick and Nancy Jackson together they encouraged us to put in practice what we learned. Keep digging!

Finally, my pastoral readers. Pastor Chuck Slocum, who leads our church, who agreed to read my work and make sure I haven't strayed too far from orthodoxy. He is a man who puts his faith to work, leading his flock in loving obedience. I thank Brent Emery of Torah For Today, a Jewish follower of our Messiah who I asked to keep my scribblings consistent with Jewish tradition and teaching.

Preface

The most rudimentary reading of the Bible will acquaint the reader with the title: "The God of Abraham, Isaac, and Jacob." The fact that God chooses to identify with these men, is both telling and amazing. Their story makes up the better part of the book of Genesis. What we read about them is often not very flattering. These were men who failed often and badly. They repeated sins again and again. That is what makes them so very real and relevant. The New Testament provides important commentary on why God identifies with these patriarchs. They are all inaugural heroes in the "Hall of Faith" we find in the book of Hebrews. But their fame precedes the New Testament writer. Moses, in his sermon that is Deuteronomy, reminds the Israelites as they are about to enter the promised land, that the land they will enter is the land promised to them and to Abraham, Isaac, and Jacob. He tells them that they, like Abraham, Isaac, and Jacob, are people chosen by God, people, who attest that He is their God.

What the New Testament so clearly teaches us is that God identifies with them because of their faith. The true children of the patriarchs, according to the apostles, are those with faith in God. But even more important is the declaration that it is this faith in God, which they apparently exhibited, that made them righteous in the eyes of God. This is life-changing because the Bible makes it abundantly clear that men are sinners and separated from God. All sin leads to death and atonement must be made. Jesus, we are taught makes this atonement, but His atonement can only be applied where there is faith.

Biblical fiction allows us to meditate on the Biblical account. My purpose is to provide fictional characters who can ask, probe, and reflect on the words and actions of the fathers, to consider their struggles to come to a saving faith. By filling in the blanks and putting words into the mouths of fictional characters, I hope to bring New Testament commentary and interpretation into the Old Testament story. I intend this as an aid for study. Whenever the Old Testament speaks I try to remain literal. I do not delete or edit their words or the Holy message God gave to them. I write this story from the perspective and lifetime of an amazing woman, Deborah, Rebekah's nurse. She is mentioned but twice in the Bible, but most telling is the report of her death. Long after the death of Rebekah, she is serving in the house of Jacob. Her death brought great mourning. The tree under which Jacob buried her was named "the Oak of Weeping." I chose Deborah because she was loved. I surmise she was loved because she knew how to love others.

This story is a search for understanding faith, true faith that saves, faith that comes from loving God with all of your heart, and all of your soul and all of your mind and all of your strength.

-David Martyn

The Hall of Faith

The Oak of Weeping

The Story of Rebekah and Deborah

David Martyn

Chapter One

Then Rebekah arose with her maids, and they mounted the camels and followed the man. So the servant took Rebekah and departed.

Genesis 24: 61

The air was hot and still. The only sounds she heard was the crunch of the dust and sand under her camel's padded feet, and the high-pitched buzzing of the flies which circled about, endlessly evading the swishing tail and shrugging furry coat. An occasional snort punctuated the steady cadence of her mount as it effortlessly carried her south along the caravan road.

The journey which began with such excitement a week ago in Haran had become a monotonous grind, hour upon hour seated high on the camel's back trying to allow any semblance of fresh air to make its way beneath the great robes which shielded her from the sun. When the breeze came up she choked on the dust. When the air was still, the heat became unbearable. She learned to adjust an opening in her robe throughout the day on her shaded side to capture just a little more air. She noted that the view which had not changed since they crossed the Euphrates at Carchemish, to the right low hills rising to a mountain range, to the left arid plains edging a great desert, began to show areas of green. Vineyards and olive groves now dotted the low hills, with an occasional village set off, away from the noise and dust of the caravan road. Small streams could be seen coming down from the mountains, meandering along the road and watering fields of grain.

Deborah glanced ahead to her close friend and now mistress, Rebekah, riding ahead of her. How strange for her to be silent, she thought. *Was it just the heat and monotony of the journey that has finally silenced her, or is she having second thoughts about marrying a stranger, a relation yes, but one she has never met or even knew of a little more than a week ago? And the distance, starting life in a land far from home; would she ever see her family again? Has her adventurous nature and strong will led her down a path of regret? Did I let her down? I could have said something. How many times have I cautioned her in the past? Not this time. This time I followed her. Did I allow my own desire for adventure to cloud my judgment with her to be bear all the risk? It all happened so fast. Did any of us think it through?*

Deborah's thoughts were interrupted by Abiel riding back through the parade of camels, stopping briefly alongside each person and speaking a few words. As he spoke to Rebekah, she could see her head nod in understanding. Rebekah sat up straight, shook the dust from her head scarf and turned and smiled at Deborah brightly. "Damascus tomorrow," she shouted.

Abiel came alongside Deborah and in his perfunctory manner said, "Eliezer wishes you to know we will arrive in Damascus tomorrow. We will enter the city where you can rest and refresh for two days at the house of his brother, Keshet. If there are any items you will need or you believe your mistress will need in the house of Abraham and Isaac, you are to inform me tonight. He will make the necessary purchases in the market. Do you understand?"

"Yes Abiel," she answered. "How much longer will we travel today? I need to sit with my mistress and go through her belongings to prepare a proper list. This would be far easier in daylight."

"I will share your concerns with Eliezer; I am sure he will consider them."

As Abiel rode off down the line, Rebekah waved for Deborah to ride up alongside. All of Deborah's concerns for Rebekah faded as the irrepressible spirit of Rebekah returned in force. "Do you believe it," Rebekah began, "Two days in Damascus! And I am permitted anything I want from the market! Eliezer is such a strange man, always in a hurry and now this! Remember how he was in such a hurry to leave Haran once I agreed to marry Isaac, and he has never stopped at any of the cities along the way. Every morning is a rush to get moving. I think I shall never want to ride a camel again! And now he surprises me with two whole days in Damascus. I hope his brother's house is respectable. I will not share a one-room hovel with all of these men. But two days in Damascus and then only a few more to Canaan."

Deborah smiled and said, "Yes, a bath and rest will be most welcome. Abiel did say we must provide a list tonight for Eliezer. We must go through your things and make sure you have everything you will need in the house of Abraham and Isaac. Like your family, they dwell in tents and are not near the great market of Damascus. You must make the most of this opportunity."

Rebekah paused and thought. She began curling her red hair around her finger, a habit since childhood. "Yes, I will need a wedding robe and, and what else does a bride require? You must help me, Deborah, what does a bride need? And a wife. I must dress as a wife! Jewelry? Does that come from my husband? I should have asked mother or grandma Milcah these things. I never really thought about being a bride, and Isaac lives in such a faraway land. We left in such a hurry. So many things I don't know!"

"You know I will help," Deborah replied, "And Isaac's mother is sure to help as well. You are a beautiful woman Rebekah, we will find something in Damascus perfect for you, and Isaac will love you all the more."

Rebekah thought for a moment and said, "Eliezer will send Abiel for the list. You must ask him about Isaac. I know so little about him."

Deborah replied, "He says so little. He is just a younger version of Eliezer, always courteous but never betraying any information on his master. Nothing excites or upsets either of them. They just maintain the same consistent manner. Their patience alone astounds me! I don't think I have seen half a smile between the two of them! Do you think they have ever laughed? And yet, somehow I trust them to do the right thing."

Deborah sighed and said, "I'll try to find out what I can."

That evening they stopped an hour earlier than usual. Evidently, Eliezer got the message intended for him. Rebekah's tent was the first one set up and servants quickly unpacked all of her belongings from her pack camels. Deborah and Rebekah immediately began going through her things and preparing her list.

When the two young women emerged from Rebekah's tent, the sun was setting behind the mountain to the west. Only the last rays of daylight were diffused onto the arid plain to the east. The eastern horizon was now merging with the indigo eastern sky, where the first stars appeared overhead. Torches were lit about the camp and the smell of roasting meat and simmering lentil stew guided them to the cooking tent.

Abiel, ever efficient and attentive, met them as they approached. Bowing slightly to Rebekah, he asked, "Deborah, would your mistress take her food in her tent this evening?"

Rebekah, slightly peeved replied, "Run and tell Eliezer, as you always do, but Deborah and I will enjoy the evening and eat here. There seems to be plenty of room. I have been a shepherdess my whole life and I have labored in the company of men most of whom had the honest smell of sheep about them."

"Certainly, mistress Rebekah, I will lay out a clean rug for you," Abiel replied and he began to retreat into the cook tent.

Deborah followed Abiel into the tent and then said, "Abiel, please do not think my mistress does not appreciate all of your efforts to protect her and her reputation, but Rebekah has been indulged by her father and grandmother to enjoy the freedom to learn of the world about her. She has not been restricted to her mother's tent. She is a curious, adventurous and most able young woman. She has been taught that a wife should complement her husband, sharing in his life as Eve most surely complemented Adam."

Abiel stopped and looked at Deborah, "I make no judgments on God's chosen wife for my master, I merely offer her the respect due her as the betrothed wife of Isaac, son, by God's promise, to Abraham. And I pray she becomes the complement and helping wife she aspires to be. You say she is adventurous and most able, these are qualities that will help her in the days ahead. Here are the rugs. Shall I spread them or would your mistress find that too servile?"

Deborah smiled, "I'll take them. Oh, and I would like to discuss my mistress' list with you later."

"You will find me here, or one of the servants will know of my whereabouts." Abiel walked off into the darkness.

Deborah returned to Rebekah and spread out the rug. "I'm surprised he trusts us to spread a rug," Rebekah mumbled.

"Rebekah, don't be hard on Abiel. You are his master's intended bride. Imagine his fate if anything were to happen to you. He means only to afford you respect and service. If you want to learn more about Isaac, show him respect as well. You never treated any of your father's shepherd's or hired hands with such disdain."

"My father's shepherds let me be me. I could do as I pleased," Rebekah replied.

"Did they have any choice? They did as they were told, and Laban was responsible to look after you. I'll be back with your dinner."

Deborah walked to the food tent and filled two bowls with lentil stew and warm roast lamb. Both young women were naturally active and maintained hearty appetites. Returning to Rebekah, Deborah said, "When you finish this there are some lovely figs as well."

Sitting down, Deborah glanced at the night sky above, and half to herself said, "How papa loved the night sky. He could read the stars and the moon and tell the seasons. He used to say the voice of God speaks through the stars and moon, the sun above, the mountains and the creatures of the earth. What did he say? Yes, 'Only man in all of creation chafes against the Most High God's created order, having some dominion and authority but man will always be less than God.' I miss Papa. I wish I had listened closer to all of his stories."

After a few moments, Rebekah answered, "My father always held him in high esteem. He insisted we pray and consider all of our sins before making the sacrifice of atonement. I never saw my father treat any other man of such humble birth with such great respect and affection. But I miss your mother, Leah. She convinced me I would not be restricted to my husband's tent and that a husband and wife are to be one. Each shall make the other stronger and that they should walk together as Adam and Eve in the garden."

The night breeze began to stir, bending the flames in the camp torches. Staring into the darkness, Rebekah spoke again, "My mother feared my father, though I never saw him treat her with anything other than kindness and love. Grandma Milcah instilled doubt. She complained constantly that men forget the wives of their youth when they can no longer bear children. She was so bitter towards Nahor for taking Reumah his second wife. Nothing could appease her."

Turning to Deborah she asked, "Were Leah and Zimri-Ruel as close as they appeared? For all of their teaching were they really happy?"

Deborah put the spoon back into her now empty bowl. She leaned back, staring into the darkness. "They really are one. They are different in so many ways but yes, they seem to fulfill each other. Papa is always focused on God, he sees lessons everywhere on how we should love God and love all whom He loves. Papa has a big heart and tries to love everyone. Momma is more practical. She understands people much better than papa. That's why she insisted on teaching the women. She said papa would never do it or certainly not well. Momma knows how to bring Papa back to the right path when his mind wanders. I never saw either of them cross with each other except when my brother Adniel died. Papa mourned and mourned. He could not be consoled. He was so angry with God. Momma challenged him harshly. How could he challenge God only when it was his son that died? She reminded papa that God protected the guilty Cain when he killed the innocent Abel. She reminded him that God is a giver of second and third chances. And then she offered the most wonderful hope. She said that if Enoch walked with God and then was no more, and if God's heart is to walk with men, would not the God who loved Adniel take him to walk with Him as well."

Deborah lowered her yes and sighed, "Forgive me, I ramble on."

Rebekah also looked down and softly said, "I hope I am the wife to Isaac Leah taught me to be."

Deborah brightened and her voice strengthened, "You will be, I am sure. Never forget that God called you to be Isaac's wife. That is why we left in such haste. Now, let's go back to the tent. I must take your list to Abiel. And I will start questioning him about Isaac. Remember, nice!"

Deborah went over the list one last time with Rebekah and made her way to the cook tent. The torches were still lit, but the camp quiet, all the servants and trained men apparently off to sleep. The night breeze was blowing stronger, perhaps even a little chilly. She saw the silhouette of a man standing in front of the cooking tent. "Abiel?" She asked softly.

"Yes Deborah, you have the list for me?" Abiel answered. "Perhaps we should go over it together, it is most important to get it right."

As Deborah went through Rebekah's shopping list, Abiel interrupted, "This won't do. I have traded in the markets of Damascus, Canaan, and Egypt, but I have never purchased most of these items. You must come with me to market."

Deborah replied, "Rebekah would very much enjoy shopping herself. I would come along with her of course, and you could chaperone."

"That is not possible. Rebekah is now a great lady; Isaac is as a prince among men. Great ladies do not bargain in the markets. It would bring scandal to his name."

He paused for a moment and then looking softly into her face, said, "Excuse me, I'm sorry if you and your mistress take offense. She is young, bold and adventurous, very admirable traits, but she will have to make some adjustments. Perhaps after they are married, Isaac will make allowances for her. He is a very kind man and seeks to please those he can. Some things must wait for a husband's decision."

Deborah looked at Abiel and saw the sincerity of his words in his eyes. "You like your master very much. I am pleased to hear of his kindness. Rebekah knows so little of him, only that he is the son of Abraham, uncle to her father Bethuel. You must be able to tell us something about him."

Abiel thought for a few moments. "I can tell some things, but is it not better that she learns for herself of her husband's secrets?"

"Oh, I would not have you betray any secrets. Is he young? Or old? Is he handsome? You say he is kind. Tell me why you say that."

Abiel laughed lightly.

"So, you can laugh! Tell me all about Isaac," Deborah said brightly, never realizing she could flatter a man.

"He is neither young nor old. Isaac is forty years old. As a man I do not find him uncomely, but then, I could not judge. He is a serious man, and hard working. His father Abraham is now very old and looks to Isaac, his heir, to lead his people. But the real reason he is a serious man is he knows that he is the son of promise and called by God to be the father of nations. The promise of God Most High to his father, Abraham, now falls upon Isaac. He has mourned the death of his mother, Sarah. He was her only child. He has seen his older half-brother, Ishmael, sent away at Sarah's request because of the jealousy she bore for Hagar, Ishmael's mother. Oh, Abraham loved Ishmael and knew God would bless him, but Abraham sent Ishmael and his mother off with only a small supply of bread and water. Isaac always desired to know his half-brother, to know the love of a brother. And now Abraham has married Keturah and fathered more sons, as each son comes of age, Abraham will send him off just as he did to Ishmael. Perhaps without the jealousy of Sarah, he may grant them gifts."

"Does Abraham not love his other sons? This is most strange." Deborah commented.

"Abraham loves all of his sons, it grieved him to send Ishmael off, but he sees this as obedience to God's will."

Abiel paused, "Eliezer would be better to tell you about Abraham, and Abraham keeps no secrets of his past. He has been blessed, yes, but he was sorely tested by God. A test that Isaac will never forget. A test which made Isaac the man he has become."

Abiel was about to go on but suddenly stopped. "It is late, I have kept you from your mistress far too long. I must remember your reputation as well. We shall speak more. After we arrive in Damascus I will call for you to attend the market with me. May the Most High God keep you safe."

As Abiel began to walk into the darkness, Deborah said, "Rebekah fears the house of Eliezer's brother may be a hovel unfit for women to share with men."

Abiel did not stop or even turn but immediately said, "Then perhaps her bravery and strong spirit will carry her though," and laughed to himself.

Chapter Two

And Abram said, "O Lord what will You give me since I am childless and the heir of my house is Eliezer of Damascus?"
Genesis: 15:2

Rebekah and Deborah were slow getting packed in the morning. Abiel had a line of servants waiting to pack their camels. They moved slowly through the cooking tent, drowsy eyes betraying a late night of talking. As they finished breakfast, the camp was already broken down and loaded for the day's journey to Damascus. Finally, they climbed on their camels and the small caravan began making its way south. As Abiel rode by her, Deborah looked for signs of impatience. His steady countenance was worn as a mask that always hid his thoughts. The patience of Abiel and Eliezer truly amazed her.

Rebekah was still drowsy and sat on her camel in a state between sleep and disinterest. Deborah, now feeling refreshed, looked out beyond the road ahead. The day seemed different; the air was fresh and the dust did not rise about her. She noticed how much greener the fields had become. The low hills were now filled with vineyards, olive and fig trees. She could hear the distinct sound of running water. She saw a river of clear water beyond the first hill, running along the road. It grew wider as the day went on as stream after stream joined it flowing down from the mountains to the west. The sun was at its zenith when she first saw Damascus, the white city walls rising above the hills. She could see the river running right into the city, entering beneath the city wall. With the city now in sight, Rebekah cheerfully waved for Deborah to ride alongside. "It is a beautiful city to behold is it not?" She began, "So much grander than Haran and all the cities we passed along the way. And such a market! Damascus is renowned for its market!"

"I did not know you went into Haran? Damascus will be the first city I visit. It does look grand, such a large city and only two days to see it."

"Well father never did take me to Haran, but I'm sure it isn't so grand as this. Are you certain Abiel will not allow me to shop in the market? Oh, I must see the market, who knows when I will have another chance. Please convince him, Deborah, he will listen to you. You can be so persuasive. Did you not say you made him laugh? He must like you! Please ask him."

"I will try. But you must remember to be nice to him, he has more to say about Isaac, I am sure of it. And Eliezer too, he is the one charge."

As they neared the city gate, Abiel came alongside. "Eliezer thought perhaps you would enjoy a walk through the market as we enter the city. We will dismount outside the gate and the servants will lead the camels. You will walk to the humble dwelling of Eliezer's brother."

As Abiel rode off again, Rebekah spoke, "It is a hovel just as I feared!"

"Rebekah," Deborah scolded, "You are the woman who enjoyed the fields in the company of men with the honest small of sheep! What difference where we stay, we will see the market together!"

When it was Rebekah's turn to dismount, Eliezer elegantly took her hand and helped her down. "Welcome to Damascus, mistress Rebekah, my home. I believe you will find everything prepared for you. Come, let us walk through the market, you have seen nothing like it on the plains of Nahor."

As they walked, Eliezer explained how the market was organized. "Everything in the market is planned for the buyer. The merchants make it easy for their customers to find what they need in an orderly manner. You will notice that the livestock is near the gate and the outer wall, far away from the fruits, vegetables, and spices. Next to the livestock are found the sellers of firewood, lamps and lamp oil. Next, you will find the armorers, no need for you to wander there."

The young women could only half listen, as the sights, smells, and the sound of the market encompassed them. There was an excitement in the air as patrons and merchants haggled and argued only to come to an agreement and act as long-lost brothers once the purchase was made.

Deborah could now hear Eliezer explaining, "Now we are entering the food seller's market. Here are the stalls for staples, you have grain and flour, both wheat and barley. And over here are dried figs and raisins. And of course, lentils and dried beans of every variety. Those large jars are filled with fresh olive oil, and those contain wine; the smallest ones are filled with the sweetest honey. In that row are the butchers, any meat you can imagine, fish from the mountain streams and Lake Merom, waterfowl and game birds. Now we see the fresh produce: onions, scallions and garlic; olives, figs, grapes, and raisins; apples, pears pomegranates and fruit you have never before seen!"

The young women gawked at the men and women garbed in every manner carrying baskets, smelling, touching and sometimes tasting the foods before them. Eliezer stopped in front of a covered stall and politely waved them over. "A small treat until dinner, warm cakes just cooked in oil and sweet fig cakes, try some, please." The warm cakes were like the ones she made as a little girl, but the almonds and honey drizzled across the top made them a wonderfully sweet treat that paired perfectly with moist fig cake. Eliezer slipped a coin to the woman attending the stall, and moving on said, "Now we come to my favorite area, the spices! Breathe in deeply, such pleasing aromas! Spices from Egypt and Sumer and Ur; spices from the islands in the great sea. Learn these spices and your husband will grant you your every wish!"

As they sniffed, sampled and smelled their way through the spice merchants, Eliezer said "Now the secrets of the great ladies! Spices and oils, perfumes and salts for the bath, body, face and the hair. Here you will find everything to enhance your beauty. But be not swayed; a warm heart, spirit, and goodness are the truest highlights to beauty."

Rebekah stopped to linger among the exotic lotions and oils, but Eliezer was once again moving on. Realizing she was about to be left behind, she quickly turned and rushed to catch-up, colliding with a woman in a black robe and scarf, who unceremoniously flung her basket of figs in the air.

"Clumsy girl, the woman screamed, "Look what you have done! Look at you, you don't belong here, I should..."

Eliezer immediately appeared, recovered the figs, and bowed in apology to the woman.

The woman was alarmed by the nobility of Eliezer, took the figs from him and said, "Thank you, my lord, I meant no disrespect for the young lady."

Eliezer continued his narration. Pointing to another row of stalls, he said, "Here you will find medicinal herbs, lotions, ointments and treatments for any malady or wound. There are fresh herbs for poultices and roots and potions for chronic conditions. You can find a cure for anything that ails you, and if there is no cure they will sell you one anyway!"

He paused and pointed to another stall, "It is only fitting that incense, myrrh and spices for the dead are sold there as well!"

Not slowing his stride, Eliezer kept walking, the strong odor of myrrh hanging in the air.

"Now, Rebekah, you will find jewelry in this next area, but the best is never sold in the market. No, you must find your own master jeweler and he will make such creations that will flatter you only. And here are the robes and scarves; they are perfectly acceptable when riding a camel through the desert, but a great lady wears only the most select and she must choose the material and their maker carefully."

Slowing his pace and turning to Rebekah, beaming brightly he said, "As a son of Damascus, I am proud of my city and its market, No doubt you have seen other markets but certainly none so grand or so well provisioned. Thank you for bearing with an old man, I hope you were not bored, but here is Straight Street. The palace square is ahead and my brother's humble home is just down this street to the left."

Rebekah could not help but look back at the magical market scene behind her. Her eyes open wide and her mouth agape she shuffled along behind Eliezer as he gracefully glided around the corner. They crossed another street and walked a short distance. Eliezer entered an open gate in a high wall where the camels were all there being carefully unloaded by the other servants. Most of the belongings were moved to a storeroom across the compound. As they entered, Rebekah's belongings were being set down.

Rebekah turned to Deborah and exclaimed under her breath, "It is worse than I feared! He lives in a stable!"

Eliezer did not stop in the courtyard but kept walking to a gate at the far end. As he approached, the gate swung open and an immaculately dressed man bowed low and said, "Master Eliezer, welcome home!"

Eliezer clasped the man's arm and said, "Will you not just call me Eliezer, I am a servant, no more than you."

"No master Eliezer, you will always be master here. Your guests are with you I see, all has been prepared, I have sent for your brother, master Keshet."

Rebekah and Deborah were ushered into a whole new world. Beyond the gate was a courtyard garden with a fountain of running water, potted palms, lush cedars, fruit trees, large ferns and exotic plants. The air was cooler and the noise of the market was not to be heard. Birds were singing! Caged songbirds competed with sparrows and doves flitting about the garden. A large open dining hall welcomed them on the far wall, draped in scarlet and white awnings. The great table was set with grapes, figs, and olives. A large bowl of wine was surrounded by drinking cups and flanked with fresh flowers, unlike any either of the women had seen in Nahor. Apartments surrounded the courtyard, and a young servant girl directed Rebekah and Deborah to one prepared for them.

She bowed and said, "Welcome to the house of Keshet. You will want to wash away the dust of your journey and perhaps rest awhile. The garden will be so much more pleasant come evening."

In their apartment, baths were filled and waiting, the scent of bath oils and perfumes invited their indulgence. Flower petals floated placidly on the clear water. Deborah spoke first, "As you said, a hovel indeed."

As Rebekah soaked in the bath, she mumbled, "Why is such a wealthy man, a servant?"

Why indeed? Deborah thought to herself and then answered Rebekah, "If you are comfortable here, I think I will take a walk about the garden, the songbirds reminded me of the mountain village I knew as a little girl." Deborah dressed in the clean fresh garment laid out for her and softly made her way out.

Chapter Three

Serve the Lord with gladness; come before Him with joyful singing.

Psalm 100: 2

The garden was even more beautiful than at first impression. As she slowly wandered about she saw ever more detail and careful planning. There were sculptures set among the plants, shrubs were trimmed to fanciful shapes, color coordinated paths intersected in tiled mosaic reliefs. The combination of singing birds and trickling fountains made it a place suited for contemplation and pleasant conversation. Why did Eliezer leave this for a life of service to a wandering herder?

Her thoughts were interrupted by the gate from the outer courtyard swinging open. Abiel was coming in. "A wonderful garden, is it not?" He said as he saw her watching his entry. "Mistress Rebekah is resting comfortably I hope."

"And you let her believe she would spend her days in a hovel!" Deborah replied.

"Sometimes doubts are best faced, not argued by others, especially if a trust has not been established first."

Deborah asked, "And where have you been? Eliezer led us on a tour of the market. What wonderful things! Such excitement. Such sights and smells!"

Abiel answered, "I have given your mistress' list to someone more expert than myself or you. No doubt Eliezer told you that the finest goods are not sold in the market. We shall make her purchases tomorrow."

Deborah sighed and said, "Abiel, I now know my mistress and I can trust you and Eliezer, can you not trust me as well? Since I entered this garden I have been pondering why a wealthy and truly noble man like Eliezer would choose to serve another man."

"Eliezer finds joy and reward in serving Father Abraham. He finds in serving his master, he also serves the Most High God."

Deborah nodded, "I have also noted how you care for your master Isaac. I think, now, you and I are alike. We serve the interests of our master and mistress because we care for them. We see something special in them and we in no way diminish ourselves in serving them."

Abiel smiled at her and said, "I saw the servant's heart in you the day we left Haran, you were determined to come beside your beloved Rebekah whatever Eliezer would say. Of course, Eliezer saw this as well. And why not? Your father, a priest, has a servant's heart and I would suppose your mother does as well."

Abiel paused then said, "What most people never realize is that the Most High God who made us, gifted us to serve. The question is only who or what we serve. If we do not serve God, and we do not serve others, we serve only ourselves, and there is no fulfillment in that."

Abiel smiled and gestured about the garden, "Eliezer enjoys this garden as much as any man, yet he chose to serve God first and one chosen by God to be the Father of Many Nations. For many years his brother, Keshet, did not understand Eliezer's decision and Keshet served money. Now

Keshet was a good, kind and honest man, indeed, he learned his skill form Eliezer. But Keshet could not love God. He blamed the patriarch Shem, a priest of God, and the Most High Himself, for calling Eliezer into service. Keshet found no fulfillment in money or in this garden. When you meet Keshet ask him what he enjoys most in this garden today."

Deborah looked at Abiel and said, "You are very good talking about other people you respect and honor, but what about you, Abiel, why do you serve Isaac?"

Abiel looked at her and said directly, "It is my calling from before I was born."

Deborah stared at him and said, "Trust me, I need more than that!"

Abiel shrugged, "It is true. My mother lost my older brother, and my older sister was stillborn. She and my father traveled to Salem in hopes of a blessing from King Melchizedek, Priest of the Most High God, on my safe delivery. Well, in short, Melchizedek did bless her and me. He gave me my name, Abiel, 'God is my father' and prophesized that I would serve the Most High God throughout my long life. And once God brought us to Damascus and the house of Keshet, a business partner with my grandfather, father, and uncle, the patriarch Shem received a word from the Lord that I would serve Abraham's son, Isaac, as Eliezer serves Abraham. He said Keshet would teach me the skills he learned from his brother Eliezer. It is just as Melchizedek and Shem have said."

Deborah thought a few moments and said, "So you believe that the Most High God has called Eliezer, Keshet, and you to serve Abraham and Isaac. So, is your service to God or Abraham?"

Abiel smiled and replied, "What does God expect of man but to love God with all of his heart and all of his soul and to love all whom He loves. There is no division in loving God and loving Abraham and Isaac. God loves them and has laid a calling before them; of course, I, that is, we love them. You must see that they too are servants of God's will."

Deborah sighed. She breathed in the floral scents freshened by the evening air. "When you say we are to love God with all of your heart and all of your soul and love all whom He loves, you speak the very words of my papa," Deborah replied as a sweet smile formed on her face.

"A servant of God who has taught his daughter well," Abiel replied.

The doves cooed softly as the songbirds sang accompanied by the soothing song of the fountain waters. The sun was below the walls of the city and evening was falling. The heat of the day had lifted to the sky overhead. Abiel and Deborah enjoyed the moment.

Abiel broke the silence, "The others will be about soon. I must wash and prepare for the evening. And you should see to your mistress Rebekah."

As Abiel began walking off, Deborah reminded him, "You still have more to share with me and my mistress about Isaac, the more we share the better equipped we will be to serve them."

"As Eliezer is a master in this house and we are his guests, you are certain to learn more," Abiel replied as he went into his room.

When Deborah returned to Rebekah, she was dressed in a white gown, brushing her long red hair. "There you are Deborah, please help me with my hair, it is still a little wet and tangled. Should I cover it tonight? I never did at home, but mother and grandma Milcah always covered their hair for meals with guests."

Deborah took the comb from Rebekah, "Your hair is beautiful but it is a gift for your husband, Isaac. Why not wear your sheer white headscarf, and we will let just a few locks peek from underneath, and perhaps wear the green garnet pendant your father gave you which highlights your beautiful light green eyes. Let everyone speak of the beautiful intended wife to the fortunate Isaac."

Rebekah instinctively began to curl the hair above her right ear around her index finger; Deborah brushed it away, "None of that tonight. You are now a great lady, remember?"

As the young women got up to leave, Deborah said, "Remember nice! Eliezer is our host here. We were wrong about him, and I believe there is more to Abiel as well. As your husband's steward and chief servant, he can be an influential friend."

Rebekah replied, "Nice."

The last light of dusk left shadows about the courtyard garden broken by torches just off the paths leading to the dining pavilion. The silhouettes of others could be seen enjoying an evening walk about the garden, low voices punctuated by laughter brightened the women's already light, expectant mood. They made their way to the pavilion which was wondrously prepared for the feast to come. Abiel was talking to a man wearing elegant, but not ostentatious clothes. Both were laughing when they approached.

Abiel bowed slightly to Rebekah and said to her, "Mistress Rebekah, may I introduce your host, master Keshet, younger brother of Eliezer."

Keshet bowed to Rebekah and said, "Mistress Rebekah, you are most welcome in my humble home. It is a blessing of the Most High God to meet the woman called to be the wife of master Isaac and Mother of Nations. I have heard that you are bold and spirited, but now I see you are beautiful as well. As beautiful as Sarah, the beloved wife of Abraham and mother to Isaac."

Turning to Deborah he said, "And this is the wise and fearless Deborah, no doubt called by God to serve you. You too, Deborah, are my honored guest. I remember well when your father visited here. He came with Jared and Abaigael, father and mother to Abiel. He was anxious to return to his village in the hills above Khalab, zealous to serve those who enslaved him."

Deborah answered, "You are most gracious master

Keshet, my father serves the people of Dabar El'Elyon to this day, but they now live with the tribe of Nahor. Sir, I could not help hearing you laugh as we approached, I hope we have not interrupted your conversation."

Keshet smiled, "Abiel just learned of the small joke on him I have placed in my garden. At risk of embarrassing him, I will tell you. You may have noticed the small statues placed throughout my garden. I assure you they are not idols! No, I have made statues of those whose company I enjoy. A master craftsman carves them in their likeness. Since my friends cannot always be here to walk with me, I have them as a sweet reminder of their company. This evening Abiel came across my newest addition. It is a pair of statues, an old man, and a young boy, and I was just reminding Abiel of the name he is called by in the market. The statue is me and my shadow, Abiel. Ask anyone in the market if they will remember Abiel as Keshet's shadow."

Abiel was red with embarrassment and said, "It is true, I am truly blessed, it is like having two fathers who love me. My father Jared…"

"A fine man, a man of God, truly," Keshet interrupted.

Abiel continued, "And master Keshet who taught me and trained me to be steward and chief servant to Isaac."

Deborah asked, "What has he taught you?"

Abiel thoughtfully answered, "Keshet taught me the ways of the marketplace."

"Tell us please," Rebekah asked, "Tell us the secrets of the market!"

"Abiel looked to Keshet and then began, "He taught me how the many market stalls in the city selling the same goods mean prices will be stable with little variation in price and then only for freshness or quality. He taught me buyers buy from the same seller building relationships of trust."

Abiel looked again at Keshet, who stood beside him smiling, then continued, "Again, and again, he emphasized that trust is the most valuable possession of a merchant. Once a merchant loses the trust of his buyers, he is bound to fail. Keshet taught me how relationships built on trust support a merchant and his customers in times of shortage, either from drought or war. Prices will rise, but fairness and trust must continue, otherwise when normal times return an unfair merchant will be remembered."

Both Rebekah and Deborah listened closely, as Abiel for once spoke with enthusiasm.

Abiel went on, "For all of his understanding of the market, Keshet owns no stalls in the markets of Damascus. Master Keshet, like Eliezer his brother before him, deals with kings, governments, and ministers. He establishes trades based upon needs and mutual interests. Indeed, my father, uncle, and grandfather were workers in bronze and when we were forced to leave Hazor in Canaan after my mother prophesized against the priests of Baal, it was Keshet who arranged for us to supply newly designed bronze spearheads to the kings of Egypt and Tyre; bronze made from Egyptian copper and tin imported through Tyre. Keshet insisted that trust is the bond that makes trade possible."

Rebekah blurted out, "Your mother is a prophet? And your family was forced to flee Hazor in Canaan? Is she a prophet of the Most High God?"

Keshet laughed loudly and hugging Abiel said, "Abiel is humble as ever. Yes, his mother is a prophet of the Most High God, a fearless woman, who with her husband has taught my shadow, Abiel, to love God with all of his heart and all of his soul and to love all whom God loves. He is an expert in strong women!"

Abiel added, "Yes. It was God who led my family to safety and prosperity in Damascus where I was born and He speaks His words through my mother, Abaigael, a prophet first in Canaan and now in Damascus. The Most High God has guided my path ever since. He has blessed and prepared me for His service. He touched the hearts of my father and mother who follow Him faithfully and they have taught me how to love

God with all of my heart and all of my soul. They have shown me the truth of loving all those whom God loves, for if we do not love whom God loves, how can we love God?"

Rebekah and Deborah stared at Abiel, their faces expressing puzzled thought.

"My mother loved and nurtured me; but more than that, she taught me by her bold confrontation against all idolatry and the detestable acts of temple priests and prostitutes. She was ever fearless in proclaiming the word of the Most High, for she would say she was only being obedient to God. With all of her strength and boldness, she remained humble, a loving and obedient wife to my father. My father taught me to always support God's servants. He bore no jealousy to my mother's calling. He loved her and stood beside her and led our family in worship and sacrifice to the Most High God. His faith was unshakeable. There was never a doubt from either of them that I would serve the Most High God as Melchizedek prophesized. And when the patriarch Shem gave them a word from God that I would serve the promised son of Abraham as Eliezer served Father Abraham, they gave me to the teaching of Keshet, brother of Eliezer and the most successful and influential merchant in Damascus."

Deborah looked differently at the man standing before her and saw both strength and a tender heart. With a soft smile, she said, "Earlier you spoke of trust. How wise to value trust in a relationship. I hope to earn your trust as well."

Keshet motioned towards the great table and said, "I see my brother Eliezer has arrived, come, it is time we sit at the table. All is ready and I would hear from my brother his news."

Chapter Four

Now the Lord said to Abraham. "Go forth from your country, and from your relatives and from your father's house, to the land which I will show you."

Genesis: 12:1

They were led to the great table with a sumptuous feast set before them. There were several kinds of roasted meats, green vegetables, dishes with beans and lentils, sweet figs and dates, loaves of fresh bread, cheese, olives in oil and a great bowl of fine wine. The table was surrounded by fragrant flowers and palms. The light evening breeze mixed the aromas into a pleasing, inviting, sensual delight.

Keshet sat Rebekah in the place of honor with Deborah on her right. Eliezer was across from her with Keshet and Abiel on either side. Keshet said, "I thought an intimate dinner appropriate this evening after your long journey. I have invited friends who long to meet you tomorrow."

Rebekah looked surprised, "Who in Damascus would long to meet me?"

Eliezer answered for Keshet, "Damascus is the home of

the patriarch Shem, a priest of the Most High God, and others, brothers and sisters who follow the Most High God. We have hope in the promise of God to father Abraham and his son Isaac. You have been chosen by God as a mother of nations. To welcome you will bring joy and thanksgiving to God and his plan for all men."

Rebekah did not know what to say. After staring ahead a few moments, she decided to taste the food before her.

Eliezer allowed her to eat before continuing, "The patriarch Shem is too old and feeble to leave his bed. He has asked that you visit him tomorrow. I believe he has a word from the Lord and a blessing for you. Deborah, you are asked to come as well. Perhaps after you return from the market? I will call for you in the afternoon."

Then to Keshet, he said, "Brother, I see your cook is widening her use of spices! This dish is truly new and wonderful, may I have some of this spice to take with me for Abraham's table?"

Deborah asked, "Eliezer, my mistress and I wonder how you, a man of wealth and stature, came into the service of father Abraham?"

Eliezer smiled and thought for a moment, "I met Abram, for that was his name then, oh, let me remember, yes, it was sixty-five years ago. When Abram entered the city with his great flocks, many camels, donkeys, servants and trained men. He was welcomed by the people who offered to make him king. He spent many days with the patriarch Shem, priest of the Most High God, who taught him of El'Elyon, whose voice called to Abram. The patriarch Shem, too, heard the voice of God after God saved him, his father Noah and his family from the great flood on the ark. Shem has lived a very long life as God's priest, interceding for the people."

Looking at the patient faces of Rebekah and Deborah, Eliezer said, "I must go back to the beginning and recount the story of Abraham, then called Abram. Abram was the son of Terah, the son of Nahor. He traveled to Ur of the Chaldeans with his father, Terah while his brother, Nahor, your grandfather, Rebekah, remained on the plains of Nahor, named for his grandfather. Abram and his younger brother, Haran, took wives while they dwelled in Ur; Abram married Sarai, his half-sister, and daughter of Terah. Haran took a wife and she bore him a son, Lot, in Ur. Terah, his sons, and their wives, were in Ur but not of Ur. They remembered the stories of El'Elyon recounted through the generations, but they neither knew Him nor worshipped Him. The people of Ur worshiped idols and practiced detestable rituals before them. After Terah witnessed the death of his son Haran, he gathered his family and traveled up the great river, Euphrates, to the plains of Nahor and the city of Haran. The long journey from Ur to Haran was just the beginning of a lifelong journey of Abram and earned him the name, Abram the Hebrew, for he was a sojourner in the land, who lived in tents."

Rebekah replied, "I can remember no other brother of Nahor, or any house of Nahor leaving the plains other than those who chose to dwell in Haran. I have heard stories of Terah. He was called the "Goat who wanders," but he was loved by all who knew him. I knew his son, Abram, took his nephew Lot with him on his journeys. Please, tell us more."

Eliezer nodded politely and continued. "Now the voice of the Lord said to Abram while he dwelled in Haran, 'Go forth from your country, and from your relatives and from your father's house, to the land which I will show you; and I will make you a great nation, and I will bless you and make your name great; and so, you shall be a blessing; and I will bless those who bless you, and the one who curses you I will curse. And in you, all the families of the earth shall be blessed.'"

Only the sound of the garden fountain could be heard as Eliezer paused for a moment.

"Abram obeyed the voice of the Lord and gathered up his all of his possessions, for he was a very wealthy man, and took his wife Sarai, and his nephew Lot, and set out for the land of Canaan. Abram was seventy-five years old when he departed

Haran; not too old to begin a life of obedience to the Most High God! Just as you did, Rebekah, Abram and his host followed the Euphrates north and west to the city of Carchemish, where they safely crossed and followed the caravan road south along the mountains past Khalab (Alep), here to Damascus. Abram was a very old man when I came into his service. Indeed, his son by the promise of God, Isaac, was born when he was one hundred years old, and his wife Sarai, beyond ninety years old, was well beyond the age of bearing children. The birth of my master, Isaac, whose name means 'Laughter,' was the fulfillment of this promise by God, who is forever faithful. The joy of his birth led Sarah to proclaim, 'God has made laughter for me; everyone who hears will laugh with me.' And she said, 'Who would have said to Abraham that Sarah would nurse children? Yet I have born him a son in his old age.'"

Rebekah interrupted, "Sarah must have been elated by the birth of Isaac. Truly a joy and blessing from God. Tell more, please."

Eliezer smiled. "Father Abraham would not count God as slow to answer his prayers or fulfill His promise, though he followed the voice of the Most High God for many decades before his son, his pride, Isaac, was born. It was here in Damascus that Shem gave Abram and me a word from the Lord to serve Abram's as his steward and chief servant. And I joined him on his journey."

Rebekah said, "My journey has been but a week or so and it has been so tiring, yet exciting now that we are seeing new places, Damascus is so different. Tell more of your journeys." She then took several quick bites of the tasty dishes before her. Deborah, too, was happy to listen and learn. She politely continued her meal.

Eliezer nodded and continued his story, "Abram continued his journey and came into the land of Canaan as far as the city of Shechem, to the oak of Moreh and camped there. There the Lord appeared to him and said, 'To your descendants, I will give this land.' Abram built an altar there and worshipped the Lord God. But Abram did not stay in Shechem; he proceeded towards Bethel and made camp on the mountain to the east, between Bethel and Ai. There, too, he built an altar and worshipped God."

"Abram, the Hebrew, continued his sojourn throughout the land, south towards the Negev desert. Through all of his journeys, Abram was in the land but not of the land. He camped outside of the cities and lived apart from the people. He took great pleasure in negotiating with the kings of the land for permission to graze and water his flocks. His great wealth and host of trained men brought respect and fear to the kings of Canaan. Once permission to camp was given, my job was to trade wool and tents for food and provisions for all of Abram's host."

Eliezer paused, "Surely I speak too much! I would not bore you or distract you from this wonderful meal my brother has prepared in your honor..."

Rebekah answered, "No please, we are not bored, I want to hear more of my father-in-law, and my betrothed. Deborah, too would hear more, is that not so, Deborah?"

Deborah nodded her agreement. Abiel smiled and Keshet gestured for his brother to continue and said, "The night is pleasant, the food most tasty and the wine agreeable. Our guests do not know of the long journey of Abraham following the voice of God."

Eliezer replied, "If you insist. Now, when Abram traveled to the south of Canaan land, towards the Negev, the land he entered was in drought. Abram determined to travel to Egypt and sojourn there. The king of Egypt was unlike the kings of the cities of Canaan. The king of Egypt had a great army and did not count the trained men of Abram as a danger or the wealth of Abram as too great for a man, not of royal birth. Abram feared the king of Egypt, and in his fear, he sinned greatly!"

"Abram's wife, Sarai, was a most beautiful woman and

Abram feared that when the Egyptian officials saw her they would kill him and take her for the harem of the Pharaoh, King of Egypt. Not trusting in the Most High God, Abram told Sarai to say she was his sister if asked by an Egyptian (as you know, Sarai was indeed his half-sister, a daughter of Terah by a different wife than Abram).

Well, Abram entered Egypt with his flocks, servants and trained men. He watered his flocks there and led them to good pasture. When he pitched his tents, the officials of Pharaoh, King of Egypt came to inquire of him his intentions. Abram welcomed them and provided hospitality befitting such noble visitors. When Sarai served them, saying she was sister to Abram, they saw that she was a beautiful woman and they spoke of her beauty to Pharaoh."

Eliezer's face turned serious and he said, "In this, Abram sinned greatly against God and his wife Sarai; he condemned her to the harem of the Pharaoh in return for his life and added riches. For the Pharaoh sent for Sarai and took her into his harem and rewarded Abram with sheep, oxen, goats, donkeys, camels and servants, both male and female."

Eliezer pounded his fist on the table, "But God would not permit this injustice! The Lord struck the house of Pharaoh with plagues because he took Sarai. When Pharaoh learned Sarai was wife to Abram, he sent her back to Abram, condemning him for his lies saying she was his sister and not his wife. Pharaoh, King of Egypt sent soldiers to escort Abram, with Sarai, and all that he owned out of Egypt."

Rebekah looked shocked. "Abram did that! Really? And she agreed? But God saved them! That must have changed them forever."

Eliezer looked into Rebekah's eyes and answered, "Trust is a hard lesson. Abram had followed the voice of the Most High God from Ur of the Chaldeans, north to Haran, into Canaan, the Negev and all the way to Egypt. But Abram did not believe the promises of God, he had not learned to trust in the Most High God. Even so, the Most High God knows that we are but dust and loves us even when we are weak in faith, sinful and commit the most ugly deeds. The Most High God had chosen a broken vessel, of common vulgar use, to be the father of His chosen people. Abram was obedient to God's voice, available to follow him and would learn to trust the word of God and be taught what it means to love God and love all whom He loves."

Eliezer paused again, "I think that is enough for this evening.You have had a long day and must rest. Tomorrow will be just as busy."

Rebekah was captured in the story and replied, "I am not tired, please continue, I want so much to hear the story of Abraham and Sarah and so much more about Isaac."

Eliezer warmly smiled, "And you will. We have many more days of travel and nights to hear more stories but I must tell you about tomorrow. You will meet with the patriarch Shem, as I mentioned."

Turning to Abiel he asked, "Is all arranged for your market visit with Deborah?"

Abiel answered in his perfect servant voice, "Yes, I have arranged for a local expert on fine women's things to accompany us. We will return in time to accompany mistress Rebekah to the house of the patriarch Shem."

Eliezer nodded, "Good." And then smiling said, "God be praised, what a glorious night. How I do love your garden, brother!"

Deborah interrupted the silence, "Master Keshet, I am reminded that Abiel tells me I should ask you what you like most in your garden."

Keshet looked at Abel with a smile and turning back to Deborah said, "So my shadow would have me give up my secrets!"

Then his face settled into a different kind of smile, one that was directed to thoughts and memories rather than the present company. "There are two things that make my garden precious to me. It is nights like this spent with those I love in warmth, tranquility and intimate conversation which warms my heart. That is why I memorialize my friends with the statues."

Deborah said softly, "You said two things; what is the second?"

"Ah, the second is even sweeter than the first. I come into this garden alone to pray. Here there are no distractions and I can open my heart to God."

Rebekah asked, "Master Keshet, you have everything the heart could desire. What do you pray for?"

Keshet laughed lightly and answered, "Child, I pray to hear. I pray that I would hear what God would say to me. To know His will, yes, but more to know His heart. Knowing God is worth more than all of my possessions, or my health. It is what I live for."

Eliezer broke the silence, "Mistress Rebekah, so much has happened to you so quickly. God called you to marry Isaac and the next day you were on the road here. You have many questions about Isaac and Abraham and Sarah, but you must have questions for the Most High God Himself. Might I suggest you spend some time in this garden tomorrow listening for the voice of God? He has called you, He will listen to your questions and answer your prayers."

Keshet stood up, stretched and said, "Friends it is late. God keep you this night."

Chapter Five

Charm is deceitful and beauty is vain, but a woman who loves the Lord, she shall be praised.

Proverbs 31:30

Early the next morning a servant girl gently tapped on the doorframe before entering and suggesting Deborah dress and have some breakfast before her appointments in the market. Rebekah could rest if she wished, breakfast would be available at her leisure.

Deborah found the garden most cheerful in the morning light. The birds still sang along to the melodious fountain, but the song seemed more fresh, expectant and eager for the new day. Glancing about she saw no one else in the garden. The pavilion table was set with fresh flowers and fruits. Then she caught the aroma of cooked cakes with figs and nuts.She indulged herself on several of the hot, fresh cakes and a raisin cake as well. She surprised herself by taking a fresh pear and enjoying its sweet and juicy meat, leaving the core in a common jar at the end of the table. She was wiping the last drops of pear juice from her chin when the gate at the end of the garden creaked open.

Abiel held the door open for a nobly dressed, aging woman. The woman, followed by Abiel, made her way through the garden to the pavilion. As she walked there was an elegance about her, a confidence, or rather grace, in her movement. Her clothes clearly fine, were not showy. About her neck hung but one jewel, a large shining blue stone set in fine gold. She wore little make-up, no overdone black outlines about her eyes, nothing to diminish her natural beauty. Her dark hair and brown eyes were warm complements to her fair face not burned and browned from the sun.

As they approached, Abiel said, "Deborah, this is Abaigael, my mother, and our guide in the market today."

Abaigael walked slowly to Deborah, took hold of her forearms and said, "Deborah Bath Zimri-Ruel, daughter of Zimri-Ruel, priest of the high hills above Khalab?"

Deborah, surprised, nodded her head and said, "Yes."

Abaigael leaned in, hugged her tight and gave her a kiss on the cheek. "Welcome Deborah Bath Zimri-Ruel, may God's blessing be upon you, daughter of my dear friend. There is so much I would hear from you of your father's house."

Then stepping back, she looked at Deborah from head to foot and said, "Abiel has told me of your beautiful servant's heart, but he never mentioned that you are a beautiful young woman, a complement to the mistress Rebekah, well known for her beauty. But your mission, well, come along we can talk as we go. We must find everything a noble lady will need. Isaac is certainly blessed by God, and everyone who sees Rebekah will know of it."

Abaigael led the way to the market, entering first the row of apparel dealers. She stopped and purchased several headscarves and light linen robes. "These are well suited for the dry dust of Canaan. Sand is less a problem there. She will still need some warm woolen robes for the winter."

As they walked Abaigael asked, "How did you come to live on the plains of Nahor? And your mother, tell me about your mother, your father was so dedicated to serving the Most

High God, how did he meet your mother?"

Deborah briefly recounted the story of her father being mauled by a great lion while watching the flock at night and how Leah, her mother nursed him back to health. She mentioned Zimri-Ruel's vision while unconscious of Melchizedek telling him not to fear to ask Leah to marry him and of Leah's mysterious visitor, said to be Melchizedek, telling her mother to marry Zimri-Ruel when he asks her. She told of their life in Dabar El'Elyon and how they fled the Amorites. The warmth between them grew as Abaigael led them through the market stalls.

Several stops later, Abiel had wished he had brought more servants to carry packages, but a few words to a merchant and several young men arrived to relieve him from the load. In the apartment of the best robe maker and seamstress in Damascus, Abiel sipped on his spiced wine as Abaigael had Deborah model robe after robe, assured she and Rebekah were close in height. Abaigael was shown fabric after fabric and promised the finest embroidery with additions of jewels and gold thread.

While they were alone, Deborah asked Abaigael, "Tell me how God called you and Abiel to serve him. Was it difficult to send him off to serve God?"

Abaigael looked warmly at Deborah and said, "It was not a difficult thing, I could do no other. The Most High God sent His priest, King Melchizedek, to my husband, Jared and me, as we were leaving Salem. He knew everything about us. He knew my pain of losing a young son and the stillbirth of my daughter. He knew I was carrying Abiel, though the light was poor and I was covered under a great robe. With love and authority, he spoke to us. He told us I would bear a son, his name would be Abiel, for God is his father, and Abiel would serve the Most High God throughout his long life. Everything he said and more has come about. He has made me His prophet; the angel of the Lord comes to me in visions and instructs me on what to say. I obey because I trust the Lord yes, but more so because I love the Lord, the Most High God. He has heard my prayers and the prayers of my husband. I find joy in serving Him and joy in knowing my son, Abiel, loves and serves Him as well."

Looking again at Deborah modeling the fine robe she said, "I don't know your story, Deborah, but I feel you have been called by God as well. How did you come to serve your mistress, Rebekah?"

Deborah looked down at the finely embroidered robe and said, "I'm not sure I know. Papa said something about God telling him to send me along with mother when she was asked to help Rebekah's mother when Rebekah was born. Momma would help, but mostly she was always instructing the women, and then Rebekah and me. She told stories how El'Elyon wants to walk with us as He did with Adam and Eve in the garden, how we are to love God with all of our heart and all of our soul and to love all whom God loves. She told all the women that it is God's will that a man and wife be one flesh, that they complete each other. Rebekah and I were permitted to know the world of men as well as women. Her father Bethuel and her grandmother Milcah supported everything momma taught. So, when Eliezer came and spoke of how the Lord showed him Rebekah was chosen to be Isaac's wife, and when she asked me to come with her, I just knew I must come. And papa and momma knew as well."

After Abaigael made her selections, Abiel was called to pay the price agreed. Robes, gowns, and clothing purchased, the trio led their train of bearers to the shop of a goldsmith and jeweler known to Abaigael. As they entered, the jeweler greeted Abaigael. "Ah, Abaigael, I have what you ordered yesterday," and he gave her a wooden box.

Abaigael looked at Deborah and said, "Mistress Rebekah will be given all of Sarah's jewels. She will be known for her beauty and wealth, and the calling God has given her." Turning towards Abiel, she handed him the box of jewels. "These are Isaac's wedding gift to Rebekah. She will be given them to wear on her wedding day and is not to see them before. Isaac loved his mother greatly but he knows his wife is loved by God and will walk with him as one."

Deborah turned to Abiel and said, "You promised to tell me more about your master Isaac, what kind of a husband will he be to my mistress, Rebekah?"

"It is as I said, he will be a kind and loving husband, anxious to please," Abiel replied.

"What will he expect of Rebekah? Everyone speaks of their calling, this will surely bring expectations on her."

Abiel replied, "Isaac will expect what every husband expects, the love and support of his wife, and submission to his authority and…"

Abaigael interrupted her son, "Isaac is a man, a kind, and good man, but he will expect love, respect, honor and obedience and in return, he will give Rebekah his love and provide her all of her desires to the best of his ability. It is how men think, it is not how women think, but until trust is established it is helpful to meet his expectations. It is wise for Rebekah to understand Isaac's world, his concerns, his obligations and his promise from God. As Isaac's expectations are met he will become open to her counsel and advice. They will grow into one. She must be wiser than Isaac and know his heart better than he knows it himself. From the start, she must recognize Isaac's distaste for confrontation. She must also remember how Isaac has witnessed God's testing of his father Abraham."

Deborah replied, "Twice now I have heard of God's testing of Abraham. How was he tested? And why is it so important to Isaac?"

Abiel answered, "Have Rebekah ask Eliezer of Abraham's lessons from God. She will understand."

Abiel paused, "Our last stop. Mother will help you select a lady's beauty oils, salts, and spices. Be sure you are instructed in their use."

Their final purchases made, Abiel said, "We must return to

the house of Keshet straight away. You are to join Rebekah on her visit to the patriarch Shem."

Abaigael said, "I leave you here. Until tonight; God keep you until then."

When Deborah returned to Keshet's garden, Rebekah was pacing impatiently along the otherwise serene pathway. "Deborah, I am so glad you are back, I need to talk to you."

"And I have more to tell you of Isaac," she replied.

Rebekah said, "Yes, Isaac. What do I really know about him? And everybody talking about God's calling. I have been thinking all day and I am only more confused. I even tried praying, but I don't hear any answers; I haven't seen any visions or signs. Do I have to go through with this? Everybody else is so sure of everything, but not me. You always seem to think for both of us, why didn't you stop me?"

Deborah hugged her friend, "That is the amazing thing in all of this. You knew as soon as Eliezer spoke of his answered prayer. I knew as well. Your family knew; my parents knew. None of this could have happened except God reached out from heaven to call you to be a mother of nations. You are prepared for this. Leah and Milcah have prepared you. And I know of your strength. God tests us. This day is but a test, the first of many to come. Trust the Most High God; love Him and He will give you the strength you need."

Deborah paused, "I learned today that you must be wiser than Isaac. I know what he expects, I know that his desire is to please you. Can it be a bad thing for a wealthy young prince to love you and want to please you? You can build the marriage you desire." Pausing a moment Deborah said, "I am hungry, let's eat before we go visit the patriarch, Shem."

When Eliezer took the young women to the house of Shem, Keshet was there tending him. It seemed strange to them that a wealthy merchant like Keshet was helping him to sit up, fluffing his pillow and asking what else he could get him. When Keshet saw them standing at the entrance to the room, he spoke softly, "They are here patriarch, mistress

Rebekah, and her nurse Deborah. Are you ready to receive them?"

Keshet bent low, his ear just in front of Shem's tired and creased face. Shem's eyes were a cloudy blue; clearly, he was now blind. Thin white hair enclosed his head and fell onto his white beard. "Yes, I can stay if that is your desire." Then motioning to the young women, Keshet waved them into the room.

The patriarch raised his arm in a blessing; with a weak but authoritative and audible voice, he said. "God's blessing on you Rebekah, you shall be a mother of nations. God is working His plan. He has made a covenant with Abraham. A better covenant than He made with my father Noah. He has promised to be God to the nations of father Abraham and his descendants forever. I have been His priest like my father before me, but my priesthood will soon end. God is preparing a new priesthood whose ordinances will be ordained by God Himself. With Isaac, you will be blest by all generations of God's promised people, for Isaac is heir to God's promise to Abraham. I see that you are a strong woman whose heart fears the Most High God. Your strength will be tried, but God will be with you. Trust Him and persevere."

He lowered his arm and said, "And Deborah, daughter of that mountain goat, Zimri-Ruel, it is a blessing to me in my old age to see the daughter of a man with a steadfast spirit." Then raising his arm again, he said, "Hear my blessing, you shall steadfastly serve the Most High God and his called mother of nations, Rebekah. You shall serve her and her children throughout your long life. You will love and be loved for that is your calling."

Shem settled back against his pillows, his blind eyes focused and opened wide, he spoke softly almost past them, "Daughters of God Most High, your hearts have been sealed to His calling. You shall love God with all of your heart and all of your soul. Love Him for He is always faithful; His word will never change. Trust the Most High God and He will comfort you and bring salvation in a trial. Show Him your love with obedience and see if He does not pour out blessing upon blessing to you and your children for generations to come. His mercy endures forever."

As Rebekah walked back to the house of Keshet, she turned to Deborah and softly said, No more doubts."

Chapter Six

By loving the LORD your God, by obeying His voice, and by holding fast to Him; for this is your life and the length of your days, that you may live in the land that the LORD swore to your fathers, to Abraham, Isaac, and Jacob, to give them.

Deuteronomy 30:20

That evening Rebekah and Deborah were joined by Abiel's family: his father, Jared; mother, Abaigael; and his uncle, Obed. It was clear that they were close friends with Keshet and frequent visitors to his garden. Keshet made the introductions. Jared, a small, handsome man, immaculately groomed and dressed in a fine robe, graciously bowed to Rebekah and said, "Both Abiel and Abaigael have told me of your beauty and grace but now I see their words fall short of the lady who stands before me. Isaac is truly blessed. May God bless you and Isaac with sons and grandsons, but even more with His joy and peace. Walk with Him in His love."

The elegant, but warm and open, Abaigael, reached out and hugged Rebekah saying, "My husband greets you with sweet words, but I would greet you with a hug. Know that

God loves you always and forever. Isaac will love you as well, you two shall be one."

Obed, a large man with massive arms and hands, who looked out of place in his fine clothes self-consciously said, "I am very pleased to meet you."

Rebekah gracefully thanked them for their warm greetings, "My visit to Damascus and the house of Keshet and you his good friends has given me assurance of God's gracious calling to Isaac and me."

Abaigael turned to Deborah and said, "Husband, this is Deborah, daughter of Zimri-Ruel. Truly a blessing from God. She has told me so much of our dear friend and his wife. May God bring us together once more! How I long to see him again and meet his dear wife."

Jared replied, "Welcome Deborah. It is true, Abaigael and I began our walk with the Most High God along with your father. We all had been blessed by King Melchizedek, priest of the Most High God, but your father was truly a disciple of Melchizedek and we learned together to trust God. Tell me, does he still sing sweet songs of praise? What joy to join him in his songs!"

Deborah smiled, "Papa would burst if he could not sing his praise songs. They are always welcome among our people, a constant reminder of the salvation God brought to us."

Keshet and Eliezer ushered them to the table prepared for them even more grand than the night before. Again, Rebekah was seated in the place of honor, with Deborah by her side. Abaigael was seated on her other side and Jared next to her. Obed took a seat with Abiel, Keshet, and Eliezer across the table.

Eliezer politely said, "I hope our stop here in Damascus was successful, and you will have everything you will need in Canaan."

Rebekah answered, "Deborah assures me that no queen could be provided better. But it is your love that is most sweet to me."

Keshet asked, "Did your time in the garden this morning serve you well?"

Rebekah thought for a moment and then said, "You were right to suggest I seek answers from God, but it was the blessing and words of the patriarch Shem that brought me the answers I sought."

Eliezer and Keshet both smiled. Keshet answered, "The patriarch is God's priest. He intercedes for God's people. But know that Shem is very old and longs to walk with the Most High God. He would not close his eyes until meeting you, mother of nations, and with Isaac, an heir of God's promise to Abraham, God's covenant with Abraham and promise to his people."

Rebekah nodded and the said, "You must tell me more of father Abraham and my husband to be, Isaac. Last night you promised to tell more." Turning to Jared and Abaigael she said, "You don't mind hearing the story, please tell Eliezer to continue his telling..."

Jared said, "Mistress Rebekah, you are the honored guest, we will gladly hear Eliezer's telling of father Abraham's story with you."

Eliezer smiled and said, "You mean the wonderful food and perfectly spiced dishes do not make the evening special? For certain I will continue the story, now please enjoy my brother's table."

Eliezer took a few bites of the aromatic dish in front of him and then began, "Where was I? Yes, I recall, Abram traveled north from Egypt and returned to Canaan and the city of Bethel with all of his flocks, servants and trained men. Abram was very wealthy and his flocks were greater than any in Canaan. His nephew Lot traveled with him, bringing his great flocks. Arguments arose between the shepherds of Abram and the shepherds of Lot over water and the best pastures for grazing. The combined flocks of Abram and Lot were too great for the land to support. Abram and Lot climbed to the ridge of the mountains of Canaan and Abram said to his nephew Lot, 'Please let there be no quarreling between you and me. The whole land is before you, please separate from me; if you go to the left I will go to the right. If you go to the right I will go to the left.'"

Rebekah interrupted, "This I understand, shepherds always argue when watering their flocks, each wants to be first so he can get them early to the night fold. Unless the owners agree and are firm in their instructions, the shepherds will squabble. I have seen this while shepherding on the plains of Nahor."

Eliezer smiled, "Your experience will serve you well with your husband, Isaac. Now Lot looked out from the mountain and saw the green valley of the Jordan river. It was well watered throughout with lush, green pastures. Lot chose to take his flocks east to the Jordan valley and pitched his tents near the city of Sodom, a wicked city of exceedingly sinful men. Abram stayed in Canaan, west of the mountains."

"After Lot had separated from Abram the voice of the Lord God said to him, 'Now lift your eyes and look from the place you are, northward and southward and eastward and westward; for all the land which you see, I will give it to you and your descendants forever. And I will make your descendants as the dust of the earth; so that if anyone can number the dust of the earth, then your descendants can also be numbered. Arise, walk about the land through its length and breadth; for I will give it to you.'"

"Having heard the promise of the Most High God again, Abram listened to the voice and moved his tents and dwelled by the Oaks of Mamre, which are near Hebron. There he built an altar to the Lord and worshipped."

Again, Rebekah interrupted, "Is that where we are going, the Oaks of Mamre?"

"Abraham is indeed fond of the Oaks of Mamre; it is his favored grazing land," Eliezer answered. Continuing in his unhurried, calm and dignified voice he said, "Now Sodom was as wicked a city as ever there was. Lot was not concerned with the wickedness of the city. For him life was good. He had green pastures and water in abundance for his flocks and he was able to trade for anything he or his servants might need or desire. Lot enjoyed the deference afforded him for his great wealth. He was unprepared for the War of the Nine Kings that was about to ensnare him."

Deborah could not stop herself, "Lot was unprepared for war? Who is prepared? I remember what it is like to run from soldiers, hiding in caves, worrying if you would be slain or starve to death. It was horrible... I'm sorry, please go on."

As always, Eliezer waited patiently before he continued, "For twelve years, the kings of Sodom, Gomorrah, Admah, Zeboiim, and Zoar served Chedorlaomer, King of Elam. In the thirteenth year, the five kings rebelled. King Chedorlaomer and his allies the kings of Shinar, Ellasar, and Goiim, came and defeated the kings of the Jordan River valley and turned to battle the five kings in rebellion. The armies met in the valley of Saddim where the Jordan enters the Salt Sea. The valley of Saddim was covered with many tar pits and the kings of Sodom and Gomorrah fell into tar pits and died. The army of the five kings fled before King Chedorlaomer and his three allied kings. Sodom and Gomorrah were sacked and everything of value and all of the food was carried off. They also took Lot and all of his flocks and possessions and returned to the north towards Elam."

"Abram was camped at the Oaks of Mamre when he was told of the capture of his nephew Lot. He led his trained men, three hundred and eighteen of them, in pursuit of King Chedorlaomer to the far north of Canaan, north of the Sea of Chinnereth (Galilee). Abram divided his forces in a night attack and defeated Chedorlaomer and his kings. He pursued the fleeing king further north of Damascus where he rescued Lot and recovered all that was carried off from Sodom and Gomorrah."

Eliezer again paused, took a few bites of food and then continued softly, "It was this victory that taught Abram a great lesson. It was not the bravery of his trained men or the battle plan of Abram that brought him this great victory; it was the power of the voice he followed. The victory belonged to El'Elyon, the Most High God. And Abram realized the plague that came upon the house of Pharaoh and Pharaoh's decision to send back Sarai and allow Abram to leave Egypt wealthier than when he entered, was also the work of God. Abram learned that the Most High God who was speaking to him, promising a great blessing, was shielding him, encompassing him and his house in a fortress of protection and blessing him beyond measure. It became evident to Abram what others had already realized; the God of Abram was protecting him and blessing him unlike any other man on earth."

Eliezer looked around the table, his gaze settled on the enraptured eyes of Rebekah and he continued, "Returning with his nephew Lot and all that was recovered, Abram did something most unexpected. He acknowledged all that he recovered belonged to God and a gave a tithe, one-tenth of everything he recovered back to God and the remainder back to the people of Sodom and Gomorrah from where it had been taken. Abram traveled back to Sodom by way of Salem where our paths crossed for the first time."

Now it was Jared who interrupted, "We were there! Abaigael and I were on the walls of Salem and we watched the great tribute that was brought into the city. We heard King Melchizedek bless Abram. Deborah's father, Zimri-Ruel was there too. I will never forget it. Abram must have known Melchizedek was God's priest and he knew the victory was God's and returned his tithe in thanksgiving."

Keshet smiled at his brother and then said, "Herein is the lesson; there are many reasons to be obedient. A slave who is obedient to his master brings no honor to his master. The obedient slave is fearful for his very life. A soldier who is obedient to a king is little better than the slave who is obedient to his master. Where is the honor in that, or in the obedience of a debtor to his lender? Obedience in the face of obligation is little more than survival. How much better is the obedience of a child to a parent! An obedience based on trust. Is not the child wiser than the man in seeing the better way? An obedience based on trust is the first step in an obedience borne of love."

Eliezer nodded and continued, "Abram's obedience may not yet have come from trust and likely not from love, but God, in His grace and mercy in order to strengthen and assure him, came to him in a vision saying, 'Do not fear Abram, I am a shield to you; your reward shall be very great.' But Abram replied, 'O Lord God, what will You give me since I am childless and the heir of my house is Eliezer of Damascus?' Abram complained, 'And You have given me no offspring to be my heir.'"

Rebekah in her surprise asked, "You were Abram's heir? How did you feel when you learned of this?"

Eliezer answered, "I was always, and remain, honored to serve father Abraham. I have no need or desire to be his heir. I know the heart of my lord Abraham and rejoiced with him in the promise of God. For the word of the Lord answered him and said, 'This man will not be your heir; but one who is born by your own body, he shall be your heir.' Then the voice took Abram outside and said, 'Now look up to the heavens and count the stars if you are able to count them.' Abram looked up, and the voice said, 'So shall your descendants be!' Abram believed the Lord and the Lord reckoned it to him as righteousness. And the Lord said to him, 'I am the Lord who brought you out of Ur of the Chaldeans, to give you this land to possess it.'"

And the Lord made a covenant with Abram saying, "To your descendants, I have given this land. From the river of Egypt as far as the great river Euphrates."

Eliezer stopped. "God's promises to father Abraham were made to him many times, over many years. In all of this time, Abraham listened; Abraham obeyed God and followed where the voice of God sent him. Shall not all men follow where the voice of God sends them? We should but follow. Patiently. God would have us be patient. This is a good thing, for He is ever patient with us."

Looking up brightly, he changed the subject, "Brother, how sweet are the times at the table with friends in the beauty of this garden! And what a night the Lord above has given us! It is fresh and fragrant with hope. Nor do we not have hope in our God? Look at the beauty of His handiwork."

Keshet said, "As you say, brother; and if Zimri-Ruel were here he would indeed be singing God's praises this moment. But you and our honored guests must depart tomorrow. Rebekah and Deborah should rest. You have days of travel ahead to finish your story."

Rebekah replied, "The evening is yet young. I know what awaits us on the caravan road, please continue the story. Surely the others are enjoying the telling as much as I am. Obed, you have been listening intently, would you hear more?"

Obed replied, "Listening is one of my favorite things to do. If you would hear more, I will be pleased to stay and listen. Eliezer tells the story so well."

"There you have it, Eliezer," Rebekah said, "Obed enjoys your storytelling as much as Deborah and I do."

Keshet chuckled and said, "Brother, you must continue, there will be no disappointing of guests in this house!"

Eliezer sighed. "The story becomes hard here. I must share a hard trial for Abram and Sarai. Now, after this time, Sarai said to Abram, "The Lord has prevented me from bearing children. Please go in to my maid, Hagar, perhaps I shall obtain children through her."

So, Abram listened to Sarai and took Hagar, the maid as his wife, and Hagar conceived. When Hagar saw she conceived, she despised Sarai. Sarai blamed Abram for taking Hagar as his wife and treated her servant poorly. So, all three who violated God's perfect plan for man and wife bore the fruit of their sin. The house of Abram was filled with strife and pain to the point where Hagar fled from Sarai. Is this not always the case when men take additional wives and concubines? But God is patient and, in all ways, loving. He sent the angel of the Lord to Hagar to comfort Hagar and promise her that she would bear a son whose name would be Ishmael, "God Hears," because the Lord had heard her affliction. Abram was eighty-six years old when Ishmael was born. Ishmael grew strong in the house of Abram his father.

Rebekah said, "I know full well the pain and discord in the house of a man who takes another wife. Grandma Milcah was very bitter when Nahor took a concubine. After all the sons she bore for him, why did Nahor need more sons and daughters? Strife, oh yes strife. Deborah's mother, Leah, taught us that this is not what God intended when He walked with Adam and Eve in the garden. This lesson I have learned."

Eliezer continued, "Even so God reminded Abram of His promise to him. When Abram was ninety-nine years old, the Lord appeared to him and said, 'I am God Almighty; walk before me and be blameless and I will establish my covenant between me and you and I will multiply you exceedingly.' Abram fell on his face in the presence of the Lord and God said to him, 'Behold My covenant is with you, and you shall be the father of many nations. No longer shall your name be Abram, but your name shall be Abraham; for I will make you the father of many nations. And I will make you fruitful, and I will make nations of you, and kings shall come forth from you. And I will establish My covenant between Me and you and your descendants after you throughout their generations for an everlasting covenant, to be God to you and to your descendants after you.And I will give to you and your descendants after you, the land of your sojourning's, all the land of Canaan, for an everlasting possession; and I will be their God.'"

Eliezer stopped to fill his wine cup and continued, "As a sign of this covenant, Abraham, his son Ishmael and all of the men of his house were circumcised. Every male born of Abraham and his descendants to this day is circumcised according to this covenant. After Abraham was circumcised, God said to him, "As for Sarai your wife, she shall no longer be called Sarai, but Sarah shall be her name. And I will bless her, and indeed I will give you a son by her, and she shall be called a mother of nations; kings of people shall come from her."

"God told Abraham that Sarah would bear Abraham a son and his name would be Isaac and God would establish his covenant with Isaac for an everlasting covenant for his descendants after him. God did not forget Ishmael but blessed him and made him the father of princes and a great nation."

Eliezer paused and drank some of the fine wine from his cup. A light night breeze had settled in over the garden. The cloth shades over the pavilion lifted and fell gently with a soft ruffling sound. The fountain water sang quietly in the shadows as the flames of garden torches danced along playfully. No one dared disturb the serenity of a special evening.

"God sees time differently than you or I." Eliezer continued, "He is patient to know our heart has learned to trust Him. Abraham and Sarah heard the promises of God for many years before they were fulfilled. It took them many years of obedience and waiting to grow the trust in God He desired for them. But, all of this came to pass just as God promised. God shielded Abraham and blessed him with great wealth and honor. God delivered kings into the hands of Abraham. God spoke to Abraham and made His covenant with him. Abraham obeyed God and followed his voice for many decades. Abraham believed God and God credited him with righteousness"

Then raising his voice Eliezer said, "And still Abraham sinned! He sinned again against his marriage and against Sarah his wife; but worse, Abraham sinned against God by not trusting in Him and having little faith."

"It happened that Abraham traveled towards the Negev

following the destruction of Sodom and Gomorrah and settled in Gerar. Once again, Abraham said of Sarah his wife, "She is my sister," and Abimelech, King of Gerar sent and took Sarah. God came to Abimelech in a dream of the night and said to him, "Behold you are a dead man because of the woman you have taken for she is a married woman." Again, God restored Sarah to Abraham and brought more wealth and riches upon him. This time Abraham learned the lesson. We know this because God tested him."

Rebekah said, "The patriarch Shem told me that God is patient and I must be patient and persevere. If father Abraham repeated the same grievous sin even after all of God's promises, who can obey? Is anyone strong enough to obey God? Or to trust Him totally? I think God is patient with us to learn to trust Him. And He will test us only when we are prepared."

Keshet answered, "God has given you wisdom, mistress Rebekah. God knows we are but dust. Even our ability to trust God is a gift that He gives, for truly no one has the strength to overcome sin. That is why we sacrifice to Him. That is why we must love Him, for He loves us and does for us what we cannot do for ourselves."

Abiel added, "In the days ahead Eliezer will share with you the final test of Abraham. And I will share with you Isaac's role in this test. It has shaped his heart and his mind."

"Mistress," Deborah said, "It is late, this has been a most eventful day. There is so much to consider in what we have learned. But truly, you must rest for the journey."

"Yes," Rebekah offered. "I am tired. I think I have heard enough today. Thank you, Keshet; thanks to all of you for sharing your love and your wisdom."

Abaigael spoke, "Mistress Rebekah, hear this word. 'Your marriage to Isaac will be tried, but Isaac's love for you will not fail and your love for Isaac will bring him strength.'"

Chapter Seven

The north and the south, You have created them; Tabor and Hermon joyously praise Your name.

Psalm 89: 12

When Rebekah and Deborah finished their breakfasts, their belongings had already been packed on the camels. Leaving the tranquility of the garden with its singing birds and trickling fountain they entered the noisy bustling outer compound with snorting camels and busy servants. Deborah noticed that another camel had been added to their caravan to accommodate their purchases in the market. Keshet, Jared, Abaigael, and Obed were waiting. Obed was giving Abiel a bear hug and Abiel could be heard saying, "Yes, uncle, I will be careful for mother's sake."

Jared gave his son a hug and said, "Go with God and with my blessing."

Abiel replied, "I will visit again, as soon as I can."

Abaigael gave her son a warm hug, then kissed his cheeks, his forehead and cheeks again and said, "Only God can love you more than me, my son. You are my joy; serve your master Isaac well just as you serve our God. Walk with God, my son, never stray from Him. Now go in love before I start to cry."

Tears streamed down Abaigael's face; she rubbed them away with both hands and smiled the smile only a mother can bestow her child.

Keshet was first to notice the young women. "Mistress Rebekah and miss Deborah honored guests; I hope your visit was pleasant. The Most High God keep you in his hand and deliver you safely to master Isaac and father Abraham. Please carry my warm greetings to both of them."

Abaigael took Rebekah's arms and then hugged her saying, "God has chosen a strong woman of beauty and grace as a mother of nations. May He strengthen your heart and your mind even more as wife to Isaac, heir of God's promise."

To Deborah, she said, "I treasure our time together, I know your heart to serve. Teach love in all your service, it is your gift. Now one last hug!"

The small caravan made its way through the back streets of Damascus and out the gate. The skies began to fill with clouds and the air grew moist. They joined the caravan road south, each refreshed and in good spirits. Rebekah had regained the hope and excitement she had when they left Haran but was now buoyed by the fondness she had developed for Abiel and Eliezer. She more than trusted and respected them, she liked them and saw them as friends and allies. She laughed as she remembered only a few days earlier thinking there was not half a smile between them.

Eliezer rode beside Rebekah and said. "Mistress Rebekah, do not be alarmed but I expect some weather later today. You will witness one of the storms that keep the fields of Damascus green. We will make an early camp if need be."

As they traveled south, the skies continued to darken. The tops of the mountains to the right were shrouded in cloud. Suddenly, a cloudburst into white light and a thunderclap reverberated overhead. More lightning appeared, piercing the gray cloud cover as again and again the thunder violently sounded its displeasure. Then the rain came, cold and heavy, forcing all to squeeze under the protection of their robes. The camels continued their methodical pace, splashing through the mud and puddles, unconcerned with the rain, the lightning, and the thunder.

The lightning moved along its eastbound track, the thunder lowered its voice and followed. The rain lessened and the cloud cover rose. Patches of blue sky appeared once again. The mountains to the right seemed to grow smaller, and then, ahead of them appeared a majestic mountain, its three peaks covered in snow, aglow in a shaft of afternoon sunlight. Mount Hermon, the great and high mountain cluster that anchored the long range they had been traveling alongside since Carchemish, came clearly into view.Beyond Mount Hermon lie a gap which opened a way across the mountain range and a road to Hazor.

They continued their journey and Mount Hermon grew larger, yet still appeared far-off. Two hours before sunset, Eliezer chose a campsite for the night. The tents were erected and fires lit with drying lines rigged for the wet robes and clothes. Their damp clothes changed, a warming fire took away the chill that had gripped them since the storm. Bread and the hot stew was the favored dish as Rebekah and Deborah settled next to Eliezer.

Eliezer spoke, "We should reach the end of Mount Hermon tomorrow afternoon and turn east towards Hazor and enter Canaan. Then we will begin a slow ascent before descending into the Jordan river valley. We will follow the river to Lake Merom and to the city of Hazor and will pass above the Sea of Chinnereth, a beautiful lake in a deep valley surrounded by mountains; indeed, Mount Hermon fills the lake and the lake waters all of Canaan with the Jordan River."

"And this is of the land promised to Abraham and Isaac?" Rebekah asked.

"Canaan is indeed promised to father Abraham and Isaac, but the promise is even greater, for it includes all of the lands from the river of Egypt to the Euphrates river. Abraham has come from the Euphrates and for many years he has traversed Canaan to learn of it and know his inheritance."

"You sound as if you love the land as much as Abraham and Isaac," Deborah added.

"I do love this land, and somehow feel God's promise to Abraham extends to me. Not that I am his heir, like Isaac, but that I, or we are being blessed through Abraham. It is a joyful thing to be a servant in God's plan."

Rebekah said, "Eliezer," and then paused. "Eliezer, twice I have been told that father Abraham was severely tested, and Isaac lives in the knowledge of this testing, tell me how Abraham was tested."

Eliezer nodded and said, "Yes, you should hear this story, it will help you understand how Abraham has become the man you will meet, and how Isaac understands his calling. It happened after Hagar and Ishmael were sent off. Abraham was living near Gerar, a city ruled by King Abimelech, a Philistine with whom Abraham had made a covenant. God spoke to Abraham and said, 'Take your son, your only son, Isaac, whom you love and go to the land of Moriah; and there offer him as a burnt offering on a mountain of which I will tell you.' So, Abraham saddled his donkey and took two of his young men with him and Isaac his son. He split wood for the burnt offering and went to the place God told him."

Rebekah could not stay silent, "Did God really expect Abraham to sacrifice Isaac? He can't be that cruel!"

Eliezer did not answer her; he continued the story, "On the third day, Abraham looked up and saw the place from a distance. Abraham told his young men, 'Stay here with the donkey, and I and the boy will go up the mountain; we will worship and return to you.' Abraham took the wood for the burnt offering and gave it to Isaac to carry. He carried the fire and the knife. And the two walked off together. Isaac asked his father, 'My father,' and Abraham answered 'I'm here.' And Isaac said, 'I see the fire and the wood, but where is the lamb for the burnt offering?' Abraham answered, 'God, will provide for Himself the lamb for the burnt offering, my son.' So, the two of them walked on together. Then they came to the place of which God had told him, and Abraham built the altar, and arranged the firewood, and bound his son Isaac, and laid him on the altar on top of the wood."

Turning and looking directly into Rebekah's eyes he said, "And Abraham stretched out his hand and took the knife to slay his son."

He paused again, still looking intently at Rebekah, then said "But the angel of the Lord called to him from heaven and said, 'Abraham! Abraham!' and he said 'I am here.' And the angel of the Lord said, 'Do not stretch out your hand against the boy, and do nothing to him; for I know that you fear God since you have not withheld your son, your only son, from Me.' Then Abraham looked up and saw a ram caught by the horns in a thicket, and Abraham took the ram and offered it up for a burnt offering in place of his son." Abraham called the place, 'The Lord will provide,' as it is said to this day, 'In the mount of the Lord it will be provided.'"

Rebekah was about to speak, but Eliezer said, "There is more. Then the angel of the Lord spoke to Abraham a second time from heaven and said, 'By Myself I have sworn declares the LORD, because you have done this thing, and you have not withheld your son, your only son, indeed I will greatly bless you, and I will greatly multiply your seed as the stars of the heavens, and the sand on the seashore; and your seed shall possess the gate of their enemies. And in your seed, all the nations of the earth shall be blessed because you have obeyed my voice.'"

Rebekah finally spoke, "Indeed a hard test for father Abraham, and a hard lesson for Isaac."

Eliezer smiled and said, "God knew Abraham was prepared for this test. He knew Abraham would pass the test and it would seal his faith forever."

"Why do you say that?" Rebekah asked.

"Remember how Abraham answered Isaac, "God will

Himself provide the lamb for the burnt offering. Abraham trusted God! And if Abraham did sacrifice Isaac, his son, his son of the promise, Abraham trusted God to raise him from the dead! Whatever was to happen, Abraham trusted God. God tested Abraham but not beyond his ability. God knew Abraham's heart and Abraham knows he can trust God always. Because God loved Abraham and fulfilled His promise, Abraham loves God and obeys Him in love."

Deborah spoke, "And this lesson now lives in the heart of Isaac as well. Isaac knows he can trust God. Does he love God as his father Abraham?"

Abiel answered, "My master loves God and trusts him, but that does not mean he will not face trials of his own. Abraham's life has instructed Master Isaac in his faith, and he knows that trials and sufferings bring about perseverance; and perseverance, proven character; and proven character, hope; and hope does not disappoint because the love of the Most High God has been poured out on him."

Deborah asked. "Does God, then, test all who follow Him?"

Abiel answered, "What does God require of us, but to love Him with all of our heart and all of our soul and to love all whom he loves? Is not love always tested? Love that cannot stand a test is no love at all. But God in His love for us is merciful and gracious not to test beyond our ability. The tests of God build us up in strength and assurance. It is proof to us that our faith and our love is real. God loves us, He can do no other."

Rebekah said softly, "I am reminded of the words the patriarch Shem said to me, 'Your strength will be tried. Trust Him and persevere.' I must remember this lesson. Please, Deborah, help me remember."

"Mistress, you are surrounded by those who love you, and none more than God Himself. You will persevere and you will be all the stronger wife and blessing to Master Isaac." Deborah replied.

Then looking up at the clear, star-filled sky above, Deborah said, "It grows cold, would you return to the tent now?"

Rebekah replied softly, her eyes staring into the fire, "No, I will stay here for yet awhile."

"Then I shall bring you a warm cloak," said Deborah as she got up and went back to the tent.

Rebekah sat before the fire, listening to the snapping and crackles of the burning wood and asked softly, "Eliezer, did Abraham and Sarah have a good marriage, one of love? Did they walk as one as God intended for Adam and Eve in the garden?"

Eliezer poked at the fire with a stick, "Abraham and Sarah did not live in the garden. No one has since Adam and Eve before they sinned. Father Abraham would freely say he sinned greatly against Sarah. And Sarah would say she sinned in sending Hagar to Abraham when she grew impatient with God's promise. Yes, they sinned, like all of us. But did they love each other? Oh yes; they loved and walked as one. They each sinned, they were each forgiven by God and blessed by God because they trusted Him and obeyed. God in His patience waited for their trust."

Rebekah sat silently still gazing into the fire and then said, "I am tired, I think I will go to my tent after all. Good night Eliezer and you too Abiel."

The next day, the sun had already moved to the western sky before the small caravan rounded the bottom of Mount Hermon. The caravan road forked and they traveled the road to the right, the road through Canaan. Just as Eliezer had said, they began a slow ascent in a rocky terrain. Mount Hermon loomed above them like a giant sentinel; a high ridge could be seen ahead in the distance. Once they crested the low ridge, they could see a green valley below them with a river running along the base of the next ridge, much higher than the ridge they just crossed. Here the road forked again, straight ahead, down a steep descent, was the city of Laish, built at the falls which form the headwaters of the Jordan River, where the valley abuts the great mountain. Eliezer took the fork to the left and began a steady descent to the southwest.

After an hour or so a lake came into view, the river running into it. And then a larger lake farther south could be seen, glimmering in the late afternoon sun. With both lakes forming a beautiful panorama, Eliezer called the journey to a halt and set camp for the night in small meadow within the thick forest.

When Rebekah and Deborah left their tent for the evening meal, they saw Abiel standing alone watching the sunset. Rebekah stood beside him and said, "The sunsets in the mountains are so beautiful."

Abiel said, "Ah, yes, the sunset. No, I was looking at Hazor, there beyond the first lake a bit farther south on the other side. It is the city of my parents. My mother's family still lives there. We will pass the city tomorrow on our way farther south."

"We will not stop there?" Rebekah asked.

"No reason to. In fact, I have never been in the city. I was just thinking how pleasant Hazor looks from here, standing on its rocky tell, overlooking Lake Merom, you would never know the kind of place it really is," Abiel said not turning from his view.

"What kind of place is it? Rebekah asked.

Abiel said, "Unrepentant."

"Unrepentant? Rebekah asked.

Still looking at Hazor, Abiel said, "Hazor is a place that says it is wrong for one man to take another man's wife and it wrong for a woman to be unfaithful to her husband but in their practice of religion they perform the must detestable, debauched things. It is a city that worships Baal and Asherah, two gods of the Canaanites.

"It is a city where temple prostitutes, both women and boys, are available to anyone and the pleasure is called worship, not sin. It is a city where religious festivals encourage everyone to engage in any sexual pleasure with any partner and call it worship and not fornication or adultery. It is a detestable city where the priests of Baal and the temple prostitutes forever seek new paths to sexual pleasure.

"They say these acts and those of the people arouse the gods to their own sexual acts and brings fertility to the land. But in their hearts, they know it is a lie, it is merely a license to their own debauched, sex-crazed lifestyle that they believe must never be denied them. Who can abide such a people?"

Deborah asked, "Your mother, Abaigael, prophesied against the city, didn't she?"

Abiel looked down for a moment, and then turned to Deborah and said, "Mother confronted the priests of Baal with a word from the Lord at a festival. Father had to save her from the crowd who demanded she be given to the priests for the detestable, sex-crazed, worship practices. That night they left Hazor for Damascus. None of us have ever entered the city again."

"And they remain unrepentant," Rebekah added.

"She prophesied that Hazor will be destroyed and that all who live in the city will die by the sword; but God is merciful and will spare any who return to the Most High God and follow Him," Abiel replied.

Then he said, "That was forty years ago and the city still stands. The people still sin."

Deborah said, "God is patient. He loves even the people of Hazor and wishes they repent. But God is righteous and sin that has not been atoned for must be punished. What about you Abiel, do you want them punished for what they did to your mother or do you want them to repent and live?"

A half smile crossed Abiel's face and he said, "I will have my dinner."

After Abiel walked off, Rebekah turned to Deborah and said, "Remember, nice."

The young women followed Abiel to the cooking tent, filled their bowls with goat cooked with plums and raisins, bread, and ripe olives in oil and sat on the rugs laid out for them.

Eliezer was speaking to Abiel, something about the trained men.

When the young women sat, Eliezer said, "A beautiful valley. Tomorrow you will see not only the lake but its other guardian, Mount Tabor, beyond. It is a most beautiful mount, standing alone, sheltering the lake from the western mountains and showing the way into the heart of Canaan."

Rebekah finished her meal, got up and said, "I think I will have a cooked cake. Do you think they could find some nuts and honey to drizzle on it, like the ones in Damascus?"

Eliezer smiled, stood up and said, "Come we shall have our cakes in the style of Damascus!"

As they walked to the food, Deborah turned to Abiel and softly said, "I know what it is like to flee for your life. I remember the fear, though it was many years ago and I was a little child; I still remember the fear.

"But I also remember my father. You see, when the Amorite soldiers took our village, the men, including my father watched them from the hills. When all but one left to bring the rest of their company, Papa was watching him.

"When he lost sight of the soldier, he tried to find another vantage point. But the soldier found him instead. Papa would not tell the soldier where we were hidden and the soldier lowered his spear and was about to run him through, when Dov, our village elder, slew him from behind.

"Once all the soldiers had left our village after taking our flock and all of our crops, filling our well and destroying our groves, and we were forced to leave our village, after all of the fear, pain, and destruction, my father asked Dov, 'Did God love the Amorite?' He worried for a man for whom God's patience had passed.

"When my brother was taken, after much mourning my papa and mama had the same questions for the Assyrian soldiers who slew him."

Abiel said, "I did not know you had a brother? And he was slain? Such pain your family has suffered. And yet you speak of God's love and His patience."

Their conversation was interrupted by the arrival of five men on donkeys.

Chapter Eight

Deliver me, O Lord, from evil men; preserve me from violent men.

Psalm 140: 1

A band of five men mounted on donkeys stayed just out of the light of the campfire and torches. One slowly rode his donkey forward and loudly called out, "No need for alarm, friends we will merely take what we have come for and be on our way. You will be free to travel on."

Eliezer walked forward, "Come before me and we shall talk."

The man rode forward and into the light. He wore the hat and robes of a priest but also a fine, ornate, bronze sword strapped to his side. His donkey was covered in a rich blanket embroidered in gold with the head of a bull.

Eliezer said, "What is it that a priest of Baal would take from us?"

The priest said, "A young woman travels with you. A fine young woman with hair as red as the fire and green eyes that can haunt a man's soul. She travels with her maid, a bit old perhaps, but a comely face. They will come with us to the great temple of Baal in Hazor. We have the need for such women and our people will pay a great price for them as temple prostitutes."

Eliezer spoke, "You would abduct two young virgins into prostitution? May it never be! You will return to Hazor while you have legs to walk and arms to guide your mount."

The priest said, "Consider your words, I will call my men and they will put all of you to the sword and we will take the virgins all the same. A virgin is of even higher value."

"Call to your men," Eliezer replied.

Turning his head to the side, the priest shouted, "Take them!"

The night was silent. Nothing moved. No one spoke.

Again, he yelled, "Take them. Take them now!"

Eliezer said, "Your men are silent before you, as silent as your mute stone idol. Perhaps they know more than you. Look behind you, priest."

Turning around the priest of Baal saw a man behind him with a spear pointed at his back. Then he saw his four men, each being held from behind with a knife to his throat.

The priest turned back to Eliezer, "Did I say take them, I meant to say we will take them for a price. I can bargain. Fifty pieces of silver for the maid and ten gold coins for the red-haired virgin. More than fair. I will pay and leave you this night."

"The young woman is betrothed to my master's son and the maid is her nurse. They travel under my protection," Eliezer said.

"You want more, I can pay more. I can make you a rich man, your master will never know. I can make you so rich you will never need to return to your master," the priest replied.

"Priest," Eliezer replied, "You appear to be in no position to bargain. Give me your oath that you will return now to Hazor and interfere with us no longer, and I shall permit you to live."

The priest looked about and then said, "If you change your

mind, the offer stands, just send them to me in Hazor." Then, to his men, he said, "We go now."

The man behind him stepped back half a pace, his spear still at the ready. The trained men lowered the knives from the throats of the priest's men and allowed them to mount their donkeys. They could be heard riding off into the darkness.

Abiel walked up to Eliezer and asked, "Can we trust them?"

Eliezer replied, "No."

Eliezer than said, "Rebekah and Deborah listen. Go back to your tent with a torch. The torch outside your tent will be extinguished, once this happens, extinguish your torch and make your way in the darkness, fully covered in a dark robe, to the tent of Abiel. It too will be dark. You will not leave Abiel's tent until I call for you in the morning. Do you understand? You will be safe in Abiel's tent."

Rebekah said, "I understand. Give me your knife."

Seeing the look on Abiel's face she said, "You forget I am a shepherdess, not a princess."

Eliezer gave Rebekah his knife and said, "Abiel, you and Jachin, a trained man, experienced with weapons and warfare, will wait in Rebekah's tent. You should expect an unwelcome visitor."

Abiel and Jachin sat back to back in the middle of the tent. Jachin faced the closed curtain of the tent door and Abiel faced the back. Both held a fine bronze sword in one hand and a spear in the other. Each had a knife sheathed to his side. Two trained men patrolled silently outside and the other servants, each armed, waited in a nearby tent. Eliezer slept across the door outside of the Abiel's tent, another servant across the back.

The time passed slowly, only the normal sounds of the night could be heard, the occasional screech of an owl and the distant growl of a great cat. It came about the time the mind begins to play its tricks, that time of the waiting when the sound of your own breath and the beating of your heart pounds in your ears; your mind wants to wander, just to catch itself and question if it hears something, or imagines it hears something. It came when the overextended senses fused with imagination, a slow movement on the curtain and the faint sound of cloth being cut; but only briefly and then the instant realization that the curtain was thrown open, and the rear of the tent being sliced up to reveal the black silhouettes of three men rushing into the tent.

Abiel and Jachin leveled their spears at the black figures rushing in. Screams could be heard as two of the intruders were impaled. The third figure continued towards Abiel, slashing with a sword. Abiel parried the first slash but was off balance with the weight of the dying man on the end of his spear. Before he could let go another slash caught him across his shoulder and chest, he immediately followed with a thrust and slash which put the third man down. A light appeared, a torch in the hands of Eliezer with his trained men, a yell could be heard from outside the camp and the sounds of a man running. The torch revealed the two men run through by the spears were in the throes of death; the intruder with the sword lay wide-eyed on the ground, blood spurting from his chest and running from his mouth.

Eliezer called out, "Abiel is hurt, quickly, the herbs, aloe, and bandages. He must be bound tightly to stem the loss of blood."

Bringing the torch near and lifting the bloody cloak from the wound he said, "Your wound does not appear deep. We will stop the bleeding and dress your wound. God willing you should recover."

Rebekah and Deborah appeared standing behind Eliezer. Deborah spoke first, "Abiel, you're hurt! No! No! You must not die!"

Rebekah tore strips from her robe and immediately set about wrapping him tightly. "The herbs and poultice can wait, first we must quench the bleeding. Eliezer is right. If we can stop the bleeding he should recover."

Rebekah glanced at the three other men bleeding in the tent, "What about them?" She asked, "Can they be saved?"

Eliezer was kneeling over the man with the sword wound, both hands over the wound to stop the blood. He answered, "Those two are dead, this man may survive. Bandages!"

Jachin picked up Abiel's sword from beside the dying man. Deborah immediately began to tear her robe and went to work wrapping the wounded intruder while Jachin removed the spears from the two dead and dragged the bodies from the tent. Deborah did not notice her patient stop breathing or his blood stop flowing. Eliezer put his hand on her shoulder and said, "He is gone. Take Rebekah with you and clean yourselves. You have done all that you could."

Deborah looked down at her bloodied hands and arms. She stared at them as if they were foreign objects. Then holding her arms out in front of her, she nudged Rebekah with an elbow and said, "Come, let's wash. Abiel is safe, you have done well."

Abiel said softly, "Thank you mistress Rebekah, praise God you are safe! And you too Deborah. God's blessing be upon you."

With the danger over, Rebekah just stared at Abiel, and then her bloody hands and without saying a word followed Deborah outside the tent.

Abiel turned to Eliezer and said, "It all happened so fast. I did not think, even after his sword cut me; I did not think; I watched as if I were a bystander to the fight. But now, now, I feel the pain."

Eliezer said, "Can you sit astride your camel? We must move soon."

"I can ride," Abiel replied.

"Rest now until all is prepared. I shall see to it a support is made for your saddle."

When Eliezer stepped out of the tent, a servant was waiting for him, "One man escaped. We chased but lost him in the woods. But he must travel on foot for we have captured their donkeys."

Eliezer commanded, "We break camp and go on. No cook fire; bread, cheese, raisins cakes and fig cakes for everyone. Load quickly, we have little time. See to a back support for Abiel's camel, he will be bound to his saddle. Roll the dead in their robes and blankets, bind them to the backs of their donkeys."

Looking at the clear night sky, he added, "We have but one or two hours until daylight. I want to pass Hazor before they have much time to prepare to meet us."

In less than an hour the small caravan, now longer by four donkeys, carefully made its way down the road. Abiel joined Eliezer and Jachin at the front. Eliezer was giving orders to Jachin for the deployment of his trained men and servants; he finished saying, "Have everything in order, as soon as the light is sufficient I will put the camels to a fast pace."

Abiel said, "Eliezer, perhaps one more deception may help us. We send Jachin and two trained men dressed in the robes of Rebekah and Deborah ahead. They ford the river towards Hazor and we continue south on this side of the river putting time and distance between us."

Eliezer replied, "Your plan puts Jachin and his men at risk, and the army of Hazor would surely pursue us. The Most High God has protected us this far. He will see his chosen mother of nations safely to Isaac. Trust God, Abiel, no more deceptions; we will expose the evil of Hazor's priest of Baal to the sunlight, that all may see God's salvation of His people."

Abiel said, "Your plan then is to..."

"My plan is to move quickly and trust in the Lord."

At dawn, Eliezer motioned for his camel to a faster gait, almost like the cantor of a horse. The caravan was now moving faster than a man could jog and they were recovering the distance between them and the escaped attacker. Three hours later, the road and ford leading to Hazor at the bottom of Lake Merom, could be clearly seen. Barely half an hour's ride ahead was a lone man running slowly, near exhaustion towards the city gate. Within minutes of entering the city, trumpets could be heard calling the guards to arms. They continued down to the river ford and watched armed men forming just outside of the city gate.

As Eliezer led the caravan across the Jordan river towards Tel Hazor, the rocky mount on which the city stood, a captain appeared and brought some semblance of order to the armed men. They had just formed a battle line when the small caravan finished crossing the river. As Eliezer began to lead the caravan down the road past Hazor, the King of Hazor with the Chief Priest of Baal beside him, rode forward on saddled donkeys.

Eliezer stopped the caravan and called for the donkeys bearing the dead attackers to be brought forward. Eliezer called out, "King of Hazor, I send you the bodies of three men who attacked our caravan in the night. Three of four men and a priest of Baal who tried to catch us unaware earlier in the night, seeking my master's mistress and her nurse as temple prostitutes of your detestable religion. When their trap failed the priest attempted to bribe me and purchase them. I sent him on his way having heard his oath to leave us in peace. I ask you King, is this not treachery in your city? Is not Hazor a trading city? Does not the King of Hazor protect the caravan and show hospitality to the traveler. Now, O King, show justice and punish your priest."

The Chief Priest responded, "Do not listen to his lies my great king. It was this very man who sent his messenger ahead saying he would sell two virgins to the temple of Baal if we would testify that thieves and robbers stole them by night. My priest agreed to buy the women at a fair price but would not be party to his lies. It was then that their trained men fell upon my humble priest and his servants, and stole their money. Only my priest was able to make his escape. I demand the young women, bought and paid for by the temple be delivered to me and I demand justice for our slain brothers!"

Eliezer said, "I will deliver the woman chosen by the Most

High God, safely to my lord Isaac, her betrothed, son of my master, father Abraham the Hebrew. You, O king, remember how Abraham defeated the four kings who took his nephew prisoner when they sacked Sodom and Gomorrah. He defeated them near Laish, not far from this city and pursued them as they fled beyond Damascus. If Abraham pursued the four kings, and God gave him a great victory, how much more will Abraham, a man who negotiates with kings, a man who has made a covenant with Abimelech, King of Gerar, pursue and put to the sword the man who abducts the betrothed wife of his only son, his son by the promise of God? Will not the Most High God give him an even greater victory?"

The chief priest spoke," Abraham will not pursue if no one lives to tell him. The girl is from far off, and he will never think to look among the temple prostitutes for his daughter-in-law. Your people will find new pleasure and thank you for your gift."

Abiel struggled to sit straight and called out, "Men of Hazor, you have been cursed by the Most High God. Has not a prophet of the Most High God, a Canaanite and a daughter of your city prophesied that Hazor will be destroyed and every man woman and child in the city will be put to the sword. But God is merciful and will spare anyone who departs from the detestable practices of your city and follows the Most High God. God has been patient, He has waited for you to repent. How much longer will he bear your evil deeds? Repent and return to El'Elyon the only true God."

The king's face turned red in anger, he turned to his captain behind him and said; "Captain give the order to... "

Before he could finish his sentence, the ground under him began to move, his donkey stumbled and the king fell to the ground. The ground continued to shake and he watched in horror as the tower and the city gate began to crumble. The carved likeness, the Bull of Baal and the likeness of Asherah holding her crossed poles, crashed to the ground burying the unfortunate guards at their post.

Eliezer shouted, "The Most High has spoken!" He signaled for Jachin to leave the dead bodies and four donkeys, and the small caravan resumed its journey south.

Chapter Nine

The LORD is my strength and my shield; in Him my heart trusts, and I am helped; my heart exults, and with my song, I give thanks to Him.

Psalm 28:7

They made their way south along the western side of the Jordan River. The river bank was lined by green fields and meadows. Rebekah asked, "What are all these poles planted along the river bank? I noticed many more along Lake Merom?"

Eliezer answered, "Asherah poles. They are 'eyes' for the voyeuristic goddess Asherah to watch the ritualistic sex of her worshippers. Canaanites are obsessed with sex. Abiel is right to say that sex as worship is a delusion. He believes it is the people who desire no restriction in their insatiable desires. I believe people become what they worship. If you worship a god of sexual lust and incest you become addicts to the same depraved practices. And in the end the desires of the flesh are never fulfilled; man can only find fulfillment in loving God."

Rebekah replied, "Now I understand why Nahor and my father would not allow foreigners and their gods to abide with us. Father asked Zimri-Ruel to be a priest to us and sacrifice to the Most High God, but there are still some who keep household idols. Tell me Eliezer, are all the cities of Canaan as bad as Hazor?"

"Sodom and Gomorrah were worse. God destroyed them but all worship the detestable gods of Canaan. That is why father Abraham does not dwell in the cities of Canaan but makes his camps far away from the city walls. And it is why he would not allow Isaac to take a wife from among the Canaanites. It falls to Abiel and me to enter the markets to trade. We are familiar with their detestable ways but are treated fairly in the market. Even in Canaan, trust rules in the market. Even so, some cities are less debauched, and still provide hospitality and protection for the sojourner, the foreigner and the for followers of El'Elyon."

Rebekah rode in silence a while and then asked, "Sarah was Abraham's half-sister, what about his other wives? Were they Canaanite?"

Eliezer replied, "Hagar was Sarah's maid, she was Egyptian, and honored Sarah and Abraham by not worshipping the gods of Egypt. As I told you, God heard the cries of Hagar and blessed her. Likewise, Keturah is a Hittite; she too honors and obeys Abraham and worships only the Most High God."

Rebekah asked, "If Canaan is the inheritance of father Abraham and Isaac, what will become of the Canaanites in the land? It seems father Abraham will have no relations with them."

Eliezer looked at Rebekah and said, "God will provide the inheritance as He wills. Have you not heard the prophecies of Abaigael?"

Jachin rode up alongside Eliezer and reported, "The king has returned to the city. He has put his soldiers to work clearing the rubble of the gate. No one follows us."

The road took a small bend and rose over a bluff. At the crest, the Sea of Chinnereth, or Galilee, came into view. It was a beautiful lake, gleaming in the early afternoon sun, with waves shimmering in the fresh breeze that snaked its way between the mountains. It was the most beautiful place Rebekah and Deborah had ever seen. Barren, white, rocky, mountains pocketed with forests of deep green ringed the lake. They descended to fields of golden grain, soft green pastures, and vineyards which fell to shining silver sparkles on the dark blue water. Boats could be seen with men struggling to haul nets from the choppy lake. The view made no impression on the camels which kept their steady pace on the still descending caravan road.

The road turned to the west skirting the city of Chinnereth which gave the lake its name. They traveled along the north shore of the lake until they rounded the western shore and again turned south. They stopped between the lake shore and the city of Hamath and set camp. Eliezer purchased a basket of fresh fish from fisherman returning to Hammath with their catch. Once he delivered the fish to the cook he asked Deborah to help him with Abiel.

A poultice was made of moss, aloe, wine, and spices to apply to Abiel's wound. Deborah applied the poultice and wrapped Abiel's chest in clean linen bandages. Abiel was clearly fatigued and in pain from the day's journey. Deborah tenderly wiped his brow with a cool damp cloth and found the coolest water in the camp for him to drink. As she sat silently dabbing his forehead, he looked up at her and said, "All day I have been thinking about what your father said about the Amorite soldier. Until today, as you surmised, I was more interested in God's judgment on Hazor than His patience for their repentance. But three of them are dead at our hand, two men I have killed. But God did love them. Everything I know about God tells me He loved them. And now their opportunity to repent is gone. They face only God's judgment and His wrath. And it is at my hand. It is a very hard thing, indeed."

Deborah looked into Abiel's eyes, "It was God's will. His patience for them ran its course. Just as it did when the earthquake brought down the gate of Hazor. We each are accountable to Him only. As you said it was forty years ago that your mother, Abaigael, prophesied against the city and still God waits. Do not condemn yourself Abiel, you love God and you love men. It is not easy to love all whom God loves."

Returning to dabbing his forehead with the cool cloth she said, "Eliezer has bought a basket of fresh fish. Are you strong enough to eat some?"

Abiel smiled, "Eliezer never misses a chance to eat the fish of this lake. Yes, I know they will be very good."

The smell of the cooking fish drew Deborah from Abiel's side. While she prepared his plate, Rebekah, seated next to Eliezer asked, "Would Abiel enjoy some company tonight? We would not stay too long or interfere with his rest."

Deborah said, "I think he would enjoy the company of friends tonight. His spirit is as wounded as his body."

Abiel was happy for the company. Rebekah ventured, "What shall we discuss tonight, it has been a most eventful day. A day I have seen God's salvation, but you Abiel have paid a price."

Abiel was still too troubled to talk about the encounter with the priest of Hazor and his thugs; he offered, "Rebekah, you still have more to hear of father Abraham and your husband to be, Isaac. Perhaps Eliezer could be persuaded to speak of Sarah, beloved by husband and son?"

Eliezer smiled and began, "There are times in life you can bargain, and there are times you must pay the full asking price.I learned this truth, not in the marketplace of Damascus, rather I was taught this truth by my master whose wisdom came from patient obedience, and faith in the Most High God. Father Abraham, a man who loved to bargain, even to the point of bargaining with the Most High God, learned this truth after many years.He fulfilled it when his beloved wife Sarah died."

Rebekah asked, "Abraham bargained with God?"

Eliezer looked at her and said, "We all try to bargain with

God. It is a very foolish thing we do. But yes, Abraham tried to bargain with God when the stench of the sin of Sodom and Gomorrah rose before God's throne, God determined to destroy the cities and warned Abraham. Abraham tried to bargain with God to save the city of Sodom. To God, we are as little children and in His love, he patiently listens to our childish bargains and then acts as the wise and loving father. In the end, even Abraham's bargained number of righteous people living in Sodom was insufficient to save the city. But I was speaking of Abraham's understanding of this lesson when Sarah died."

Rebekah said, "Yes, please continue."

"Sarah died in Kiriath-Arba in Canaan. She was one hundred and twenty-seven years old. Abraham wept bitterly and mourned her death. He went to the sons of Heth, Philistines, and asked for a place to bury Sarah. The sons of Heth told Abraham, 'You are a prince among us; bury your dead in the choicest of our graves; none of us will refuse you his grave for burying your dead.' Abraham bowed before the sons of Heth, acknowledging their respect and said, 'If it is your wish that I bury my dead in your lands, ask Ephron son of Zohar for me, that he sell me the cave of Machpelah at the end of the field he owns; for the full price let him give it to me in your presence for a burial site.'"

"Now Ephron, the Hittite, was sitting at the gate of the city among the sons of Heth, and he answered Abraham, 'No my lord, I give you the field and I give you the cave that is in it. In the presence of the sons of Heth, my people, I give it to you; bury your dead.'"

"Abraham bowed and said, 'I will pay the price for the field, accept it from me and I will bury my dead'"

"But Ephron answered, 'My lord, listen to me; a piece of land worth four hundred shekels of silver, what is that between me and you? So, bury your dead.'"

"Abraham weighed out four hundred shekels of silver and he purchased Ephron's field which was in Machpelah which faced Mamre, the field and the cave that was in it and all the trees which were in the field, all of it was deeded over to Abraham for a possession and Abraham buried Sarah, his wife in the cave."

Rebekah said, "Love cannot be bought, but love requires we pay a dear price."

Eliezer smiled and said, "This was three years ago. Abraham mourned Sarah, yet he took Keturah as his wife. But Isaac also mourned Sarah without consolation. Isaac parted from Abraham and went into the Negev, to Beer-Lahai-Roi. Abraham knew Isaac should marry and find comfort in his wife so he sent me to your father's house. God is both our salvation and our comfort. Today you have seen His salvation. You often speak of a wife's calling to walk beside her husband as one, sharing his life. Truly your calling is one of blessing and comfort to your husband, but so, too, has Isaac been chosen to be one with you in the inheritance of the promise the Most High God first made to Abraham and Sarah. You must know that Isaac's heart is still heavy with grief and the weight of not knowing the trials that lie ahead and the burden of his calling."

Rebekah sat quietly, her head bowed down in thought, only her right index finger moved, curling her red hair on and off her finger just below her ear. Then slowing nodding her head up and down she said, "Yes, my husband must know that he need not face trials and carry his burdens alone, but will he let me help him?"

Abiel had been listening quietly, eating the tasty fish of the lake; he sat up straight with a small groan from the pain and said, "Has God not chosen you? Has He not this very day shown to you the power of His salvation? He has moved the earth and shaken the foundations of the gates of Hazor! Mistress, I know my master's heart—"

"Now it is mistress again, Abiel?" Rebekah interrupted.

"Yes," Abiel answered back, "And so it must always be so, but hear me mistress, if you open your heart to my master and affirm the desire of your heart to walk beside him as one, as Eve walked beside Adam in the garden, sharing every trial, bearing every burden together, he will welcome you as wife and companion and trust in your strength and hear your words. Is this not God's will? Does not God love you and Isaac? If you can trust in God's salvation can you not also trust in His love? Learn from father Abraham, there is no need to bargain or beg favor with God; you can know His love for you is that of a perfect father, who desires only good for you. Remember His love and you will behold His blessings. You are strong in spirit, become strong in faith. Let your strength strengthen my master Isaac."

Again, there was silence. Finally, Deborah spoke, "It is true no one should bear a heavy burden alone, and mistress, you and master Isaac are surrounded by helpers who serve you with love."

"Tell me, Eliezer, how many more days?" Rebekah asked and then said without waiting for an answer, "How did the priest of Baal come to know of me?"

Eliezer said, "We are not more than a week's travel from the Oaks of Mamre. As for the priest; the priests of Baal constantly prowl about to buy or capture young women to prostitute for their temple. Do you think fathers bring them their daughters? No, the priests have their thugs. They look for the young women, they watch the caravans, they sit and watch in the markets. They are paid to procure young women like you and Deborah. I would guess they have been following you since our walk through the market.

After leaving Hammath, Eliezer led the small caravan past Mount Tabor, a tall solitary mountain in the middle of a gap which opened the way from the lake to the coastal plain all the way to the Great Sea. The road to the west led to Megiddo and the heart of Canaan. But Eliezer continued south climbing a ridge along the Jordan, journeying past Dothan, Shechem, and Salem to the Oaks Mamre.

Chapter Ten

Now Isaac had come from going to Beer-lahai-roi; for he was living in the Negev.

Genesis 24:62

The Negev was a lonely place but for all of its desolation, it was still a place with its own beauty, a place where God could be heard. Isaac loved the Negev. He loved the isolation and the peace it afforded.

After the death of his mother and his father's marriage to Keturah, a young Hittite woman, Isaac bade leave from his father to explore the wilderness on his own. Abraham loved Isaac and could see his son was troubled, so he gave Isaac two donkeys and all that they could carry and his permission to wander the Negev.

Isaac took the donkeys and slowly walked south. When he came to Beersheba, the 'Well of the Oath,' named by his father for the oath Abraham made with King Abimelech of Gerar, he rested under the tamarisk tree planted there in commemoration.

The water of the well was sweet and he lingered, pondering the stories he heard. *How could father let Abimelech* believe Sarah was just a sister? How could he watch the wife he loved to be taken off to the king's harem? After all, God had done for father, how could he fail to trust. Or did he just believe God would save her? He did not hesitate to sacrifice me, convinced God would raise me up. But he was condemned for letting my mother be taken and father said it was a sin. Surely, he loved mother?

Fear. Fear must be a terrible thing. And mother complied! Did she act in love for my father or in fear as well? Then, after God's salvation, after all the gifts from Abimelech and the squabbles between the shepherds over wells, it was settled here with a covenant. A covenant of peace, but not friendship. Father would never befriend a man dwelling in Gerar, the city of Abimelech, or any city of idolatrous Canaan.

Before following the wadi south, Isaac filled all of his water bags; this was the gateway to the Negev and water would become far more precious than anything else he brought.

The rainy season was ending, but the risk of flooding in the wadi remained. The rocky hills were covered in wildflowers just unfolding their blooms. These flowers joyfully lived for their short season of beauty and would soon die in the summer heat only to be born again with the winter rain.

Two days later Isaac came upon Beer-lahai-roi, 'Well of the Living One Who Sees Me.' The very well where God heard the cries of Hagar and told her to return to Sarah and submit to her authority.

Isaac's mind was spinning as he remembered the story, *The Angel of the Lord promised she would bear a son and name him Ishmael, God hears, for He has heard her affliction. Ishmael would be a wild donkey of a man and live east of his brothers. God spoke to Hagar here. God spoke to mother, telling her I would be born. He spoke to father many times reminding him of the promise to make him a father of many nations.*

I have never heard from God. He doesn't speak to me. I am the one with questions. I am the one with doubts. I am told over and again the promise God made to Abraham will come through me. Why doesn't God answer me?

Isaac pitched his tent at Beer-lahai-roi. Isaac thought, *if God saw the needs of others at this well, perhaps God will see me and listen to the cries of my heart.*

For days Isaac looked into the stillness of the Negev. He wandered among the dry rocks, baking under the silent sun. He explored the crevices and caves not aware what he was looking for.

Sliding to the ground he lifted his tired sweating forehead, scanning the ridge facing him. The dry reddened cliffs seemed to scowl at him. Then in pain, he began to yell, "Are you there? Answer me El'Elyon! Speak to me Elohim! Answer me God of Abraham! Don't you hear me? I was told you know me and I am the son of Your promise? You speak to others, why don't you speak to me?"

Isaac lowered his eyes to the ground as the sounds of his voice echoed through the rock-rimmed wadi. Again there was silence, but then came a calm voice, "Who is it that scares my game away? Why can't you just draw water and go on? Leave this place in peace!"

Isaac looked up to see a brawny, hairy, dusty, bearded man in rough clothes lacking even a headscarf come walking towards him leading a donkey with an antelope slung across it's back. The man's steps could not be heard, only the plodding of the donkey. A bow and half a quiver of arrows were slung over his shoulder and the hilt of a knife in a leather sheath strapped to his side.

As he approached, the burly man said, "You come all the way here to yell at God? Trust me, friend, you can argue with God from your own tent."

Isaac stared at the man a few moments and answered, "Friend, I have not seen another person for days, and my heart is troubled, forgive me for disrupting your hunt."

The man walked close to Isaac, looking into his face and said, "I have meat for my table. It is not my hunt you disturb, but my tranquility. Tell me, why bring your troubles here?"

"I mourn my mother, and my father has already married again, a woman much younger than me! I have come to the Negev to find peace, but everywhere I travel I come across reminders of stories I have heard from my father; first at the well of Beersheba and now the well of Beer-lahai-roi. The stories tell of God speaking to the afflicted, bringing salvation and promises of blessings. I am told I am a son of God's promise, but God never speaks to me."

The man walked around Isaac looking at him as if he were an animal to be purchased. He then walked over to the donkey's and examined the packs. Returning to Isaac he said, "I was saved by the Most High God near this very spot. I was still a boy, nearly a man, traveling with my mother. Our food and water gone, my mother told me to rest under a bush while she went a short way off. Later she told me she prayed to God that she would not see me die. And then an Angel of God called to her and said, 'What is the matter with you, Hagar? Do not be afraid, God has heard the voice of the boy where he is. Return to him and hold him by the hand, for I will make a great nation of him.' Then God opened her eyes and she saw this well of water and went and filled the skin and brought me water to drink."

Isaac cocked his head, thought for a moment then looked wide-eyed at the man and said, "Ishmael, my brother, it is me, Isaac! How I have longed to find you!"

"Isaac?" Ishmael said quizzically, "But you are Abraham's heir, the son he loves, the son of the promise. When you were born I became nothing in his eyes and my mother was scorned by Sarah. Why do you now search me out?"

"Brother," Isaac began, "You have always been loved by our father. To this day he loves you and his heart longs for you. Our father has been sorely tested by God, and Sarah is buried. Father has changed, he no longer bargains with God, he no longer negotiates with kings. He lives humbly, one day at a time, trusting the Most High to direct his path."

Ishmael still pondering, said, "The day is getting short. Come with me."

Ishmael led Isaac and the donkeys a short way down the wadi and then turned into a gap in the rock walls. They followed a well-worn path which snaked its way through the mountain. Exiting on the other side they followed another wadi winding its way west towards the setting sun. Ishmael led them towards a crevice in the rock; this time he stopped to pick up a dead bush at the side of the trail.

"Go ahead," he said. And after they passed, he deftly removed their footprints. "My road sign to my sons," he said lightly. "When it is on the road they know I am out. To everyone else, it is just a dead shrub."

As they closed on the crevice Isaac could see they were entering a small gap, once inside Ishmael left the bush. Beyond the narrow entrance, the gap turned and snaked its way out of sight of the wadi road and opened into a wide canyon with a green tree-lined oasis at the far end beneath a small waterfall. A few sheep and many goats grazed the canyon floor and half a dozen goat hair tents were set up on a small grassy plateau above the pool of water at the base of the fall.

As they entered the camp, a statuesque woman in Egyptian dress met them. "Fresh game, and a friend to stay with us," Ishmael said as he led me to her.

The Egyptian woman clapped her hands and two servants quickly came out. "Make a roast from a hind quarter and hang the rest in the larder," she said and turning to Ishmael, "It will be prepared in two hours husband."

A servant took the donkeys to a pen and Ishmael led Isaac to a tent. "We can wash here. Don't worry about your clothes; I have something you can wear."

Both men washed with several pails of water from the pool. Ishmael gathered his wet, dark hair behind his head and combed his beard before dressing in fine Egyptian linen and a light robe. He gave similar garments to Isaac and soon, clean and refreshed, they appeared as two Egyptian noblemen dressed for the court of Pharaoh.

"My wife, Halima, "Gentle," is Egyptian and favors this dress, and who can argue it is not comfortable in the Negev? But I must hide my rough and dirty hunting clothes lest she be tempted to burn them! You see, brother, hunting is my one passion and good game on my table is a joy."

Isaac said, "I admire your bow, it is also of Egyptian design?"

"It may resemble an Egyptian bow, but it is far superior; it is Nubian. See, it is longer and the grip wider; it pulls harder. Notice also, that I use bronze arrowheads rather than the Egyptian copper.Even hardened copper is inferior. Without a good bow and the skill to use it, fresh game would be hard to come by in the Negev. The country is too open and too quiet for other hunting weapons."

Isaac said, "I see sheep and goats; surely you have enough food?"

Ishmael laughed, "Brother, I enjoy eating game! It is real food and requires skill and cunning to take. No, the sheep are for wool, the goats provide hair for tent making and milk for cheese, though my wife and her maids do prefer goat meat. Tonight, after you have sat at my table, tell me you can again go happily back to goat or lamb!"

Ishmael said, "Come, you must see my pool and fountain before the sun sets. I permit no man to approach the pool after dark. It is only for the beasts to enjoy after dark. They know they can drink of its water without the threat of any man."

Isaac was amazed at the clear water of the pool. Reeds and green grass grew along the shore, but the real beauty was the falling water that fed it.

"I cannot see the water at the top." Isaac offered, "It looks as if... "

Ishmael finished his thoughts, "As if it just appears to come from the mountain itself! Yes, the water does not come over the top, it spills from within the mountain. The river flows from within the mountain and sends us cool, clear water. It is a miracle of God!"

Isaac stared at the mountain astounded by what he saw.

Ishmael put an arm on his shoulder and said, "Come, taste my game and let us leave the oasis to our wild friends."

Isaac asked, "Do you ever hunt-"

Ishmael cut him off, "I will permit no hunting here. This is a sanctuary we share."

When they had returned to the tent, the table was set and dinner waiting. As they entered, two young men stood up. Ishmael said, "These are two of my sons, Mishma and Dumah. They are not yet married. I have four older sons who have established camps of their own in the Negev. And three more sons too young for my tent, and many daughters! God willing, more sons will come! Isaac, sit here in the place honor."

When the men had settled on the cushions around the table and poured wine, Ishmael's wife appeared with bowls of food and a handsome roast. Ishmael took a jewel-encrusted knife from his belt sheath, and sliced hearty portions of roast meat for Isaac, his sons and himself. He then filled his plate with a hummus of peas, olive oil, and garlic. As he cut and tasted of the roast antelope, he would scoop up his meat drippings and hummus with warm fresh bread.

Isaac and Ishmael's sons wasted no time in following Ishmael's lead. After his third or fourth mouthful, Ishmael said, pointing with his knife, "Truly good, is it not? But tomorrow, tomorrow we will have my favorite. Hard as it is to imagine anything tastier, tomorrow Halima shall prepare the game in a stew. Slow cooked, all day. My wife will prepare a meat that is tender beyond imagination! And the lentils, beans and onions and garlic, so many good vegetables that will slowly absorb all the goodness of this magnificent antelope! Sons, tell me, am I not speaking truly?"

Mishma replied, "It is just as you say father, tender and delicious!"

They finished their meal and sat back to enjoy another cup of wine. Ishmael said, "So brother, you come to the Negev and yell at the Most High and you think this will bring you peace?"

Isaac said. "I do seek peace in the Negev, away from the cities of Canaan and the many flocks contesting for pasture and water. It has always been a place of peace and well suited for thinking."

Then sighing, Isaac said more as a realization, "And no, yelling at God does not bring peace, but the release of the fears and doubts that trouble me."

Ishmael replied tersely, "So Sarah died and father Abraham has a new, young wife. Well, she should be much happier than Hagar with Sarah gone. Sorry, brother, you say you still grieve her loss, but she bore no pity for me or my mother. And Abraham only sought to please Sarah with no thought of us."

"It is true father sought to please my mother," Isaac answered, "But God spoke to him and told him to send you off. The Most High made a promise to father, that He would make a nation from you, and with all of these fine sons, it seems his promise will be true.Just look about you; such blessings! God has sent a river of crystal water flowing from a mountain to sustain you in this Eden."

Isaac thought for a moment and then continued. "Brother, were you not circumcised with father as a sign of God's covenant? Is that not proof that you too are blessed with father? Are you not of the promise that the Most High will be Your God if you follow Him? Father is promised to be a father of many nations, are you not destined to become a nation?"

Ishmael thought and then answered harshly, "Abraham loved me until you were born. Then it was you who became the son of promise. You became the only heir. Is not all the land from the river of Egypt to the great Euphrates promised to Abraham and to you?"

Ishmael banged the hilt of his knife on the table and roared, "Well, I will not leave this land. My sons, too, will make this land our home. Know this, little brother, you shall not send me from this land!"

Isaac replied softly, "I do not seek to send you from this land. I am your brother. I, too, was circumcised to the same covenant. Our father has not and will never raise his arm against you. I know what it is to be subject to our father's obedience to the word of God. You, he sent off; me he laid on an altar of sacrifice and lifted the knife to slay me."

Ishmael's eyes widened, "What? Did father try to sacrifice you on an altar? As a burnt offering? You and I, brother, are more alike than I thought!"

Isaac continued, "Yes, God told him to sacrifice me and he fully intended to. At the last moment, God told him to stop and not harm me. It was a test of his faith. Father told me he fully trusted that God would provide another sacrifice or he would raise me up again. He trusted God's promise and was obedient to His command."

Ishmael replied thoughtfully, "Too hard of a test, too hard."

Isaac said, "So this is how our father now lives, humbly, obedient to God. He trusts God in everything and fathers more sons with Keturah."

Ishmael said, "And you Isaac, you fear the trials God has before you?" Then pausing for a moment, he continued, "Why don't you marry? Father sons of your own. Find a wife who can bring you pleasure and comfort." Ishmael laughed, "With a wife, you will no longer have time for worries and yelling at God! She will demand your attention and only an occasional hunt in the desert will bring you peace."

Isaac smiled, "This is my last chance for peace then, my brother, for father has sent Eliezer and my servant Abiel to his kinfolk in Paddan Aram to find me a bride. Come with me brother! Come to the wedding feast. See father once more; it would bring him such pleasure."

Ishmael sighed and said, "No brother. I will not come. I will not see father again. I have been sent off because you are the son of promise. You must go back and follow the path the Most High has established for you."

Both men fell silent. Then Ishmael said, "Brother, come with me tomorrow and share the joy of a hunt. Perhaps I can make an archer of you before you leave."

Isaac smiled, "Yes and I must taste your antelope stew."

Chapter Eleven

Now Abraham took another wife whose name was Keturah.
Genesis 25: 1

God did not speak to Isaac at Beer-lahai-roi. Isaac returned to his father's camp at the Oaks of Mamre, near Hebron, still saddened by his mother's loss but with a clearer understanding of his father's faith. His defense of Abraham to his brother Ishmael mocked his own anger with his father. He decided his disapproval of Abraham's marriage to Keturah was wrong and selfish; the reconciliation he sought between Ishmael and Abraham betrayed the need of his own reconciliation with his father.

When Isaac entered the camp with his two donkeys lightly loaded, he saw Abraham slowly walking towards him, his head covered in a robe as white as the long beard on his weathered face. He steadied himself with a long shepherd's crook, and as he drew near a smile could be seen on his tear-stained face. Isaac began to speak, "Father forgive me, I... "

Abraham simply placed a finger to his lips for silence and stepping forward hugged his son."Isaac, my son, come sit at my table; a feast awaits. You can tell me of your adventures in the Negev."

He commanded a servant to take the donkeys as he led his son to the tent, his arm across Isaac's shoulder, smiling and walking slowly with the gait of a very old man.

As they reached Abraham's tent, Abraham paused and said, "Wash away the dust and heat of your travels, my son, put on the clean robe laid out for you and join me. Your return brings me great joy!"

When Isaac entered the open receiving room of Abraham's tent, a grand table was set before him. His father motioned to him, "Sit my son, here in the place of honor."

As Isaac settled onto his cushion across from his father, he noticed his favorite stew was prepared along with the normal varieties of figs, raisins, olives, and bread and a large bowl of wine.

Abraham asked, "What did the Most High tell you in the Negev?"

Isaac said, "I called out to the Most High, but He did not answer me. But my brother Ishmael heard my words and found me. He is well, father, though you do not ask. God has blessed him with many sons and a splendid hidden oasis in the desert watered by a river which falls from within the mountain. A truly beautiful place of green among the reddened hills."

Abraham's white bushy eyebrows rose, his eyes widened; he nodded and said, "Tell me more."

Isaac answered, "He tells you he will never leave the land, neither he nor his sons who have settled nearby whatever the promise made to you by God. He is well and finds joy in the hunt. I saw his skill; as an archer he is unmatched. His wife, Halima, is Egyptian and brings him comfort. Hagar is buried."

Isaac stopped talking.

Abraham said, "It is just as the Most High said. Ishmael too is a father of a great nation. God heard Hagar and saw Ishmael and blessed him. His promise is ever true as I have trusted, yet the news is still sweet to my ears!"

Isaac said, "Ishmael still does not forgive you for sending him away when I was born. I told him you were obedient to the voice of God and trusted God to bless him. I urged him to return with me, but he would not. He refuses to see you again."

Abraham said, "It grieves my heart not to have him beside me, but God means it for the good and has different paths for you and Ishmael. And how did you and Ishmael get on?"

Isaac replied, "Father, I told him I do not ask him to leave the land and said you would not raise your arm against him. It was not my right to speak for you."

Abraham said, "You spoke from your heart. No, I will not raise my hand against Ishmael. I have not raised a hand against the Hittites or Canaanites, except to rescue my nephew Lot, so why would raise an arm against Ishmael or his sons?"

Isaac said, "I enjoyed the company of my brother. We have both suffered pain when you were put to the test. The trials God placed before you, speak to us of what may come. We share that knowledge and know that it will shape us."

Abraham smiled and said, "And you say God did not answer you! God's voice speaks to us when we do not see or hear him; He speaks through others he sends to meet us. Others we can listen to, like a brother."

As Isaac tasted the stew made especially for him he said, "And Ishmael has given me a new favorite dish! Not to disappoint you father, for I see this wonderful stew before me, but Ishmael has his with wild game!"

Abraham laughed and said, "I will remember that. What else does he tell you?"

Isaac replied lightly, "He tells me I should put my mourning behind me and find a wife to comfort me."

Abraham smiled and said, "There is much hope for Ishmael! Soon you shall have your bride and she will bring you comfort."

Isaac laughed and then his face turned serious once more.

"What will become of my other brothers, the sons of Keturah?"

Abraham looked with love into the eyes of Isaac and said, "Isaac, my son, you are the son of God's promise. My only son of promise. You are my heir and will inherit all that I own, and through you, all of the promises of inheritance from the Most High will pass. Though I love all of my sons, only you are the son promise, you are the son by which all men will be blessed. As for the sons of Keturah, God will bless them and I will be generous with them, but they will not grow old in my house."

Father and son sat silently. Keturah quietly entered and picked up the empty plates. "Husband, is there anything else you wish?"

Then turning to Isaac, she said, "Master Isaac, there is more stew warming, you usually eat so heartily."

Isaac answered her softly, "No, I will just sit and join my father in another cup of wine."

After she left the room, Isaac softly said, "I am still troubled. I thought you loved my mother more than all else other than the Most High, why did you remarry?"

Abraham answered, "I loved Sarah with all of my heart. We walked as one nearly a century. Nothing will ever change that. But am I to be denied comfort in my old age? I cannot abide sleeping alone."

Isaac asked, "What will become of Keturah when you join Sarah in her tomb? Will she be like her sons? Is not each new son born to be injured when you send him away? Is this not sin, my father?"

Abraham answered, "I intend no harm to the sons of Keturah, or to her. I trust God to care for them? Where is sin in that?"

"Father," Isaac answered, "The knowledge that you will bring them pain and yet you do not stop, is that not both selfish and sinful? Is not seeking your comfort in the knowledge they will be hurt, unjust?"

Abraham said, "What life is without pain? You are my son

by the promise of God; you are my heir and you suffer pain. When I obeyed God and sought to sacrifice you as a burnt offering, was that unrighteous? No, it was righteous to obey God even though the experience brought you pain. We can only be obedient to God and accountable for our own walk with him."

Abraham reached across the table and took Isaac's hands, "My son, this is why God waited so long to give you to your mother and me. We needed to learn to trust God. Obedience without love is not trusting. From the time your mother and I left Ur of the Chaldeans, we were obedient to His calling. But we made our own choices, sinful ones yes, not trusting God. But when we learned how much God loved us, saved us, protected us and blessed us, we began to love Him back. Only when we loved God did we truly learn to trust Him. As I have told you many times, I trusted the Most High that He would not take away my son that He promised to me."

Isaac replied, "Father, many times you have told me this, but I am still troubled. My head understands your words but my heart is still with my brothers who will face the pain Ishmael feels from being sent away."

"This too is a good thing my son," Abraham answered, "You must love all whom God loves. You are called by God to love them, but you are not accountable for their choices or their walk with the Most High. It will keep you humble, my son."

Then pausing a moment Abraham added, "Be certain of this, my son, God never wastes a hurt. He uses our wounds to draw us closer to Him and to those He loves."

"And tell me father, why you married a Hittite woman, from a tribe of Canaan? But you send Eliezer and Abiel to Paddan Aram for the daughter of your nephew to be my wife? You have no dealings with the Canaanites, but you marry a daughter of Canaan?"

Abraham said, "Keturah is the daughter of a man who has served me for many years. A man who was circumcised along with me in accordance with God's covenant, a man whose God is the Lord. She does not follow the gods of Canaan nor will she permit our sons to follow the detestable idolatry of her former people. Is not your chief servant, Abiel, a Canaanite? A good man who loves the Most High God? Does not God love all men and desire they walk with Him? Does God not command repentance from idolatry and obedience to Him? God welcomes all who would come to Him. But you my son, are the son of God's promise. The father of nations. A new nation will inherit this land and it shall be taken away from the Canaanite tribes."

Isaac said, "I will think on your words father."

Abraham answered, "Sometimes we need to think less and trust more."

That night as Isaac stood outside his tent, his eyes fixed on the starry night sky above, he heard a baby cry and then the distinctive voice of Keturah sweetly, tenderly singing him back to sleep.

Chapter Twelve

Then Isaac brought her into his mother Sarah's tent and he took Rebekah, and she became his wife, and he loved her; thus, Isaac was comforted after his mother's death.

Genesis 24:67

Isaac was still considering what Abraham said to him the day before. He could not accept his father's lack of concern for the sons he was fathering with Keturah. He could argue having total trust in God but having trust should not relieve a responsibility not to harm to another. Ishmael was proof that gifts and blessings will not heal the pain of being disinherited and sent off. When his father claimed he trusted God to bless all his sons, which God would do just as a matter of justice, Isaac found Abraham's argument as convenient to his selfishness. Then there was the promise of God that Abraham would be the father of many nations, and Ishmael indeed appeared to be blessed as a father of a new nation; how then is being the son of the promise, the son through whom the promise was to be fulfilled, any different?

Isaac walked as he wondered and found himself in the field north of Mamre at sunset when he saw camels approaching. As he walked towards the camels, they stopped.

Rebekah looked up and saw a man approaching. Abiel had dismounted from his camel and was walking ahead. As he passed by Rebekah she asked, "Who is that man approaching us?"

Abiel was staring at the man and then turned to Rebekah and said, "It is my master, Isaac."

Rebekah took a light scarf and veiled her face. It was not proper to show her face to her betrothed before their marriage.

Isaac turned his attention to the veiled young woman on the camel. But she turned her head away and looked at the ground behind her. Abiel greeted his master warmly and with all of the polish and courtesy of a trusted steward. They turned and walked south, back the way from which Isaac had approached.

Abiel walked alongside Isaac, reporting on their journey as Eliezer escorted Rebekah and Deborah. Ahead of them, they saw a city of goat hair tents, much like those she knew on the plains of Nahor.

Rebekah whispered to Deborah, "Did you see him, I did not get a good look, and I have this veil over my eyes. What does he look like? Can you hear what they are saying? What happens now?"

Deborah said, "I can only see the back of his head, and no, I cannot hear them. I suppose they will take us to a tent. They must unload the camels. I'm sure someone will come and tell us something."

They walked into the center of Abraham's tent city. Isaac could be seen pointing to a large tent right by the well. Eliezer escorted them to the tent and then said, "This is the tent of Sarah, Isaac's mother. You are to stay here. Do not leave this tent until you're told. Your things will be brought to you. A meal will be brought here and there is clean water to refresh yourself from the journey. In the morning you will hear the wedding plans."

Rebekah stopped at the entrance to the tent and turned to Eliezer. She looked at him a few moments and said, "Thank you Eliezer, thank you for bringing me here safely. Thank you for helping me and, well, thank you for everything."

Eliezer bowed and said, "It has been both an honor and joy to serve you, mistress Rebekah. May the Most High bless you and Isaac. May your marriage bring you both happiness and many sons. It is my prayer that you walk with your husband as one, as Adam and Eve did in the garden."

Eliezer then turned to Deborah, "Watch over your mistress carefully as unto the Most High, and may He bless you also in your service."

Deborah stationed herself between Rebekah's room and the center room of the great tent directing servants as they unloaded the camels. As the unloading continued, she began to look at the tent they occupied. It was magnificent! A worthy rival to the tent of Milcah, wife of Nahor. The goat hair side walls were folded in and covered by layers of fine rugs. Cushions surrounded the perimeter of the room along with fine copper and bronze cups and vessels carefully set on chests of polished wood. Bronze lampstands stood guard, providing light to every corner. Linen curtains separated the side rooms from the large central sitting room. Rugs and tapestries were hung on the ceiling and walls hiding every hint of rough goat hair. There was not so much as a speck of dust or grain of sand inside.

As the last of the baskets and crates were left in the tent and the servants were walking off, Deborah dropped the entrance curtain to the center room and moved to the side room where Rebekah waited. She could hear the light splashing of water and entered to find Rebekah drying her face with a towel.

"Deborah, why don't you wash and see about our supper," Rebekah said.

"As efficient as Eliezer is, it will be here before I am dry," Deborah replied. "Look at this tent!"

"Yes, very fine; reminds me of grandma Milcah's tent, and is a bit nicer than mama's. What should I wear tonight? We're not supposed to go out, I can probably just be comfortable. Are there any women here? They can't just send men here with our supper."

As they spoke they heard a clap and then a voice, "Mistress, your supper. Should I bring it in now?"

Deborah opened the flap to find not one but two young servant girls bearing large trays of food and wine. Deborah and Rebekah sat before the trays nibbling and talking late into the night.

In the morning a servant girl requested Deborah to accompany her to Abiel's tent. Abiel greeted her warmly and said, "My master Isaac is impatient and wishes the wedding take place today. He will come for her after sunset to take her to his tent. You shall spend the day helping your mistress prepare. She should bathe in the oils and salts we purchased in Damascus. Use whatever beauty treatments she desires. Do you require the help of a woman or servant?"

"No," Deborah replied, "Rebekah is a beautiful woman, she does not need to color her face or paint her eyes, she will dazzle your master."

Abiel smiled, "Isaac will indeed find his bride beautiful. I have here the jewels gifted her by Isaac. She also has the gold bracelets and rings given to her in Nahor. Now when Isaac comes to her tent, there will be maidens outside with lanterns who will shout his arrival. When she comes out, she should be robed and veiled. There will be a joyful procession to Isaac's tent where he will declare he has taken her as his wife. The guests will begin the feast while Isaac and Rebekah retire to his room. Her things will have been brought to Isaac's tent. After their time together, they will join the wedding feast as husband and wife."

Deborah said, "Rebekah will be pleased, she too, is impatient for the wedding."

Abiel smiled at Deborah and said, "I am honored to be the

bridegroom's friend and ruler of the feast. Neither Isaac nor Rebekah will be permitted to do any work or service during the feast, so you must be ready to step in and act for her at any time. Be prepared for a long and joyful wedding feast."

"And a long and joyful marriage as well," Deborah added.

After all of their impatient waiting, Rebekah and Deborah never felt so rushed. There was so much to do! Deborah laid out clothes while Rebekah soaked. She carefully set aside clothes for the feast and packed away everything else. She helped with her hair, brushing and brushing and chose the right perfume.

As Rebekah dressed in her linen gown, Deborah brought out the gift jewels from Isaac. Both were speechless as Rebekah carefully put them on, adjusting each one to fall perfectly into place. Finally, just as the sun was setting, Deborah helped her into the ornately embroidered wedding robe. Both women were weeping happy tears as they waited for the maiden's call.

Just a moment later they could hear a commotion outside and the cheerful song of the maidens, "Behold the bridegroom is coming, go out and meet him!"

As they repeated the call a second time Rebekah, in her excitement, was about to open the tent when Deborah cried, "Wait! The veil, you must be veiled!"

Deborah quickly helped Rebekah with the veil, and then beaming brightly, hugged her friend tight. "Now, you really are a great lady. And a beautiful bride."

Opening the tent, they saw Abiel next to a handsome, smiling man in a fine robe wearing a crown of a twisted golden vine. The maidens with their lanterns were all in line singing, calling for the bride and groom to follow the happy procession. A large crowd followed behind. An old man and young woman were first in line behind Isaac and Abiel.

Rebekah thought *that must be father Abraham and Keturah. He is so noble and she is so young!*

Abiel stepped back and motioned for Rebekah to take his

place. Deborah fell in line behind Rebekah next to Abiel, and the maidens began their procession. They walked around the well circling twice before going to Isaac's tent, singing all the while; everyone was singing and laughing as they paraded. Torches were lit all along the way, their flames seemed to dance with joyful singing. The great room of Isaac's tent was completely open with grand bronze torches standing guard outside brightly shining in the dusky evening light.Smaller lampstands inside provided soft light and intimacy inside the tent. A great table stood before the tent covered with food and large bowls of wine on each end and adorned with palms and great clusters of grapes.

Isaac showed Rebekah into his tent. They were followed by the old man and young woman.

Rebekah looked fully into Isaac's face, the first time clearly seeing her husband. Her eyes saw a handsome, poised and happy man standing beside her. Isaac took a quick glance at his bride, but when their eyes met, neither could turn back and face the crowd. Only the voice of the old man broke their spell.

Abraham lifted his arms to the crowd of guests, and said with a voice of age and authority, "Friends we are here to witness and celebrate the wedding of my son Isaac and his betrothed, Rebekah." Turning to the bride and groom he said, "Rebekah, you have accepted the betrothal gifts of Isaac, do you accept him as your husband?"

Rebekah said, "I accept Isaac as my husband."

To Isaac, Abraham asked, "Isaac, do you take Rebekah as your wife?

Isaac said, "I take Rebekah as my wife."

Abraham said, "Isaac take your wife home."

As all of the wedding guests cheered, Isaac led Rebekah into his room and dropped the curtain. For several moments Isaac and Rebekah stood staring at one another, neither knew what to say. Rebekah smiled and removed her veil. Her fiery red hair fell softly past her shoulders; her green eyes looked deeply into his. Looking up, the beautiful gold crown she wore began to slip, she instantly moved it back into place, the golden leaves jeweled in emeralds from which strands of gold, glittering in the soft candlelight, fell into her long red hair. Her eyes never leaving his, she took off the white embroidered wedding robe and dropped it beside her. Isaac beheld Rebekah wearing his gifts, a jeweled necklace of large emeralds, and the golden bracelets and rings he sent in advance. Finally letting his eyes fall upon her, she stood before him wearing a gown of the finest, lightest Egyptian linen, a gown so fine as to be nearly invisible. Isaac looked at Rebekah and he loved her. Rebekah's eyes reflected the same love for her husband. She reached up to each shoulder and undid the clasps of her gown. The gown drifted slowly to the ground and the two became one flesh.

Chapter Thirteen

My beloved is mine and I am his; he pastures his flock among the lilies.

Song of Solomon 2:16

Isaac and Rebekah found happiness in the wilderness of the Negev. Upon Isaac's marriage to Rebekah, Abraham gave Isaac a third of all his goats and a large number of sheep, donkeys, oxen, and camels, and sent shepherds, servants and eighty trained men into Isaac's service. They settled at the well Beer-lahai-roi. Isaac loved Rebekah and welcomed her desire to share in his work. Moving the flocks and the camp, more than a week's travel south, was an adventure; she listened as Abiel and Jachin, the Hittite, leader of the trained men, discussed each detail with Isaac. Ensuring sufficient water and fodder for so large a number of animals in the dry arid land between wells, with no other water and limited pasture was the greatest challenge. Protecting the scattered flocks and herds against thieves and robbers as they traveled fell to Jachin and his trained men. Rebekah took to heart Deborah's counsel not to question her husband's decisions in the presence of his servants, saving all of her questions and opinions for when they were alone. Even so, the eye contact between them made their partnership known to their closest servants.

Isaac and Rebekah were both happy to be away from Abraham and Keturah. They were pleased to have the support of Abiel and Deborah and Rebekah had grown to trust Jachin who protected her on the journey from Haran. They enjoyed visiting the flocks scattered among the canyons and sparse pastures of the upper Negev. Rebekah learned the names of the shepherds and offered herself as the judge as they competed to be first at the well for watering the flocks in the late afternoon. She established a rule that each shepherd must have all of his sheep and goats at the well and report their number to her before claiming first to the well privileges; she would smile and praise them for the health of their flock and the skill in shepherding. She spent time with Deborah and her servant cook learning the secrets of the spices they brought from Damascus. She became skilled in cooking the game Isaac would bring back from his hunting, in every way she threw herself into her new role as wife and mistress of the household. She was loved and respected by everyone in the camp.

Deborah was adjusting to her new role working with Rebekah's servants. She patiently instructed them on her mistress' tastes and expectations.She was surprised to find herself lonely as Rebekah enjoyed the company of her husband, even so, both women maintained the strong bond they formed as young girls. When Isaac traveled off or enjoyed a few days hunting, Deborah would join Rebekah on her daily visits to the shepherds. She always remembered to bring along some hotcakes which were warmly received along with her friendly smile. She very quickly became known as Nediva Deborah, the Kindhearted Bee.

Abiel too became very busy managing the large staff of servants, shepherds, and trained men. Jachin demonstrated his leadership as an able assistant and Abiel left Jachin in charge during his visits to the markets. Very soon the house of Isaac was established and the handsome Isaac and his beautiful wife Rebekah brought wealth and prosperity to the upper Negev. The entire tent village that was Isaac's household awaited the birth of a son of God's promise.

A year passed and Isaac and Rebekah grew to love each other more each day. They were seen together throughout the camp, among the flocks, and at the well. They made no attempt to hide their affections, whether laughing in conversation or stealing a hug or a kiss and often a tender caress even outside their tent. It was well known that Isaac offered Rebekah Sarah's tent as her own, and she famously said I will always sleep in my husband's tent only. In order to give his wife the best, he made Sarah's tent their tent and offered his humbler tent to Abiel, his chief servant.

Isaac was happy with Abiel's choice of Jachin as his deputy. He engaged Jachin's instruction in the arts of combat and warfare and spent many hours improving his ability with the bow. Isaac may not have attained the skill of Ishmael but he also became a skilled hunter none the less. The Negev was a wilderness area, but dangers beyond the heat of the desert were always a possibility. Bands of thieves, bandits, and raiders used the Negev and its craggy canyons as camps. Isaac's scattered flocks and the riches in the camp were attractive targets. Only the presence of Isaac's trained men and their reputation defending father Abraham provided the deterrence that kept the house of Isaac secure.

Jachin would refer to the traits of predators in instructing Isaac on the tactics of attack, defense, and combat. Isaac's knowledge of the predators of the Negev helped him absorb Jachin's counsel. Whether it was the speed of the leopard, the stealth of the lion or the pack attack of the wolves and jackals, the methods had their place in combat. As each predator made the kill differently so to the trained man had a variety of weapons to use. The prey had well-developed survival skills as well. All the skills of the birds and beasts maintained a balance; somehow enough each of prey and predator survived that life flourished in the Negev.

Jachin would liken this balance of survival with the balance of nations and kingdoms. Egypt, which holds sovereignty over Canaan, fell back in a period of internal turmoil when Hittites, Hurrians, and the sea people first raided and then invaded the land. Coming with new weapons and tactics, they were as leopards, driving chariots too fast to be slowed by the lofted arrows of the Egyptian archers, and armed with superior bronze spears and javelins. They overpowered the lesser armed Egyptian infantry.

But no advantage lasts long and a defeat can be a king's or pharaoh's greatest teacher. Soon Egyptians returned with chariots of their own, but much lighter and faster than the old chariots of the Hittites and Hurrians. The Egyptian infantry too was equipped with weapons of bronze and now attacked in much greater numbers. The early Hittite victories were short-lived.But they and the Canaanite kings learned as well, a new strategy of diversion and division. They retreated to their walled cities to endure a siege while other cities and nations could strike at the Egyptians overlords forcing them to withdraw and fight another battle; the small city-states were as bees chasing the bear from its honey.

Isaac listened to Jachin as he explained the strategies of the Egyptian wars and told him to prepare plans named for the predators and prey of the Negev; he directed him to train his men according to each plan so that all that needed to be passed in an emergency was the name of the Negev bird or beast.

As they were talking one day, Rebekah, listening from the other side of the curtain came out and asked, "Jachin, it is well known that father Abraham does not associate with Canaanites, how then did you come into his service?"

Jachin replied, "It is true, many of father Abraham's men are sons of Shem, most of them, like Eliezer are Aramean, but many are Canaanites, Hittites and Philistines. Abraham is opposed only to the worshipers of the Canaanite gods or any god other than the Most High God. To everyone in Canaan he is known as the 'God of Abraham.' But you ask how did I come into his service. My father came with a raiding party to take the hill country north of Laish and stayed. The land was good and we settled there. Like all Hittite boys, I was raised to be a warrior and trained from the time I could walk in the arts and skills of combat. I had heard of how father Abraham pursued the armies of the four kings and defeated them with his small band of three hundred and eighteen trained men. Abraham was well known for his righteousness and fairness and when he attributed his victory to his God, the one God, I wanted to know this God. Such a great victory! Such overwhelming odds! When I came to Abraham's camp and asked to serve him as one of his trained men, he asked me why I came to him and if I brought any Canaanite gods. I said I used to carry the Huwasi stones, talismans of the gods of the Hittites which are too numerous to count, but I threw them all away and seek to follow only the God of Abraham, the God who brings victory. Father Abraham requires all the men of his household and service to be circumcised in accordance with the covenant God Almighty made with him; too hard a thing for any man who does not truly desire to follow God."

Rebekah asked, "And your family, Jachin, did they welcome your decision?"

"My father respects my service to Father Abraham; he knows Abraham to be a righteous man. My father trusts no god, he carries his Huwasi stones but has no trust in them. He finds my trust in the Most High as peculiar, but as I am a man and a warrior he respects my decision."

Rebekah replied, "I thank you again for bringing me safely to my husband and I am glad that you serve us."

"It is an honor to serve the son of the promise of my lord, Father Abraham, mistress Rebekah."

Isaac looked at Rebekah, smiled and said, "Thank you

Jachin, perhaps we hunt tomorrow? That is if it meets your and Abiel's schedule."

"Master Isaac, our schedule always adjusts to yours, and hunting with you brings me great pleasure. I will make the arrangements."

With Isaac hunting with Jachin, Rebekah asked Deborah to stay with her and they talked as sisters and best friends just as they did all those years in Nahor. Rebekah's voice sang with happiness as she spoke. "Isaac is so wonderful! How could I ever have doubted my happiness? He dedicates himself to making me happy. He is so handsome. Don't you find him attractive, Deborah? And of such noble spirit! I want so much to please him, but it hard to tell what he really likes. He seems so pleased all of the time. How else can I please him? He treasures my company. He praises my cooking. He enjoys our bed. You must help me Deborah; how else can I please my husband?"

Deborah laughed and said, "Mistress..."

Rebekah interrupted, "Don't call me mistress, not today, not now. It is to my best friend that I speak."

Deborah continued, "Rebekah, you are truly blessed! Your husband finds pleasure in all that you do and yet you still seek to please him more! I say to you, just continue to be yourself. It is you that he loves. He loves what you do because it is you who do it. The only thing that will make each of you happier will be your children. What a great blessing they will bring."

Rebekah thought and said, "Yes. I have been so happy enjoying the love and companionship of Isaac that I haven't given much thought to children."

Deborah said, "God wants you to become one, to grow in love and trust for each other first. He will send children. I am certain. Enjoy this special time with the husband who loves you."

Rebekah hugged Deborah and said, "I think I shall call you Nediva Deborah from now on as well!"

Isaac returned from his hunting earlier than expected.

Flinging open the tent curtain he found Rebekah with Deborah, both surprised to see him. "Isaac, husband, you are back so soon, is all well? Rebekah asked.

"All is well, or will be well now," he answered.

"Was there no game to be found?" she asked.

"Yes, there was game, and I have brought back a nice antelope, it is with the cooks, but I return in need of comfort."

"Comfort?

"The comfort of my wife," Isaac said as he swept Rebekah up off her feet sending her hips and legs above her while her red hair fell encircling both of their heads.

"The hunt brings me happiness, but I find more happiness with you!"

Rebekah laughed, "Put me down. I can wear my fine light Egyptian linen gown for you."

Isaac lowered Rebekah and slung her over his shoulder. "Too late for that, my love," and he started for the inner room.

"Goodbye Deborah, that will be all for today," she said giggling as Isaac carried her off.

"Yes, goodbye Deborah," Isaac repeated, "I will serve your mistress today."

As Deborah left the tent Abiel was approaching. "Deborah, I hear master Isaac has returned. Is he in his tent? I would have a word with him."

Deborah smiled, "Oh he is in the tent, but I would not disturb him now."

Then hearing the muffled sound of laughter from inside the tent, Abiel said, "No, now is not the time. It can wait."

Deborah's face became serious, "Abiel, are you happy?"

Abiel looked at her puzzled and said, "I find great joy and fulfillment in my service."

Deborah asked again, "No, I know you find joy in serving, but are you happy as are our master Isaac and mistress Rebekah?

Abiel's face sobered, "Truly, Deborah, there is a happiness

that not all may attain. I don't see the Most High granting me or you the happiness Isaac and Rebekah now enjoy. But I am truly happy for them."

"No, nor do I," Deborah said softly as she walked away.

Chapter Fourteen

A brother offended is harder to be won than a strong city, and quarreling is like the bars of a castle.

Proverbs 18: 19

As the years passed, Isaac and Rebekah appeared as close as ever. Isaac was content and truly pleased by Rebekah's attention. Though Isaac never complained, Rebekah could not help but worry about her failure to give her husband a son. Was not a son the one thing that would bring her husband the most joy? Was not Isaac a son of the promise of God? And was not the promise made to Abraham to be the father of many nations to be fulfilled by Isaac? Was she not chosen to be his bride in direct answer to Eliezer's prayer? Rebekah's heart became troubled by doubts that would not go away.

Ten years had passed since their marriage and no one in the household of Isaac would mention children in the presence of the master and mistress. Only if prompted would they smile and say, "You are young! Enjoy your time together. God will provide in His time." Even the hugs and assurances of Deborah did not allay her doubt.

Isaac, who was in no particular hurry to have children, sensed her growing unhappiness; and as deeply as he loved Rebekah, he was still reluctant to discuss her inability to bear a child. Isaac avoided confrontation, controversy and unpleasant conversations with the people he loved. It was a weakness Abiel had always noted and tried his best, within his station, to guide his master through.

One day, as Isaac left Rebekah wearing the look of pain, Isaac said softly, "How can I bring happiness to Rebekah?"

Abiel replied, "Master, you can only love her. You must be willing to listen to her. You know why she is unhappy; let her share her doubts and reassure her of your love and the calling of the Most High."

Isaac thought and then said, "God made my mother wait and wait. It caused her great pain. I cannot be the one to tell her she may suffer as my mother did. Perhaps I can do something for her to make her forget, at least for a while. Perhaps a journey? Yes, she is bold and adventurous, let us go on a journey. Where might we go? Someplace new and different?"

Abiel pondered and answered, "Master, we have been trading, sheep, wool and goat hair tents for frankincense, myrrh, balm, and spices in addition to silver. Now that the war in Egypt is over, Upper and Lower Egypt are again united and the new pharaoh, Amenemhat, is building his new city, Itj-tawy, with many new temples so the market for our frankincense should be strong. We could trade for fine Egyptian linen and other exotic goods. Rebekah would enjoy a visit to the markets of Egypt."

Isaac's face brightened, "Yes! We will go to the markets of Thebes and Itj-tawy in Egypt. Abiel, make the arrangements!"

Abiel inquired, "Shall I send a messenger to Eliezer and your father? They may wish to trade as well and there is safety in numbers while traveling to Egypt."

"My father is very old, too old to make such a journey. Send to Eliezer and ask if he and his men wish to join us."

Within a week Eliezer arrived with camels and donkeys loaded with trade goods, servants and a well-armed contingent of Abraham's trained men. Abiel consulted with Eliezer on the final preparations and sent Jachin ahead to Ishmael to arrange a visit enroute to Egypt. The busy preparations were a welcome distraction for Rebekah who kept Deborah busy coordinating her servants with packing, planning and lively conversation about the markets of Egypt. The presence of the camels, donkeys and caravan camp brought reminders of the excitement and suspense she felt on the journey to Oaks of Mamre years ago. Both women were looking forward to the camaraderie they enjoyed in the past and decided that Isaac would find it welcome as well.

Soon the caravan of Isaac was snaking its way along the wadi road towards Egypt. They made their way west, through the narrow canyon cut through the mountain, and went further south to the entrance of the canyon home of Ishmael, his sons waiting to escort them inside. Jachin and Nebaioth, the oldest son of Ishmael, stood at the entrance to the camp to meet the caravan and direct the servants and trained men in the care of the animals. Jachin was not smiling.

Nebaioth greeted Isaac and said, "Welcome uncle. My father will see you in his tent. Rebekah will be received in the tent of my mother, Halima. Jachin will direct your servants and trained men. If your wife is ready, please come with me."

When they came to Halima's tent, a servant girl bowed to Rebekah and said, "Welcome mistress Rebekah, my mistress bids you come in and be refreshed."

Rebekah entered Halima's tent and the men continued to Ishmael's tent adjacent to it. While Isaac waited outside, Nebaioth went in and announced Isaac's presence. Isaac then heard Ishmael say, "You may come in little brother, I have refreshments waiting."

Entering Ishmael's tent, Isaac was surprised to see Ishmael, several of his sons and half a dozen trained men armed with swords and bows. Isaac exclaimed, "Is this how you greet your brother, with men armed with sword and bow?"

Ishmael answered, "You enter my camp with Abraham's trained men, as well as your own; you have already taken my inheritance, have you come to take the land and all that I own? Do you mean to drive my sons from the land and send me and my wife to Egypt once more? I see that fox, Eliezer, is with you, surely Abraham has sent him to do me harm; you will not succeed, we are prepared. Look outside again, little brother."

Nebaioth opened the tent curtain to reveal Isaac's caravan surrounded by trained men. Jachin, Abiel and all of Isaac and Abraham's men stood with weapons drawn, ready for an attack.

Isaac spoke, "Brother, withdraw your trained men. Did I not send Jachin ahead to prepare for my visit? Have we not had this conversation before? I do not seek your land or to drive your sons from the Negev. Our father loves you and will never lift his hand against you. I have invited Eliezer to come with us to trade in Egypt for his knowledge and in respect for our father. I stop here to invite your company as well. Is not Halima Egyptian? Are not your sons and servants familiar with the markets of Egypt? No, my brother, I come to the man who showed me hospitality in the past, the man who gave me a taste for game and taught me to enjoy the hunt. I come to my brother who welcomed me to Beer-lahai-roi. I come with my wife and my household. This is not the way of a thief or raider."

Ishmael continued to look outside, making no eye contact with Isaac. "My sons tell me your flocks grow larger, you seek more and more grazing land. You trade with Egyptians going back and forth from the copper mines deep in the desert. You grow wealthy and the well, Beer-lahai-roi is to you a private water. The land can hardly contain you and us. My sons tell me our father sends off his other sons with flocks and wealth. I will not have them and you pushing us from our land."

The camp was silent. No one else spoke. Flashes of light could be seen reflecting sunlight off of the bronze weapons.

Isaac replied, "It is true we trade with the Egyptians and with anyone who will buy our sheep, wool or goat hair tents. It is true that the God of Abraham our father has blessed me, and that my flocks grow. But will you deny that the God of Abraham has blessed you, even more, my brother? He gives you streams of water here in your oasis. He has given you many sons, you must tell me how many, for I have lost count. And yes, our father sends off his other sons with gifts and blessing, flocks and wealth. But he always sends them to the east and instructs them not to interfere or encroach on your pasture lands. And as I am his heir does not their wealth come from my inheritance, not yours? Your sons report about me, have any of them seen sons of Keturah in my camp? Brother, I bear you love and not jealousy. We share the burdens of brothers, sons of Abraham. We are two men in the hands of the God of Abraham, our father."

Ishmael continued his gaze at the standoff of the two bands of armed men. He dropped his gaze, took a deep breath and then looking up again, he shouted, "Withdraw. Is this how we show hospitality to my brother's household? Bring refreshment to our worthy guests."

Returning inside the tent, Ishmael said, "Twelve. I have twelve fine sons and many daughters. Is it true, my brother, you have no sons?"

As the noise of normalcy returned outside, Isaac replied, "Yes, it is true. And it has brought grief to my wife Rebekah; that is why we travel to the markets of Egypt. I seek to lift my wife's spirit."

Ishmael smiled and said, "Rest my brother. Be refreshed and sit at my table tonight. You can bring that fox, Eliezer, with you. I would hear what he has to say. Bring your steward and your trained man, Jachin, he seems a trustworthy man; bring them as well. Yes, I will consider joining your caravan, but tomorrow, you shall hunt with me."

Turning to Nebaioth, he said, "Show your uncle to his tent. Make sure he has everything he desires."

As Nebaioth opened the tent curtain he said, "Father likes to sit his table after sunset. He walks the lake at the foot of the falls an hour before. He would welcome your company there. Is there anything else you desire, uncle?"

"Thank you Nebaioth, please ask Abiel, Jachin, and Eliezer to join me here. And escort my wife Rebekah as well. It is our practice to take our rest together."

Jachin was most upset. "Master, I failed you today. Do what you will with your servant. Only the God of Abraham protected us. I prayed for your safety and for our mistress. This morning I noted men coming into the camp in small bands and disappearing into the tents. I wanted to warn you, but I was kept in the company of Nebaioth."

Isaac answered, "My brother meant no harm. His message was to me and our father Abraham. I know of your loyalty and bravery, Jachin, I will hear no more talk of failure."

Turning to Eliezer, Isaac said, "Ishmael fears you have come to spy on him. He will bear no patience with the sons of Keturah encroaching on this land or the land of his sons. I have assured him that our father sends his sons to the east. You must remind my father that his son Ishmael will resist with all of his sons and trained men anyone who brings flocks or camps in the lands of Ishmael. My brother is like an animal with a long memory of the pain inflicted by his trainer."

Eliezer said, "It is as you say, master Isaac."

The tent flap opened, Nebaioth holding the curtain announced, "Uncle, Mistress Rebekah, as you asked."

Rebekah entered and saw the concerned faces and said, "What is wrong? What has happened?"

Isaac said, "All is well. My brother just wanted Eliezer, my father, and me to know that this land belongs to him and his sons. He will never leave it without a fight."

"We are all to sit his table tonight. He has asked me to join him in the hunt tomorrow while he considers joining us in our trading journey to Egypt. It is his practice to walk the oasis pool below the waterfall before sunset. I will join him there. It is a place he finds peace. He goes there to think and to listen."

Turning to Abiel he said, "Please see to the animals and all of our people. Pitch our tents for we will be here several days. Provide the best food and wine and reassure them that all is well. You may all go. My brother sits his table after sunset. I will see you then."

After the men left, Isaac put his arm around his wife and drew her close. Rebekah said, "Halima is a cold woman, I do not enjoy her company. Husband, don't be gone too long."

Isaac joined Ishmael by the oasis pool. The tranquility of the water streaming from the mountain and falling to the clear, cool, pool below brought the brothers together once more. Ishmael said, "I still listen for his voice. I look for his angels and I wait for his voice."

Isaac sighed and said, "I have stopped crying out for him in the wilderness, but in my heart, I know he is not through with me. But you brother, I believe he listens to you. He heard the cries of your mother and sends his tender mercies. He has blessed you, my brother, he has truly blessed you here in this garden and twelve fine sons."

Isaac paused and then asked, "Tell me, brother, did you circumcise your sons in accordance with the God of Abraham's covenant."

Ishmael answered, "Yes, I know no other way to thank him."

Both men stared into the falling water, absorbing the peace. Finally, Ishmael spoke, "Come, taste the slowly simmered stew of game Halima has prepared."

The next day Ishmael led Isaac, Jachin, and Nebaioth on a hunt. Ishmael was impressed with Jachin's knowledge of the bow and was curious to see if his skill matched his knowledge. When Isaac made the first kill of a mountain goat, Ishmael exclaimed, "Little brother, you have been practicing!"

And turning to Jachin, Ishmael said, "You have trained my

brother well! But look, there beyond the wadi in the grass to the left. Do you see him? He is yours, Jachin, if you can make the shot."

Wordlessly, Jachin drew his bow, pointing the arrow well above the target and slightly to the left. He let the arrow fly. It lofted high and drifted to the right, swiftly and silently flying towards the grazing antelope. And then the antelope sprang, running, then slowing and falling over.

Ishmael smiled and said, "I see now brother, you can become accustomed to game on your table."

Rebekah asked Deborah to accompany her to Halima's tent. Halima was silent at dinner, it was unusual for her to sit at her husband's table with his guests. She was much more comfortable serving the meal and waiting the table. But her tent was her domain and she very quickly steered the conversation to her children, "Ishmael will have no other wife or concubine," she said, "Who else can cook his game as he likes it? And what other wife could bear him twelve sons and many daughters? I tell you, Rebekah, no wife is secure until she bears her husband sons! A wife may be beautiful, a wife may be pleasing to her husband in bed, but a wife without sons will be put away, you mark my words!"

Rebekah looked at Halima coldly, and said, "You cannot speak for Isaac my husband. No husband has loved his wife as Isaac loves me. We walk as one. We always will."

Halima stared at Rebekah and then smiled and said, "Of course, I was not speaking of Isaac. Surely, he loves you. He is taking you to the markets of Egypt for gifts. He hopes to please you, I am sure. Is that because you despair not having his son? No, I'm sure you have been blessed in your marriage. But if a son does not come soon, you have a beautiful nurse you can give to your husband. She looks strong. She can bear sons for you."

Rebekah's face became as red as her hair. Just as she was about to speak, Deborah spoke softly, "Truly all blessings come from the Most High. It is well known that the God of Abraham heard the cries of Hagar, Ishmael's mother and he blessed her and he has blessed your husband Ishmael. But, so too, has the God of Abraham made a promise to Abraham, a promise which is to come through Isaac. And I can confirm that the Most High has chosen Rebekah to be Isaac's wife. God has blessed my mistress Rebekah and her husband Isaac. He has blessed them and he will bless them. The blessings of God Most High are and are yet to come."

Isaac returned from the hunt two days later and was met by Abiel. Abiel told Isaac the mood in the camp was strained. Ishmael's house found offense in Rebekah's rejection of Halima's hospitality. Isaac found Rebekah and Deborah cooking and taking their meals in Rebekah's small caravan tent. Isaac asked, "Does my brother's household offer you no hospitality?"

Rebekah smiled at Isaac and said, "Welcome back husband, sit and eat. It is good you return early, we can leave soon. I find the hospitality of your brother's wife to be beyond cold and indeed cruel. Please ask Abiel to make the preparations at once."

Within two hours Isaac's household and his belongings were packed securely on his camels and donkeys. Ishmael came out to speak with Isaac, "It is unfortunate, brother, we cannot join you on your journey."

Isaac looked Ishmael in the eye and said, "There is too much fear. Your sons and their mother fear for their land. They fear our father, they fear me and the sons of Keturah. Let us make an oath, you and I, that I keep my flocks east of the mountain that separates you from Beer-lahai-roi, and your sons keep your flocks to the west."

Ishmael answered, "What you say, brother, is good. Let us make this oath in the hearing of my sons and Eliezer."

Once Isaac and Ishmael loudly proclaimed their oath, Ishmael said, "Go in peace, little brother."

Isaac replied, "May the God of our father Abraham hear

your prayers and grant you and your sons his blessing."

As Ishmael stepped back and Isaac began to ride ahead, Halima walked over to Rebekah, smiling and said between clenched teeth, "Isaac may have taken my husband's inheritance, but you are barren. Look after Isaac's concubine who serves you. Who is the honored wife? Twelve fine sons and many daughters, never forget!"

Chapter Fifteen

Wisdom has built her house, she has hewn out her seven pillars;
Proverbs 9:1

The wonders of Egypt astounded the house of Isaac. The established markets of Thebes and the excitement of the pharaoh's new city, Itj-tawy, with its new and exotic architecture, were more than could be imagined, far exceeding their expectations. The hordes of slaves pressed into the building was a fearful sight, endless lines of men dragging stones razed from the tombs of the past divided dynasties to build the new city. Large fields of mud bricks drying in the sun covered the plains between Thebes and Itj-tawy. The new city's buildings were simple to build and very strong. Two or three rows each formed an inner and an outer mudbrick wall spaced apart by the span of a large man; the void between them was filled with rubble and the exterior wall clad in thin limestone. The work progressed quickly to the point buildings whose walls were being filled with rubble when they arrived were being brightly painted by the time they left. Pharaoh Amenemhat was building a new city for his newly reunited Egypt. He ended the long civil war by betraying one pharaoh and conquering the other. Now he was destroying their memory, dismantling their pyramids and moving his throne to a city of his own making, built on the backs of those he conquered. To secure his throne and win the hearts of his people, Amenemhat celebrated Egyptian culture and glory, building immense temples with clouds of incense rising to the new idols of the old gods.

The wonders of Egypt did not lift the spirits of Rebekah. They traded for fine Egyptian linens; comfortable cotton clothes; beautiful, intricately woven wool rugs; even finely crafted Nubian bows for Jachin and the trained men. When offered by Isaac, Rebekah refused a visit to the jeweler's market. The incredible sights could not dislodge the doubt that grew and drove away every other thought. Rebekah could not forget the cruel taunting by Halima. The fear once in the back of her mind came forward, she was barren and as much as Isaac loved her, he must have sons. The day would come when Isaac would take a concubine or worse, another wife and she would lose the oneness of their marriage.

At last Isaac allowed his love to overcome his fear of confrontation. All of his attempts to restore Rebekah's happiness had failed. As the caravan was camped along the Nile, the night sky above filled with stars and a soft, moist breeze carried the smell of fresh water, Isaac took his wife by the hand and said, "Come walk with me my love."

Rebekah got up and stood beside Isaac. He pulled her close and hugged her gently. Rebekah began to sob. Isaac just held her closer. "My love," he said, "What brings you such pain that all my gifts and attention cannot relieve?"

Rebekah sobbed, and as tears fell from her eyes she was barely able to say the words, "My husband, I bear you no sons, no children. I fear I will lose you to another, to a concubine or wife who will bear your sons and be honored in your house. I love you husband, and my spirit has become one with your spirit. I never want to lose our oneness."

Isaac kept his arms tight around her and kissed the top of

her head; "I will never give up my love for you. I will never forsake you for another. As you say, our spirits are one. Is this not the will of the God of my father, Abraham from the time he gave Eve to be wife to Adam? Do not let the words of Halima, or anyone else upset you. You are chosen by God. No more tears, sweet wife. God will provide in his time. Let us find joy in the blessings of each day. Come, let me hold you as we walk in the coolness of this evening."

Rebekah sniffed, wiped her eyes and then squeezed Isaac's hand. The darkness hid the smile on her face.

Life in Beer-lahai-roi returned to normal. Rebekah resumed her visits to the shepherds as they watered the flocks in the evening, laughing with them as they boasted among themselves as to who was the most skilled, or who had just made a foolish mistake. Her warmth extended to each of them, and each saw himself as a favorite of the mistress. Her knowledge of shepherding earned their respect and her praise for a task well done was cherished. Her nurse, Deborah, was not a shepherdess like her mistress Rebekah but was warm and generous. Deborah was known to dislike too much roughhousing and she found a way to curb any misbehavior without bruising an ego. There was nothing that any shepherd, trained man or servant in the house of Isaac, would not do for Mistress Rebekah or Nediva Deborah.

Rebekah began to question the shepherds regarding the pastures and the welfare of the flocks. They shared insights regarding ewes and their lambs: which were best for breeding and bore the healthiest lambs. The shepherds also identified the ewes most likely to accept orphaned lambs and those more apt to wander. She assumed responsibility for approving their recommendations for better husbandry of the flocks and the rotation of pastures. The shepherds respected her judgment and trusted her direction. Isaac was pleased with Rebekah's involvement and stepped away from overseeing the shepherds.

All of Isaac's sheep were shorn just before the ewes were to lamb. The sheep were brought in from the pastures and kept in folds near the well. This permitted the shepherds to shear the sheep without leaving them unattended. Once the shearing was complete, the ewes which were about to lamb were kept in the fold and the others returned to the pastures. The flocks were divided for a time and everyone was busy, experienced husbandmen attended the ewes, other servants cleaned and bundled the wool, and remaining shepherds returned the flock to the fields.

One year, as Rebekah attended the ewes, a young shepherd half ran and half stumbled back to the well of Beer-lahai-roi. He was bruised and near exhaustion and was barely able to speak.

Gasping with a dry throat he said. "Invaders, foreign flocks in our south pasture, near the canyon wadi road. They drive off and scatter our flock. The others are gathering our sheep, and I have come to warn you."

Rebekah called out, "Find Isaac and Jachin, and prepare my donkey! Abiel, come with me."

Abiel answered, "Mistress, master Isaac, and Jachin have gone to the east pastures, there have been reports of a large tribe, strangers moving towards us."

Then to a trained man, Abiel said, "Go quickly and tell master Isaac and Jachin to come at once to the south pasture."

To another, he said, "Choose five men and come with us. Have the others stay here and protect the camp and the flock."

As Rebekah, Abiel and their small band of trained men arrived at the southern pasture, they came upon a very large flock of sheep and goats coming out of the small pasture, being led along the wadi canyon road west towards Ishmael's land. Abiel approached a shepherd and asked, "Who trespasses on the pastures of Isaac? Who drives off the sheep of my master?"

The shepherd replied, "Out of my way, I have a flock to attend."

Abiel drew his sword and the trained men drew arrows from their quivers. The shepherd stopped and said, "We drive the sheep of my master, Dedan, son of Jokshan, son of Abraham who was given this land by his God. We need no man's permission to pasture our sheep. We lead them to Egypt and to market."

Abiel answered, "Has not father Abraham sent your master's father, Jokshan to the east, away from the lands of his heir and son of God's promise, Isaac? And did he not send them away from his son Ishmael who lives to the east of the Negev? Father Abraham has not gifted his land to your master, Dedan. And you will find no welcome in the lands of Ishmael."

"We go where we go. Would it not be wiser for you to find your lost sheep and let us go on our way?"

Rebekah spoke, "Shepherd, your sheep must be thirsty. You will find no water on your road ahead other than the pool of Ishmael, and it is true, he will offer you no hospitality for the arrogance of your trespass. Take your flock north to the wells at Gerar where your sheep will find water and rest, then take the road west to Egypt. Your sheep will be revived, the market price better and Ishmael will not be provoked."

As they spoke a large party of trained men on donkeys could be seen coming from the west, capturing the shepherds, one by one, accompanying the flocks ahead. As they approached, Rebekah recognized Nebaioth, son of Ishmael, leading them.

Nebaioth approached Rebekah and said, "Mistress Rebekah, go home it is not safe for you here. As for your shepherds, flock and men, we take them. Isaac has broken his oath, made in my hearing."

Rebekah answered, "This flock and these shepherds are not of Isaac's house. The flock belongs to Dedan, son of Jokshan, son of Abraham by Katura. While the flocks of Isaac were being sheared at Beer-lahai-oi, Dedan's shepherds entered our pastures and drove off our returning flock. There remains not a blade of grass in our south pasture. Indeed, I have told this shepherd his trespass will find him no hospitality in the lands of Ishmael. Do what you will with them, but the servants of my husband, Isaac you shall not touch. My husband has gone east to find Dedan and his household."

Nebaioth turned to the shepherd and asked, "Is this true? Tell me if you wish to live."

The shepherd replied, "My lord, it is just as the woman says. The sheep belong to my master, Dedan. We move them to market in Egypt. The drought is severe in our country and trade caravans are few. We move them lest we all perish. My lord, Dedan, follows in a caravan with camels, donkeys, and oxen. His trained men are with him. He is a hard master, known to take what is not his."

Abiel spoke, "Master Nebaioth, perhaps it is wiser to hold the sheep and shepherds here and wait for Master Dedan to arrive. Would you have bloodshed against your cousin's house before you speak with him?"

Nebaioth shouted to his men, "Hold all of the sheep in the canyon. The shepherds we hold as hostage."

Turning back to Abiel and Rebekah, he saw a dust cloud growing on the wadi road behind Rebekah. The cloud grew and the ground shook to the sound of many camels and donkeys moving rapidly. Out of the dust appeared a large force of trained men their bronze swords, sheathed on their sides, flashing in the sunlight as they rode. Isaac and Jachin could be seen among the leaders.

When the leaders rode forward, an angry and petulant Dedan spoke, "Is this the hospitality of the house of Ishmael, to seize the flocks and shepherds of his cousin as they pass?"

Nebaioth responded, "Should the house of my father, Ishmael, grant hospitality to one who takes and does not ask? You enter as the thief and the robber who demands redress once caught in your own evil scheme."

Isaac spoke, "Your cousin's flock are in a hard way with drought and he seeks only a safe pass to Egypt."

Nebaioth answered, "My cousin speaks for himself, uncle, he asks neither permission nor forgiveness, and enters our land with the weapons of his trained men drawn. Let the bloodshed be on his hands."

Dedan shouted, "If bloodshed is what you would have, my men will fight."

Rebekah rode her donkey between the two belligerent cousins. Looking to Nebaioth she asked, "Nephew, what do you trade with when in Egypt? Is it not wool and tents? Do you not raise sheep?"

While Nabaioth overcame his surprise at Rebekah's question, she turned to Dedan and asked, "Do you not seek to trade your flock for money and goods? How many sheep and cattle have died on the journey? How many more of your livestock will die before you arrive? Do you want your servants to die as well? I say to both of you there is a better way. Let Nebaioth buy the sheep and cattle of his cousin, Dedan, at a fair price. Ishmael has many sons and knows the pastures of the Negev and markets of Egypt. Dedan can depart with his price and leave the lands of Ishmael in peace."

Nebaioth said, "These sheep are weak with hunger and thirst, there is much risk."

Rebekah answered, "The sons of Ishmael are good shepherds and know how to husband strong sheep. Make your price fair."

Dedan much calmer said, "Release my men, I will accept a fair price for my herds. It is true, they will fare poorly if we journey any further. You can tend these sheep, I am through with sheep and shepherds. I will go my way and you will not see me again, cousin."

Abiel said, "Master Nebaioth, would you not agree that good water and a month in the pasture and these sheep will be as healthy as any in your flock, would you offer your cousins four shekels each?"

Nebaioth answered, "They require much care. Three shekels."

Dedan replied, "Five shekels is the price of a sheep."

Abiel responded, "Five would be a fair price for a strong sheep. And if you press on, how many more will you lose?"

Dedan thought and said, "Four shekels."

Nebaioth answered, "Four shekels, done."

Abiel and Jachin stayed as third-party witnesses to the counting of the sheep and the payment for the flock. Separate deals were struck for the cattle, oxen and some of the camels.

As Isaac and Rebekah returned to Beer-lahai-roi, Isaac, smiling, said proudly, "Bless the God of Abraham who has given me a wise wife! Beautiful, kind and wise!"

As Isaac and Rebekah retired to their tent, Abiel said to Deborah, "What joy my master finds in his wife! She has brought comfort and strength to him I have not seen in many years. Truly, she is his blessing from God."

Deborah replied, "And Isaac is a blessing to my mistress as well; how she blossoms in his love! Yes, it is joy, indeed to watch them become as one! Is this not God's plan for man and woman?"

Abiel looked at Deborah and considered the question, "Yes, but perhaps not for all of us."

Chapter Sixteen

How long, O LORD? Will You forget me forever? How long will You hide Your face from me? How long shall I take counsel in my soul, having sorrow in my heart all the day?

Psalm 13: 1, 2

Rebekah was confident in her abilities. She was confident in the love of her husband, Isaac. But none of her confidence could remove the doubt of giving Isaac the son God promised him. As their marriage approached twenty years she feared more than ever, that Halima, as cruel as she was, may have been right. She feared she may be barren; her years of childbearing age were fast coming to an end. Isaac expressed no concern, but surely, he too must know. He kept so much to himself, reluctant to share his feelings. Would he take a concubine?

One afternoon she returned to her tent to find Isaac holding the forearms of Deborah, both of them laughing. Suddenly the threat she never thought possible ran through her mind, *Isaac will take Deborah as a concubine or wife. Has he not always loved her? She is warm and beautiful; and so charming! Could it be my lifelong friend has stolen my husband?'*

Hiding her feelings, Rebekah smiled and said, "Husband you must share with me the joy my nurse, Deborah brings you."

Isaac motioned for Rebekah to come close. When she did he gave her a big hug, sweeping her off her feet and spinning a full circle before gently putting her down. "Wife, you indeed have caught us. We have planned something special, but you must wait and see!"

Then looking at Deborah he said, "Wife, you are truly blessed to have a servant, who is both friend and indeed sister, who sees to your welfare."

Once Rebekah was alone with Deborah she asked, "So, what are you and my husband planning?"

Deborah smiled, "I have promised not to say, but he intends to bring you joy."

Looking aside, Rebekah said, "So now you decide to keep things from me, something you have never done before."

Then turning directly to Deborah, she asked, "Tell me truly, Deborah, what do I desire before all else?"

"I know the desire of your heart is a son for your husband Isaac. In my heart, I know the Most High will provide a son, a father of a great nation and blessing to all people, just as he promised to father Abraham."

With that, Rebekah began planning. She was determined that Deborah would not become a mother to Isaac's child. "Deborah," she said, "You have so much love to give, you should have sons and daughters to love and nurture."

Deborah surprised replied, "That is kind of you to say, the calling of a mother is indeed sweet and precious, but I am called to serve you. It is God's promise to Isaac and you his chosen wife to bring God's blessing to all people. I am a servant to his great promise."

Rebekah sent for Jachin and when he arrived she asked, "Jachin, could you bring me some fresh game that I might prepare for my husband? I wish to surprise my husband with his favorite stew this evening."

Jachin answered, "I am honored mistress. I will go immediately."

As Jachin was leaving, Rebekah asked, "You are yet unmarried, Jachin, have you no desire for children to raise up to honor you?"

Jachin turned and looked puzzled. His private life had never been questioned by Rebekah, "Mistress, I indeed look forward to marriage and many fine sons and daughters. I have been promised in marriage to Hephzibah, (She is my delight), daughter of Seosamh, (God Will Multiply), a trained man in your husband's service."

Rebekah's face flushed, she replied, "Oh, I had not heard. I pray the Most High bless you and Hephzibah with great joy and many children. I shall await your return then."

True to his skill, Jachin returned with a fine young antelope which would cook tender for Isaac's stew. Rebekah carefully cooked the stew using the precious spices brought from Egypt, carefully sampling the broth to make sure it was just as Isaac enjoyed. While the stew slowly simmered, she brushed and adorned her hair, dressed in a fine, light linen and clean robe. She put on her emerald necklace and applied a sweet perfume.

When Isaac returned to their tent, he was greeted by the savory smell of the stew. He breathed in the aroma and smiled. Hearing him come in, Rebekah came to greet him. When he saw his wife adorned as she was, he opened his arms to her and said, "I am truly blessed! After hugging her, he stepped back, "Let me look at you! More beautiful than that first night we met and God joined us together!"

"More beautiful? Husband, you tease! I am twenty years older!"

Isaac opened her robe and blushing said, "Ah, I have had twenty years to learn about the beauty of your love. And truly I find no one more beautiful than you What have I done that you offer me such delight?"

Rebekah smiled, "Do not you and Deborah plan to bring

me joy? Can I not bring joy to my husband as well?"

"Aha!" Isaac laughed, "You wish to know of your surprise! You will not charm it from me! It is a secret but come, let me lead my beautiful bride to our bed."

Rebekah kissed Isaac and said, "Not before you tasted this stew I prepared for you."

"It will be a night of double delights!" Isaac hugged and kissed her once more.

Isaac sat at the table and began to enjoy his stew. Rebekah sat across from him watching him eat. Isaac looked at his wife and said, "This is good, much better than even the table of Ishmael." Then, noticing she was sitting hunched forward with her chin in her hands and her elbows on the table, he said, "Rebekah, you do not eat. Is all well?"

She sat up straight, "I enjoy seeing you happy, I have tasted the stew many times to make sure it was just right. So, it is better than Halima's?"

She paused and began to twist her hair above her ear around her right index finger, and after taking a deep breath she asked, "Husband, you love Deborah, do you not?"

Isaac continued eating, "Of course I love Deborah; she serves you steadfastly. The whole household loves her. Do they not call her Nediva Deborah?"

Then sensing something was troubling Rebekah, he added, "Of course, I do not love her as I love you. Are we not one flesh and one spirit? Why do you ask this?"

"I only ask because I have been considering all that she has done for me. And now you plan with her some kind thing to bring me joy. If you wish to bring me joy, give me your oath that you will do as I ask."

Isaac said, "I made an oath with you when I took you as my wife. There has never been a need for any oaths between us. Is it not enough that I say I will do as you ask, as I ever do to please you? Tell me what it is I can do to please you."

Rebekah pulled her finger out of her hair, took a sip of wine and said, "I have determined it is not right that Deborah is denied the love of a husband and the joy of her own children. Have we not been selfish not to repay her service? So, I was thinking we must find a man as dedicated as she is, for she will never forego her calling to serve me. We must find a husband for her who will not remove her from your household."

Isaac carefully considered Rebekah's words and then said, "The only man as dedicated to serving as Deborah is Abiel. He too puts his calling to serve above his own happiness, I have often asked him when he will take a wife, for I would not see him become as Eliezer, alone in his old age. But he always smiles and says, he will not marry, for he could not ask a wife to set her happiness behind his service to this house."

Finally, Isaac understood, "Yes, of course, they should marry! I never considered this. Once again, you prove your wisdom!"

Rebekah smiled.

Isaac gulped down his wine, got up from the table walked over and to Rebekah, picked her up and said, "Now for my second delight!"

Rebekah laughed, "Not over your shoulder again, I am a great lady!"

Isaac tossed her up with a twist and caught her in his arms. Rebekah, giggling, shook her hair from her face, wrapped her arms around his neck and kissed him passionately. She looked up into his eyes and said, "You know I love you."

Isaac smiled and said, "Yes and I will always love you. Now, come and remind me just how great a lady you are," and he carried her into bed.

Having been prepared by Rebekah, Isaac wasted little time in raising the subject of marriage with Abiel. Once again, Abiel acknowledged marriage as God's plan for man and a blessing for both man and wife. When he turned the subject of some being called to service which might prove too difficult for a wife, Isaac was prepared. "Abiel," he began, "How faithful to me you are! But is not your mother a prophet, called by God? And yet she is a loving wife, supported by your father?"

Abiel answered, "It is true, my lord, my father supports my mother, but her calling came when they were together and they are truly one in service."

Isaac said, "Being one in service is indeed a calling. So, if a man and a woman have the same calling and the same heart to serve God, or those whom God has called them to serve, your objection is removed."

Abiel replied, "If such were the case, I suppose my objection would be removed, but there still remains…."

Isaac interrupted, "And if your objection is removed, should you not consider the needs of a woman in service to have the protection of a husband? And not just the protection, but his love?

And should she not have children to care for her in widowhood? Should such an honorable woman, serving God and those she has been called to serve, should she be unloved and unprotected? Is that justice?"

Abiel stuttered and then said, "Is there such a woman?"

Isaac stood up, put his arm around Abiel's shoulder, "Abiel, how many times have I listened to your advice to see things I have not seen; or listened to your wisdom to learn what I did not know? Your eyes have not seen that such a noble woman is known by you, and already you love her as a fellow servant. Is not Deborah such a woman? Does she not serve as unselfishly as you? Who will protect her? Who will father her sons to care for her in old age? Shall she be denied the joy your mother has known? Can she not be the wife to walk with you as one? To love and comfort each other? And to take the worry from the hearts of your master and mistress? Unless of course, you know of some evil or hardness on her heart that would make her undeserving of God's plan? Well, do you know of such things?"

Abiel replied, "No, no of course not. Deborah is all the

faithful, loving servant you say. I did not think, I never considered, no, I mean yes, Deborah should be protected and loved."

And then Abiel looked with questioning eyes, "Do you think she would have me? I mean, Deborah she is such a special woman. She is so gracious and well, everyone knows how kind and special she is; and beautiful too, in body and soul. And me, I am older and just a servant dedicated to working and..."

Isaac patted Abiel on the back, "Oh I think she can be shown that her marriage to you only makes her stronger in serving God and her mistress."

It took days for the normally efficient and effective Abiel to gather the words, the strength and the courage to speak to Deborah. His's proposal was both awkward and charming. Awkward because marriage had never been in Abiel's plans and he had always held his emotions in check, charming because he realized that marriage, especially marriage to Deborah was something he truly desired. Abiel prayed to God. He told how much he had grown to love Deborah and asked God to bind them together in love and service and that he would honor God's will in the matter.

Despite all of the hints that Rebekah had made to Deborah before Abiel's proposal, Deborah was still surprised. When Abiel made the case that Isaac laid out for him. Deborah listened quietly and said nothing. Finally, Abiel said, "Deborah, do you remember when you asked me if I was happy, happy in the way Isaac and Rebekah were happy? I said the Most High did not intend that happiness for me or you. I see now I was wrong. Perhaps it was my pride speaking; pride in my ability to serve. I see now that I have enough love to serve you as well. Just as Isaac and Rebekah are one, and we serve them, can we not serve them as one also? Will not the God of Abraham bless us and grant us joy and happiness as well? Is there anyone who does not at times need another to share in their burdens? I know I am approaching my old age, but I promise to love, honor and protect you, all of my days, and who knows, perhaps God will give you sons and daughters as well. I would like to join my life with yours, marry me."

Deborah looked at Abiel, standing before her with his head bowed. She had never seen him so humble or vulnerable. She thought, *he is a good man, and kindhearted; I've always liked him, no, loved him. He has always been honest and selfless; perhaps it is true, God intends for us the blessings of marriage as well.*

Finally, Deborah answered, "Truly Abiel, your offer of marriage is a surprise. We have known each other so many years. I know you are a good man, true to your word and selfless. I too had no plans for marriage, but I find your proposal to be both welcome and confusing. I am afraid, afraid I must... I must think... Do you really think God has brought us together? Yes, you said so."

Abiel and Deborah stood silently looking at each other. They had known one another for years. But each saw the other differently for the first time. They saw a future they never imagined and both knew in their heart that their love was real, and God's special blessing was now set before them.

Tears came to Deborah's eyes, "Oh Abiel I would very much like to marry you! Yes, I will marry you."

Several days later, as was her habit, Rebekah went to meet the shepherds returning with the flocks in the late afternoon. She arrived to find the entire flock of sheep and goats roaming about. All of the shepherds were assembled wearing their finest clean white robes. Each had a colored ribbon on his crook and dispersed through the field were small pens with colored ribbons at the gate. When she arrived, Isaac was waiting for her.

"Rebekah, welcome! The shepherds have gathered to honor you. They put to you to judge them this day, and to choose from them your champion."

Turning to Deborah, she said, "So this is your surprise!"

Deborah said, "Have you not always enjoyed the

competition? And these shepherds, are they not good men with the honest smell of sheep about them, and each a friend? Isaac wants to bring you an afternoon of joy!"

Isaac addressed the assembly, "Fellow shepherds, you have each been given a ribbon for your crook to match a sheepfold. You are to shepherd one hundred sheep into your fold, no goats! Once you have one hundred sheep, you have until sunset to fleece them, bundle the wool and bring it to Abiel at the wool tent. You will be judged on the number of bundles and the weight of wool. After you leave your wool at the tent, water your sheep and shepherd them to the large night fold. After all of your sheep are in the night fold, you must shepherd thirty goats to the pens for milking and leave them in the care of the milkmaids and cheesemaker.The winner will be lady Rebekah's champion and he shall sit at my table with Rebekah as the honored guest of a feast."

Isaac turned to Rebekah and said, "Whenever you are ready."

Grinning happily, Rebekah waved her arm and shouted, "Shepherds gather your flocks!"

As the shepherd hurried off, Rebekah approached Isaac and was about to speak. Smiling broadly, Isaac immediately said, "Go, go and encourage them. They want to impress you! Mingle, talk, cheer them on. This is your competition. You are are their chief! Go!"

That night as they lay in bed in their tent, Rebekah said, "Husband, truly no man has cared for the happiness of his wife as you. I thank you for all that you do, for now, I know you act only in love. But husband, why does it not pain you that I bear no sons?It has been twenty years and I have no son."

Isaac sat up and looked with love at Rebekah, "I trust God to fulfill his promises. I have no pain because I know God will provide. But I see now your pain. I see there will be no other comfort I can bring you. You must know that I love you. You must know God loves you and has called you. If your heart's desire is for a son, and you suffer until God provides, we must ask God to provide a son for you and me."

That night while holding Rebekah tight in his arms, Isaac fervently prayed that God would give her his son.

God heard Isaac's prayer.

Chapter Seventeen

I call upon you because I know you will answer, O God; incline your ear to me; hear my words.

Psalm 17: 6

Rebekah first greeted her pregnancy with disbelief, but her growing bulge convinced her it must be true, and then she became unshakably happy. It touched Deborah's heart to see Rebekah so happy once again. Isaac was thankful and pleased; he no longer stressed to comfort his wife, but he rejoiced in her happiness. It was a joy that pushed all other questions about God's plans and promises from his mind. There was only the joyful knowledge that Rebekah would be the mother to his child.

Only after Rebekah was reminded of the planning for Deborah's wedding did she remember how she manipulated Isaac and Abiel, and even Deborah herself into a marriage none had ever planned. Seeing herself focused only on her pending motherhood when her dear friend was about to enter into a mid-life marriage, Rebekah finally spoke out. "Deborah," she began, as she slowly curled her lovely red hair around her index finger, "In all the years we have known each

154 The Oak of Weeping

other, you never spoke of marriage. And now, you are pledged to marry Abiel. Do you truly desire to marry now after all?"

Deborah was thoughtful. "Abiel's proposal was most surprising indeed. But he is such a tenderhearted and good man, and we have served alongside each other so long. Yes, I am pleased to marry him."

Rebekah lowered her head and said, "About Abiel's proposal, I must confess to you that I put in Isaac's mind that Abiel should marry you. Forgive me, it was selfish and wrong. I was so afraid Isaac would want a son that he would take another wife or concubine. You know how that has always upset me and when I saw you and Isaac together, forgive me, I feared Isaac would take you as his wife just as Abraham took Hagar, Sarah's maid. I knew he would not take you if you were married. I am so sorry and ashamed. You must know that you can be released from your pledge, I have wronged both of you."

Deborah stared at Rebekah silently, her face changing from surprise to composure until it finally formed a small smile. "I can forgive; I do forgive you. What you intended as a selfish scheme, God used to open our eyes. Abiel and I can complete each other. God put the two of us together all these years ago, but we were too prideful to see that the beauty of marriage was never meant to be withheld from us. Have you not noticed the joy on Abiel's face or mine? No, Rebekah, let go of your guilt! Abiel and I will indeed marry; pray that our marriage will be happy."

Rebekah was about to reply when she winced from two kicks from within her womb. The first of many to come. Instinctively, she placed her hands on the baby and laughed lightly, "Well, someone certainly wants his presence known! So strong! It must be a boy! Surely the Most High will give us a son, a son of God's promise to father Abraham and Isaac."

Deborah beamed with joy at her beloved friend and mistress, "Is not God good! All those years of worry are now behind you! And it was Isaac's prayer; God was just waiting for you to ask Him and trust in His mercy. Can it be so simple that we do not have because we do not ask? I am not the one to know the mind of God, but I know He has made you happy. And in all of this has worked for my happiness, and Abiel's as well."

Rebekah looked at her friend and noticed the small tear in her eye, "Oh, Deborah, I do pray that your marriage to Abiel brings you the joy and comfort I have found with Isaac. We must make it special! Yes, everyone in the household must attend. A feast, a grand feast shall be prepared; after all, are you not the beloved, Nediva Deborah? Eliezer is going to Damascus, he will surely carry the news to Abiel's family. If only we could get the news to your mother Leah. She worked so hard to teach us God's plan for marriage, and your father, Zimri-Ruel. He would be so proud of you."

Deborah sighed, "It is so far to Haran and the plains of Nahor, but Abiel's parents, surely! We could wait for them."

Rebekah replied, "You must let me arrange the feast, and you shall have my robe and gowns, and yes, my jewels! I shall make you as the great lady you are to me."

Rebekah enjoyed serving Deborah in the same way Deborah had served her when she wed Isaac twenty years earlier. Her joy was made even greater knowing she carried Isaac's child. But even in joy, the kicking and struggling within her, which only increased, began to alarm her. None of the midwives had ever seen anything like it before. Yes, kicking was normal and to be expected in a healthy baby, but the activity in Rebekah's womb worried them, though none would dare tell Rebekah they worried. They didn't have to, Rebekah saw it in their eyes.

When Eliezer arrived leading Abiel's family to Beer-lahai-roi, Rebekah was relieved that Deborah's wedding could finally proceed. After hugging and congratulating their only son Abiel, Abaigael asked to see the bride, daughter of their friend Zimri-Ruel. Deborah was waiting in Rebekah's tent. Just as Abaigael entered the tent, the kicking war in Rebekah's womb resumed and Rebekah nearly doubled over in pain. Abaigael went over to Rebekah who cried out, "Abaigael, prophet of the Most High, please inquire of God on my behalf! Why am I this way?"

The word of the Most High immediately came to Abaigael, "Rebekah, the Lord, the Most High God, has this to say to you: 'Two nations are in your womb, and two peoples will be separated from your body, and one people shall be stronger than the other, and the older shall serve the younger."

At the sound of Abaigael's voice, the kicking stopped. Rebekah stared at Abaigael dumbfounded. Deborah looking on said nothing. Abaigael smiled at Rebekah and said softly, "Were you not called for this? You will be a mother to two nations, and with Isaac, fulfill the promise of God to Abraham. After hugging Rebekah warmly, she turned to Deborah whom she also hugged. "I will have a daughter! Is not God good? He has brought you and Abiel together to love and comfort each other, You will need each other's strength to serve master Isaac and Rebekah and their sons."

A tear came to Abaigael's eye as she smiled brightly, "Can I help prepare the bride, or shall I leave you both to the warmth of your love and friendship? No, I see it best to leave you together; we will have time at the feast."

As Abaigael slipped out of the tent, Rebekah said to Deborah, "This is God's word to me, please let no other hear of it."

Rebekah pondered God's words in her heart.

The wedding of Abiel and Deborah was in every way as festive as was the marriage of Isaac and Rebekah. Isaac led the procession and acted as the bridegroom's friend. Jared and Abaigael followed Abiel and Deborah and the entire household followed along singing with joy, for they truly loved Abiel and especially their dear Nediva Deborah. As Isaac pronounced the command for Abiel to take his wife, Deborah, home, the beauty of Deborah was not captured in the exquisitely embroidered robe or the expensive jewels of Rebekah, but in the beaming face of a middle-aged woman who just comprehended the fullness of joy reserved for her in a man who loved her and was brought to her by God himself. Abiel smiled like he never had before, their two hearts and spirit joined in an unbreakable bond. They escaped into the intimacy afforded by Abiel's tent chamber and tasted the beauty of God's intended gift of marriage.

When Abiel and Deborah joined the wedding feast, they could scarcely follow the joyful conversation or hear the news of Abiel's family in Damascus. Rebekah had learned her strong and beloved grandmother, Milcah recovered in death what she lost in life; she had been laid to rest beside her husband, Nahor, and that his concubine, Reumah was buried separately. Her father, Bethuel, doted on Rebekah's mother, providing every luxury known in Haran. He took no other wife, and with her brother, Laban, enjoyed wealth and prosperity.

Zimri-Ruel still served the now united people of Nahor and Dabar El'Elyon as the priest, leading sacrifices of worship and thanksgiving. Leah was well, but the other women and girls no longer sought out her teaching of independent and strong wives. The inspiration for other village daughters lost its heart after the departure of the two amazing, strong and independent young women that were Rebekah and Deborah.

Deborah found the news bittersweet. The memories of her parents and friends warmed her heart, but O how she missed them! She imagined her papa joyfully singing a song of praise for the loving-kindness of God and her momma, lovingly giving her practical advice for her marriage to Abiel. She imagined her saying, 'Abiel is a good man and loving too, but he is a man, with the weakness and pride of all men, and therefore you must know how to guard your marriage and lead him to see he can trust in your wisdom as well. Honor him, love him and obey him, but be forthright to steer him when he strays. Remember, you are one, just as God intended'.

Deborah glanced at Abiel and said to herself, *I will momma, just as you say. I will bring the love and joy to Abiel that you have brought to papa.*

Abiel caught Deborah's glance. Seeing the love in her eyes, he leaned over and kissed her.

Chapter Eighteen

When her days to be delivered were fulfilled, behold there were twins in her womb.

Genesis 25: 24

Isaac was sixty years old when Rebekah delivered healthy twin boys. Even as they were born, they were struggling and fighting just as they had throughout Rebekah's pregnancy. The first was hairy, not just the dark red-brown hair on his head, but hairy over his body, so they named him Esau, 'Hairy.' Amazingly, the second son was born with his hand gripping and pulling on his brother's heel. He was fair with only the lightest of hair on the top of his head. They named him Jacob. Now Jacob was an unusual name, a play on words in Hebrew; it could mean 'Heel Holder' but also 'Trickster,' for he certainly entered the world performing an unforgettable trick. Isaac and Rebekah cheerfully shared with Abiel and Deborah the antics of their newborn sons.

Deborah, as usual, was the first to praise God, "Is this not a miracle of our loving God? O what joy he gives us in children! Such fine, strong sons you have! Has not God lovingly answered Isaac's prayer? And in double measure; not one son, but two!

Rebekah beamed at her friend and said. "And the two could not be more different! How could my womb, carry such different babies at the same time? Are not Isaac and I parent to both? Do they not both suckle at my breast? I can only but wonder at their difference! So clearly individuals with the unique touch of God on each of them."

Abiel smiled and said, "Truly our God and creator breathes life into every newborn child, and accounts for all of their days before the first one is known. Do you not remember, Isaac, God's promise to father Abraham? It will come through a child of yours, the promise of one, 'through him all nations will be blessed.' Open the eyes of your heart and watch the promise of God grow before you!"

Isaac, holding both swaddled babies, could not lift his eyes away from them, "It is just as you say, Abiel, and may the God of Abraham bring the blessings of children to you and Deborah as well."

A year after the twins were born, the two who never expected to be parents, Abiel and Deborah, warmly welcomed their son into the world. To show that their child was dedicated to God, they named him Lemuel. Masters and servants were united in the richness of the struggles of parenting. Abiel and Deborah flowered in a joy they never thought possible, and they loved God all the more for their many blessings. Little Lemuel was a quiet baby, with large bright eyes that watched everything and everyone around him. As he grew, he proved to be a compliant and joyful son but always quiet when in the presence of anyone other than Abiel or Deborah.

Isaac and Rebekah also found new joy in the blessings of God. The truth that there is no limit to love in any person's heart was apparent to everyone in the house of Isaac. Isaac and Rebekah's love for each other became only stronger and more evident, and their love for their infant sons was every bit as much as God intended when He established the family.

They loved, laughed, and doted on Esau and Jacob. As the two boys began to crawl Rebekah remarked to Isaac, "How different they remain! Husband, I tell you the struggles between them which began in my womb only grows."

Isaac answered, "It seems Esau grows bigger and stronger than Jacob. Look how he asserts his will over his brother."

Rebekah nodded, "Indeed, what you say is true, but little Jacob shows a surprising ability to deal with his brother's aggression. See how he hides his things or comes to me when Esau provokes him."

"Yes, he knows you will step in and separate them when Esau gets too rough."

Rebekah continued, "Did you notice his ploys to trick Esau by grabbing less favored things when Esau is present, allowing his bullying brother to take them away, and then recovering his prized possessions once Esau lumbers off."

Isaac laughed, "Our little trickster!"

Rebekah added thoughtfully, "Is it not strange, Isaac, that Esau does not pester little Lemuel when he is present? Esau directs his aggression only towards Jacob."

Isaac answered, "Yes, it is true, both Esau and Jacob seem accepting of little Lemuel, but Lemuel is quiet and passive. Our twins struggle only with each other."

As the twins grew older and parental correction harder for them to ignore, their competition became more hidden from Isaac and Rebekah. Esau continued to bully his brother out of sight of momma and papa, but Jacob was a quick learner and his survival instincts seemed to keep him one step ahead of Esau. It was no surprise that Jacob avoided the company of Esau except in the presence of Rebekah, who was always his protector. It should not have been surprising that Esau saw Rebekah's protection of Jacob as unfair to him, so whenever Rebekah stepped in to protect Jacob, Esau would go to Isaac for solace. Isaac was always troubled by conflict in his family, a sore lesson from Abraham's treatment of Ishmael and the sons of Keturah. His instinct was to sooth Esau and say, "Don't be troubled son, all is well, does not the Most High love you? And you know that momma and I love you as well."

When Esau and Jacob were old enough to draw a bow, Isaac determined to take his sons on a hunt. Esau was elated to accompany his father and Jachin on the hunt, but without the company of Rebekah, Jacob was uneasy. When the boys were given the opportunity to let arrows fly, Esau's arrow flew straight and true, while Jacob's arrow fell short and far off the mark. Esau took great delight in mocking Jacob's lesser efforts. Isaac complimented Esau. "Well done son! You will make a fine hunter!" But to Jacob, he said, "You must practice more, my son."

Isaac ignored Esau's taunting of Jacob. He saw it as the childish nonsense of no great importance. But from then on Jacob found an excuse never to join his father on a hunt with Esau. This suited Esau, as he cherished his special time alone with Isaac. Esau learned to love the hunt and with Jachin's instruction, became a skilled archer and accomplished hunter. Jacob chose to join Rebekah in her visits to the flocks and shepherds. He was fascinated with the secrets of husbanding the sheep and goats, caring for lambing ewes, and preparing wool for the market. He listened intently to discussions with Abiel on how to market the wool, cheese, goat hair tents as well as exchanging trade goods for spices, myrrh or myrrh oil, or for silver or even gold. Lemuel listened quietly, only his inquisitive bright eyes making his presence known.

As the boys reached adolescence, they had become skilled in hiding their animosity towards each other in the tent of their parents. Each chose to sit as far from the other as possible. Isaac saw this as peace, after all, they were no longer hitting and kicking each other at the table. But there was no peace between them. Rebekah knew of their disdain for each other but did not know what to do. Isaac never wanted to discuss it, he preferred to believe it was nothing; he expected it would go away once they grew up. In the back of her mind though, Rebekah pondered the prophecy from God.

Isaac always enjoyed eating game, especially in a slow-simmered stew. Esau curried favor with his father by providing game for his table. One day Esau returned from a hunt and saw his brother Jacob preparing a lentil stew. In his overbearing and demanding manner, he said to Jacob, "Give me some of that red stuff you're cooking, I'm famished!"

Jacob stirring the pot, not looking up he said, "First sell me your birthright."

Esau impatiently replied, "I'm about to die from hunger! And you pester me about a birthright?"

The aroma of the simmering stew filled the air. Jacob did not look up; his eyes watching the stew as he slowly stirred. He breathed in fully of the pleasing aroma, and repeated, "First sell me your birthright."

Esau's voice grew louder and angrier, "What use is a birthright to me?"

Jacob kept stirring the pot, and said, "First swear to me."

"I swear, now give me the stew!"

Jacob gave him bread, lentil stew and drink. Esau ate his food, got up and left with no regard for what he had done.

Esau's thoughtless and foolish selling of his birthright for a bowl of stew brought shame upon him, for he had despised his birthright. A birthright was both an honored and valuable possession that could only be lost for the gravest of transgressions or sold for a high price. A birthright gave a son two-thirds of all that his father owned.

When Rebekah heard of it she asked Isaac, "Do you know what the servants call your favorite son? They call him Edom. Isaac, they call him Red!"

Isaac answered, "So, is not his hair a red-brown?"

Rebekah said, "They mock him! Not red hair; but red lentil stew! Esau has sold his birthright to Jacob for a bowl of red lentil stew! He is without honor. To disrespect his birthright is to disrespect you and the Most High God."

Isaac was blind to Esau's selfish weaknesses; he answered, "He is impetuous and a little foolhardy, but he is young, he will grow up. And what can you say about your Jacob? How often he manipulates his brother! Is there honor in that?

Esau's disdain for his twin brother Jacob grew to hatred.

Chapter Nineteen

And Abraham breathed his last and died at a ripe old age, an old man satisfied with life; and he was gathered to his people.

Genesis 25: 8

One day, when the twins were about fifteen years old, a messenger sent by Eliezer brought news to Isaac that he should come quickly for his father, Abraham, was near death. Isaac immediately summoned Jachin and directed him to take the news to Ishmael, imploring his brother to join him at his father's death bed at the Oaks of Mamre, near Hebron. Isaac immediately left with the servant and returned to Abraham's household.

When Isaac arrived in the camp of Abraham, the mood was somber. Eliezer came out to meet him as he approached the tent. "Master Isaac, father Abraham has gone to his fathers. We are your servants now."

Isaac stopped and stared at his father's tent. He could find no words to utter. He began to sob and turning to Eliezer, he said, "I needed to tell him I loved him. I wanted to hear his blessing and affirm forever I am his son. I wanted him to know he was loved. They are words he will never hear."

Eliezer came close and spoke softly, "Master Isaac, know that he knew your love. He knew your pain too, but where would the blessings of the God of Abraham be if your faith had not been tested? And you have received father Abraham's blessing. Has he not loved you with his whole heart? Has he not shown you to be his heir to the promise of the Most High God? What greater blessing could he give than the assurance that by your seed all men will be blessed."

"Can I see him?" Isaac muttered.

"He lies in his bed. When you are ready, his desire was to lay beside Sarah, your mother."

Isaac looked into Eliezer's eyes and replied, "I have sent for my brother, Ishmael. We wait until I know of his coming."

Isaac went into the tent and saw his father lying as if asleep in his bed. The servants had clothed him in his finest robe, washed him and carefully combed his white beard. He was wearing his turban and holding a shepherd's crook as if he were about to join his shepherds. Kneeling beside his father, Isaac kissed his forehead, his tears leaving streaks in his travel dusty face.

Hours later, Isaac was still in Abraham's tent, he spent the time remembering the words of his father and falling back into fits of sobs and tears. He did not notice the tent flap open and Ishmael silently enter.

Ishmael spoke, "I came for you, little brother. I knew it was important to you."

Isaac looked up and said, "It was important to him as well. O how I longed to hear him tell you, brother, how he always loved you. You must know he asked about you when I returned from the Negev. Remember when you found me yelling to God? Father wanted to hear all about you and your family. He was proud of all that you have done."

Ishmael looked at his father and said, "I hope what you say is true. He was good to me, and loving too, right until we were driven from the camp. But as you say, God has blessed me and all of my bitterness is now past."

Isaac smiled sadly, "Will you help me bury him?"

"Of course. He is our father; we will bury him together."

The next day Isaac and Ishmael buried Abraham in the cave of Machpelah, in the field of Ephron the son Zoar the Hittite, facing Mamre, the field which Abraham purchased from the sons of Heth; there Abraham was buried with Sarah, his wife.

After Abraham was buried, Ishmael preparing to leave, said to Isaac, "Your inheritance has come to you. You are now a wealthy man, a prince of the land, little brother, with two households of servants, many trained men, and great flocks of sheep, goats, camels, cattle, and donkeys. I ask only that you remember your oath to me."

Isaac answered, "I will always remember my oath, brother. Please let me give you some sheep, camels, and donkeys to share with your sons."

Ishmael replied, "God has given me a wealth of flocks, an oasis home, twelve strong sons and many daughters. Keep your flocks. Perhaps the sons of Keturah have more need. I leave you in peace, little brother."

Ishmael left alone, his bow slung over his shoulders, riding his donkey.

Eliezer was waiting for Isaac. "Master Isaac, you have much to attend to. I will stay here until Abiel arrives and establishes stewardship in your name."

"You are leaving?"

Eliezer smiled, "I have served your father most of my life. It was my honor and calling. You have Abiel, a good and trustworthy steward. I will return to my brother's house in Damascus to live out the remaining years God Most High may grant me."

Isaac replied, "Truly I cannot remember a time you were not in my father's service. He trusted your wisdom both as a steward and a friend. Let me send you off with gifts for your faithful service."

Eliezer said, "Thank you Master Isaac, but that will not be

necessary. Service to your father and the God of Abraham has been reward enough. O what my eyes have seen and my ears have heard! What lessons to my life came, learning to walk according to the will and love of the Eternal and Almighty God! Did not father Abraham show us all how to walk humbly before God in love, and obedience? Did not his complete trust in God become his love for God?"

Eliezer paused and then said softly, "Master Isaac, you know of the test father Abraham passed through, a hard test indeed. Learn the truth of God's testing, as your father did, to trust God with all of your heart. Let your trust become love and you will walk with Him in peace and joy forever."

Isaac replied, "I will think on it. Thank you, Eliezer, faithful servant and friend of Abraham and my teacher as well."

Eliezer stepped back and took a good look at Isaac, "May the God of Abraham bless you, Isaac, son of God's promise for by your seed all nations will be blessed."

Eliezer bowed and began to walk off.

"Ketura," Isaac said, "I must deal with my father's widow and her sons."

Isaac asked, "Eliezer, what has become of my father's widow? Does not Keturah mourn her husband?"

Eliezer replied, "Indeed Keturah mourns, but she mourns away from you, the heir and son of God's promise. She would not impose on you. She knew of Abraham's desire to lay beside Sarah."

"Please send for her. No, I will go to her. Take me to her now."

Isaac was led to Keturah's tent and asked to see her. She was seated, dressed in her finest robe with a single maidservant by her side.

Isaac fumbled for words, "Keturah, forgive me, I did not seek you out before burying my father. Please know you can stay in my household as long as you live. And your sons with you here…"

Keturah immediately answered, "I knew Abraham asked

to be laid beside Sarah, I knew you did not accept Abraham's love for me. I let you, his heir, bury him. I am alone here; my sons have all been sent off by Abraham. But no, I will not stay in your house, though it is right for you to provide for me. I will dwell with my oldest son, Zimran. I have already sent for him."

Isaac was stung by her frank words. "I would like to gift sheep, goats, and camels to you and your sons..."

Again, Keturah interrupted, "Do as you please with your inheritance, but Abraham has provided for all of his sons, brothers you chose not to know."

Isaac's jaw dropped. For all of his talk of his father's sin in fathering sons just to send to send them off, he realized she was right. He chose not to know them. It was easier that way.

Keturah saw the guilt in his eyes and then she said kindly, "Master Isaac, you have not learned to walk in love; to walk with the God of Abraham."

Keturah got up and walked into her private chamber.

Chapter Twenty

Now there was a famine in the land, besides the previous famine that had occurred in the days of Abraham. So Isaac went to Gerar, to Abimelech king of the Philistines.

Genesis 26:1

Isaac directed Abiel to move his great inheritance to Beer-lahai-roi, his camp in the upper Negev. Abraham's shepherds were reluctant, "Is the pasture here not greener than in the Negev? Is the water not more abundant, with many wells for our master's flocks? This is not a wise thing, Abiel. You must advise our master Isaac."

Abiel brought the concerns of his new shepherds to Isaac. Isaac listened patiently and said, "The Negev is my home. Yes, the grass is less and the flocks will be more scattered; and the shepherd's work will be more difficult, but I also remember my father's warning against the Canaanites. We have no neighbors in the Negev but Ishmael, and there is an oath between us on where we may safely pasture the flocks. Tell Abraham's shepherds I have heard their voice but we will be one household and we will keep our camp at Beer-lahai-roi."

The first year of the combined flocks in the Negev was

indeed difficult. Even so, the shepherds were able to graze the immense flocks over a wide area of the sparse landscape. The flocks survived, but they did not thrive. The trained men were stretched thin and the threat of thieves and raiders increased. The second year brought drought. The sparse grass dried up and died. New grass could not be found within a safe distance of the well. Indeed, the well at Beer-lahai-roi was strained, the level falling every day. It was clear, even to Isaac, that he could no longer remain in his beloved Negev.

The drought worsened and was widespread, even in Canaan. It was as severe as the drought Abraham faced many years earlier. Isaac moved his flocks north, to the first well of Gerar, but the grass there was also dead and the well dry. Isaac continued to move his massive flocks north to Gerar, the city of Abimelech, king of the Philistines. He hoped the Philistine king would remember the covenant his father had made with Abraham many years ago and honor Isaac, his heir, as well. Now the Philistines were a powerful, warlike people known to take what was not theirs and they did not know the God of Abraham. As they neared Gerar, Isaac was troubled and wondered if perhaps Egypt was a safer choice.

That night as Isaac tossed in restless sleep, the Lord appeared to him and said, "Do not go down to Egypt, stay in the land of which I shall tell you. Sojourn in this land and I will be with you, for to you and to your descendants, I will give all these lands, and I will establish the oath which I swore to your father Abraham. I will multiply your descendants as the stars of the heaven, and I will give your descendants all these lands, and by your descendants, all the nations of the earth shall be blessed; because Abraham obeyed Me and kept My charge, My commandments, My statutes and My laws."

When Isaac awoke, he anxiously shook Rebekah awake. "Rebekah, Rebekah, He spoke to me! The God of my father Abraham spoke to me! After all these years of seeking his voice, now He has spoken to me! It is just as father Abraham has said! The promises! The oath! It is all true! Of course, I thought it was true, everyone said it was true, but now God has spoken to me! We are to stay here, in Gerar and wait on the Lord. We do not go to Egypt! We stay here and obey the word of the Lord."

Rebekah stared at her husband. Then puzzled she said, "God spoke to you? Here in our bed, God spoke to you? You know it was God?"

Isaac was elated, "Yes, in my sleep, He came to me! I have never been more certain of anything else in my life! The promises are real, the promises of our sons and God's blessings! The promises of all the lands and blessings to come; by our descendants, all nations will be blessed! Was this not why the Most High called you in Haran to be my wife! God affirms!"

Isaac directed Abiel and his son Lemuel to have the shepherds lead the flocks to any pasture in the land and to identify all of the wells and water available. To Jachin he said, "Let the trained men know we shall respect the people of the land. Let it be known we will protect what is ours but do not provoke the herders we encounter."

There were other flocks in the area but Isaac's shepherds were careful not to hinder them in any way. Wherever Isaac's flocks pastured, the grass stayed green and plentiful and the water in the wells did not fall.

When Isaac pitched his tents and established his folds, a delegation sent from Abimelech came to inquire after Isaac's intentions. Isaac had given no thought to Abimelech since his encounter with God, but when Phicol, commander of Abimelech's army approached with a company of warriors, Isaac was afraid. He feared Rebekah's beauty may cost him his life. Isaac welcomed Phicol and turning to Rebekah he said, "And this is my sister, Rebekah."

Immediately he felt remorse but said nothing, continuing to explain his intentions were peaceful, and his flocks would bring meat, milk, cheese, and wool to the citizens of Gerar.

Phicol reported all he learned to king Abimelech. Now

Abimelech wisely chose to keep rivals and potential rivals close, where he could watch them. So, Abimelech welcomed Isaac, but bid him live in the city.

While Isaac and Rebekah lived in Gerar with their sons and close servants, Jachin stayed with the shepherds, tradesmen and trained men in the tents outside of the city. It was at Gerar that Jachin's wife died giving birth to a daughter, Yagon, 'Sorrow.'

Gerar was Abimelech's main city, and from there, he ruled over all of the Philistines. The Philistines worshiped the gods of Canaan. Unlike the other tribes of Canaan, with whom the Philistines often warred, their primary god was Dagon, a fierce rival to his brother Baal, worshipped by their Canaanite cousins. They believed that their conflict with other tribes and nations was played out as a conflict between the gods; a conflict which was never really settled with the gods struggling for advantage but never delivering a final victory. Life was ordained by the undetermined struggle between gods. That other people had other gods was also accepted, and these foreign gods were just added combatants in the struggle in the heavenly realms, the consequences of which fell upon men.

Isaac and Rebekah detested the practices of Gerar. They understood why father Abraham determined never to live in a city of Canaan. Even so, Isaac prospered. His flocks grew and brought new traders to Gerar.

Esau was drawn to the excitement of Gerar. As a prince of the wealthy household of Isaac, he was welcomed into the homes of leading families. He was courted for influence and flattered as a wise and powerful leader. He was offered wives and alliances with leading families. Rebekah scolded him, and Isaac discouraged him from any thoughts of marriage to such idol worshipping women. Esau chose his own path.

After some time, king Abimelech, standing by his window, considered this strange new resident who grew wealthier by the day, *surely his god is with him*. Just then, he happened to see Isaac happily sweep Rebekah off her feet, embrace her passionately and playfully carry her off to his bedchamber.

Immediately, Abimelech summoned Isaac and challenged him, "The woman you say is your sister is indeed your wife! Why have you lied to me?"

Isaac stammered. "I was afraid, afraid I would be killed and she would be taken on account of her beauty."

Abimelech was furious, "What have you done? One of my people may have lain with her and brought guilt upon all of us! Go back to your wife and no more lies!"

Abimelech issued an edict to all of Gerar, "Anyone who touches Isaac or Rebekah, his wife shall be put to death."

Isaac walked back to his house, crestfallen and filled with guilt. He told Rebekah, "Surely, I have sinned against you and against God. Abimelech knows you are my wife. The God of Abraham, the God who affirmed to me every promise, has chosen to save me. Even when I was unfaithful, He was faithful. He saved me and blessed me above all men. Who is like Him? His tender mercies come even when they are unmerited. Who is like Him? Help me, my wife, to remain faithful to Him."

Rebekah hugged Isaac, "We must each be the strength for the other. God has not left us alone but has made us one."

Abiel and Lemuel came to Isaac to report on the flocks, "Master, he began, the flock flourishes and grow. The pastures stay green and the water plentiful. Yet elsewhere the drought deepens and the people have no grain. Traders come looking for food; we give them meat but they need grain. Master, I advise you to plant grain. The pastures are more than sufficient and grain is needed by all."

Isaac asked Abiel, "How much grain do we have?"

"Sufficient for the year," he replied.

Isaac commanded, "You shall sow half of the grain. We will trust in the Lord for He is the source of all our blessings. Hire men from Gerar to teach our people to tend crops. If grain is what is needed, our God will provide grain."

Isaac watched the fields he had planted. The grain stalks appeared and grew thick, full and tall. He asked Abiel, "The fields look healthy. Tell me Abiel, what is a good return on seed that is sown?"

Lemuel spoke for his father, "Master," he replied, "Indeed the grain fields appear abundant. A good return on seed is thirtyfold, but you must be patient, the grain must ripen, the water hold and no locusts, storms, lightning or fire destroy the crop. Pray to God, master, this crop survives to harvest."

The crop did survive, and so did the next and next and after that for all the years of drought. The return on seed was not thirtyfold, not fiftyfold, but one hundredfold! All of Canaan came to Gerar to buy the grain of Isaac. The people of Gerar had plenty and Isaac became wealthy, wealthier than any man in the land.

The people of Gerar did not see their plenty, they saw only Isaac's wealth and they envied him. Even Abimelech became concerned about Isaac's wealth. No man was willing to attack Isaac or his camp. They feared he had become too powerful for even king Abimelech to challenge. The men of Gerar sent their servants and shepherds at night to fill all of the wells that Abraham had dug years earlier, which now watered Isaac's flocks. Isaac was always a cautious man, a man who avoided conflict. He was never a man to seek bloodshed. How far would the men and shepherds of Gerar push him? It needed to stop.

Isaac went to Abimelech. "Have not my people done all that you have asked? Do we not provide meat, and wool and grain for your city? Yet our wells are filled and our flocks thirst. Is not justice the duty of a great king?"

Abimelech listened to Isaac and said, "The people have come to fear you; your wealth is too great. Will you take all that they own? Is there any land left for their crops or pastures for their flocks? It is better you leave here; go away from us for you are too powerful for us."

Isaac stared at king Abimelech and sternly replied. "As you

wish. Our God will supply all of our needs. We will leave Gerar assured that His blessings will follow us wherever we go!"

Isaac ordered Abiel to move the flocks south, further away from the city, in the valley of Gerar; there he pitched his tent with his people. He re-dug the wells his father, Abraham, had dug but were filled by the Philistines after he left. But when the herdsmen of Gerar heard that Isaac had uncovered flowing water they insisted, "The water is ours!"

Isaac had no heart for quarrels with the Philistines, so moved even further south and dug yet another well. Again, when he found water, the herdsmen of Gerar claimed that water also. So once, again he traveled a great distance from the city and dug a third well. But it was far from Gerar and they did not quarrel over it. Isaac named the well Rehoboth, 'Open Spaces,' and he proclaimed, "At last the Lord has made room for us and we shall be fruitful in the land."

The following day Isaac walked up to the hill, Beersheba, at the edge of the Negev, and spent the night under the stars. That same night the Lord appeared to him again, "I am the God of your father Abraham; do not fear for I am with you. I will bless you and multiply your descendants for the sake of My servant, Abraham."

In the morning, Isaac did something he had never done before. Something he had watched his father, Abraham do many times. Something which before now had only brought painful memories. Isaac built an altar and there and sacrificed to God. There was no fear, no dread, no obligation. Gone were the painful memories of being laid on the altar; Isaac had only a desire to worship God; to love Him and worship Him. Isaac called upon the Lord in thanksgiving and praise.

He pitched his tent at Beersheba, and there his servants began to dig a well.

Now king Abimelech, being a cautious man came to Isaac from Gerar with Ahuzzah, his chief minister and Phicol, commander of his army. Isaac, surprised and unhappy to see them, asked, "Why have you come to me, since you hate me and have sent me away?"

Abimelech answered, "We clearly see that the Lord is with you, so we said, 'Let there be an oath between us; let us make a covenant with you, that you will do us no harm, just as we have not touched you and have done nothing but good and have sent you away in peace. For you are the blessed of the Lord.'"

Isaac prepared a feast and they ate and drank together. They arose early the next morning and exchanged oaths and Isaac sent them away. Later, that very day, his servants came to him and said, "We have found water." So, he called the place Shibah, 'Oath' and the city of Beersheba, to this day is called the 'Well of oaths.'

Now Isaac and Rebekah were happy to leave Gerar and its people behind them. Though the God of Abraham gave them shelter and wealth, the people did not know the Most High God. But Esau brought two wives out of Gerar. He first married Judith, the daughter of Beeri when he was forty years old, and then Basemath, daughter of Elon, the Hittite. Isaac and Rebekah were deeply troubled by Esau, and his wives brought them grief. They argued bitterly, but they could not agree on what they should do.

Chapter Twenty-One

In You our fathers trusted; they trusted and you delivered them.
Psalm 22: 4

A man wrapped in robes and covered in dust slowly rode his donkey into the tent city that was the House of Isaac. He asked a servant drawing water from the well, "I come bearing news for Rebekah, wife of Isaac. Please show me to the tent of your lord, Isaac."

The servant replied, "Sir, first refresh yourself here at the well, and I will take you to my master and mistress."

The man slowly dismounted, took off his outer cloak and shook off the dust. Beneath his great cloak was a fine white robe. He unconsciously clutched a bag slung over his shoulder which hung by his side. He stomped the dust from his feet as he walked to the well, where he removed his turban and shook off more dust. The servant gave him a pail of water freshly drawn from the well. He dipped a cup into the pail for a long drink, then he scooped water with his hands and washed many miles of travel from his face.

"I pray the blessings of the Most High God upon you and all of this household," he said as he returned his turban to his graying head, and looked with waiting eyes for the servant to lead him.

When he was announced at the tent of Isaac and Rebekah, Isaac could be heard saying, "Jael from Nahor? I know no Jael..."

Rebekah overhearing her husband shouted, "Jael? Jael ben Hod?"

Isaac turned, "You know this man?"

Rebekah immediately said, "Welcome Jael ben Hod! Come in, please, come in!"

To Isaac, she said, "This is Jael ben Hod, we grew up together on the plains of Nahor. His father, Hod, was a shepherd and a friend to my father."

Jael bowed and entered the tent as Rebekah continued, "Let me look at you Jael! Truly, you do not look the shepherd! Come, sit, tell me everything of Nahor and Haran and my family!"

Jael bowed his head again and said, "I have been sent by your brother Laban and bear hard news. He tells his only and beloved sister that her father, Bethuel and her mother have gone to your ancestors and lay beside Nahor and Milcah. He tells you they lived long and satisfied lives, comforted in their love."

Rebekah closed her eyes and sobbed lightly, then recovering her composure she wiped her eyes, smiled slightly and said, "Please sit with us Jael, my husband and I would hear more. He tells me they were satisfied, were they truly happy, Jael? And the others? And your father, Hod? And Dov? And my uncles? And my brother Laban, does he have wives? Sons? Oh, please sit and tell me all."

Jael sat and smiling answered, "Yes, your father and mother found true comfort and happiness after you departed. After he returned from Damascus with his special gifts and made an oath to your mother at the well, a public oath, that he would take no other wife and..."

Rebekah interrupted, "Trip to Damascus? Oath?"

"Yes, he went to Damascus with Deborah's father, Zimri-Ruel, our village elder, Dov, my father and me..."

Rebekah said, "Wait! Deborah is not here. We must send for Deborah and Abiel! They must hear you as well."

When Deborah and Abiel arrived, Deborah, like Rebekah was overjoyed to see her childhood friend. She greeted Jael with a warm hug and tears of joy. Abiel, like Isaac, stood perplexed.

Rebekah said, "Sit and hear Jael's story. Jael was about to tell me of a trip father made to Damascus with, your father, Dov and Hod. Do go on Jael, please!"

"Yes, as I started to say, Bethuel went with us, that is, Zimri-Ruel, Dov, my father, and me to Damascus. Deborah, your mother Leah, insisted on coming as well. Of course, no one could say no to Leah."

Deborah and Rebekah laughed. Rebekah remarked, "I think Leah was the true village elder!"

Jael smiled at continued, "We wanted to see our old village in the high hills above Khalab, and Bethuel, who was troubled by your mother's doubts, suggested we visit the markets of Damascus. It was a most memorable expedition! Bethuel returned and brought joy to his wife, but not with the expensive gifts or fine jewels from the best craftsman in Damascus. No, it was a public oath he swore to her at the well. An oath of love, support, and commitment; an oath that he would take no other wife or concubine, loving only her all of his life. He then gave your brother his inheritance and spent his remaining days with your mother enjoying the stories of my father, as they had become fast friends."

Jael paused and looking at Rebekah said, "Your brother, Laban, prospers. He has but one wife and two fine daughters."

Deborah asked, "And what of the village? Was it not called Dabar El'Elyon?"

Jael sighed, "The Amorites have settled there and pretend it was always theirs. We climbed to the mountaintop and made a sacrifice of thanksgiving to the Most High who saved us by His mercy and strong hand, and settled us safely with the tribe of Nahor. It was much the same the last time I was there."

Deborah asked, "The last time?"

"Yes, you see Zimri-Ruel and Leah never returned to Nahor. They stayed in the house of Keshet in Damascus. Zimri-Ruel returned to purchase the old sheepfold and its caves above Dabar El'Elyon for a burial place. First, he buried Leah, in the very cave God first revealed Himself to him, and then Dov, and his wife Namaah, in another cave nearby. I laid your father beside Leah not a year ago. You must know, Deborah, your father and mother always walked in love. Indeed, I myself heard your father's last words, 'Do not worry after me, I just go for a walk with the Most High.' I have since longed to visit you and bring you his words of comfort."

Deborah closed her eyes and cried. Then smiling said, "That's Papa. He never wanted us to worry. O how he loved God. I feel so sorry that he was left alone after mother died."

Jael nodded warmly to Deborah, "He knew of your love for him and he found joy in your love and service to Rebekah and the Most High. Zimri-Ruel was not a lonely man. He was active and loving to his last day."

Jael sighed, "It is you who must forgive me. For though I desired to come sooner, I was delayed. I was called to Nahor when I learned my father had died. I went to see his tomb and to offer a sacrifice of praise. It was then, your brother Laban asked me to carry his message to you, Rebekah."

Rebekah smiled, "And so you have. Isaac and I thank you."

Jael turned serious. "There is more. When I returned by way of Damascus I learned that my master's close friend, Jared had also died."

Then turning to Abiel he said, "Your mother, Abaigael, asks after you. As a widow, she asks her only son to come for her and take her into your house. Jared and Obed are also gone, as is Eliezer who lived a good life. Only Keshet lives with his sons who do not walk in the ways of the Most High God."

Abiel said, "With your permission, Master Isaac, I shall go for my mother at first light tomorrow."

Isaac answered, "Of course! See to the preparations. God protect you and her on the journey."

Jael patted the bag at his side, "I have something for Lemuel, son of Deborah from her father. I have served Zimri-Ruel all the days he was in Damascus, though he would never call me a servant, rather his young friend. I listened to his stories. Such stories! They told of a man called by God to be His servant and priest. Such knowledge and hope! He spoke so much of the excitement of learning the mysteries of God from King Melchizedek, Priest of the Most High God. He spoke of the wisdom gained through a life of trusting God. And praises! Zimri-Ruel never ceased singing praise songs to the God he loved."

Deborah smiled and said, "And pouch carries…"

Jael nodded, "How I ramble on. Forgive me, but I have practiced what I would say. This is his gift to Lemuel, a son dedicated to God, grandson to a priest and grandson to a prophetess. I have carefully recorded the words and story of Zimri-Ruel, for a grandson whom he never saw yet always loved and whose name he remembered in prayer."

Deborah smiled and nodded, "You shall surely give it to our son, whom we love. Perhaps when he is ready he will share it with us."

Isaac said, "Abiel, find a place for our honored guest to rest and refresh himself from his long journey. And prepare a feast in his honor this evening. We should hear more of his stories; my sons must hear of the faithfulness of our God."

Abiel led Jael to a tent and said, "I will send my son, Lemuel, to you. You may wish to have a word with him when you present him your master's chronicles. I will return for you this evening. I must prepare for my journey to Damascus. Thank you, Jael, for bringing your messages; you are truly a faithful servant."

A few minutes later, a tall, immaculately dressed man stood outside Jael's tent. "I am Lemuel, son of Abiel. You sent for me?"

"Yes," said Jael. "Please come in, I have something to give you. Come and sit with me."

Lemuel entered the tent, moving with dignity, strength and confidence. Jael marveled at his presence, more resembling a noble than a servant. He found a cushion and sat down. Once seated he asked with all of the authority of a chief or advisor, "Please, tell me how I may serve you?"

Reaching for the pouch, Jael said, "I have something to give you. Something an old man sends to a grandson he never met. Zimri-Ruel, father of Deborah, a man of great wisdom and filled with the love of God the Most High, had in his heart to share with you."

Jael gave Lemuel the pouch, "It is a chronical of your grandfather's walk, seeking to know and to do the will of the Most High. As you are a man dedicated to God, it is right that you know the tender mercies God sent to your fathers and forefathers and the prayers and blessings that were answered in you.

"Zimri-Ruel was a man born a slave, a slave with no name. He was called Jael, "Mountain Goat,' by the masters that owned him and sent him to pasture their sheep alone in the high hills at night. God, who knows all, called him and gave him a true name, a better name than one given by a natural father, Zimri-Ruel, "My praise, friend of God." And it was a good name, for indeed, how he loved to sing praises! And he learned to walk with God as friend."

Lemuel opened the pouch and removed a scroll. He held it in his hands and looked at it with sober, curious eyes. Not looking up, he said, "He gives this to me, and not my mother?"

"Deborah remembers her father. Certainly, you can share it with her, and anyone you desire."

Lemuel looked at Jael, "You are also named Jael, as he was called."

"Yes, my father, Hod was a shepherd and friend of Zimri-Ruel. It was my father who first called him by that name. He loved Zimri-Ruel and said he would always be to him his friend Jael. He named me in his honor."

"And you served him?"

"He was a second father to me. He opened my heart and mind to the love of the Most High God."

"I will read these words," Lemuel said as he got and left the tent.

After sunset, Jael was escorted to the tent of Isaac and Rebekah where a fine table was set.

When Jael arrived, Isaac greeted him warmly and led him to the seat of honor. "Welcome to my table, Jael ben Hod. You who have faithfully served one who has blessed my wife and many of my household, sit with us and share your stories. I have asked my sons, Esau and Jacob to hear your words. Rebekah, Deborah, Abiel and I believe, Lemuel, you know. Sit now, taste the wine, and there is game tonight, a favorite of mine and a gift from my son Esau. Sit, and tell me, how does a slave become a priest? For that is what Rebekah has told me."

Jael bowed to those seated around him and sat down. "You do me too great an honor, master Isaac! Far too great an honor indeed! A slave becomes a priest much the same as a herder becomes the father of many nations; he hears and obeys the call of God Most High. El'Elyon, who made us from the dust of the earth, who knows all of our days before there is one, who plants the seed of revelation within our hearts, calls out to us, and so it was with my master. And so shall it be with you and your seed."

"With me," Isaac replied, "I am but a son of my father, Abraham, to whom God gave a promise. God has told me that by my seed will come nations promised my father, many people, as many as the stars in the sky. He has told me that by my seed all nations will be blessed. That is the only seed of revelation He has shown me. That is my only calling after a long life of seeking His voice, to bear sons of this great promise."

Jael looked at Isaac and said, "Is not a father called to be an example to his sons? How much more is a father of nations to be an example, a leader to his nations? You say you have sought His voice; what is it you seek to hear? Perhaps He has said much and you have not always heard Him speak?"

Isaac stared at Jael and thought, *'Who is this forward servant that questions me?'* Then tasting his game stew and drinking the wine set before him, he said, "But I did hear His voice when He came to me at night and I have obeyed His command. Rebekah remembers well, I was certain the God of Abraham spoke."

Rebekah's eyes moved between Isaac and Jael, sensing but not fully understanding the tension between them.

Jael nodded his head yes and said, "Yes God speaks clearly when He knows we will obey and we must obey urgently. And so, you obeyed God. But my lord Isaac, did not the Most High speak to you when you lay on the altar? He spoke to your father Abraham, and He spoke to you. It was a most hard lesson that he spoke."

The conversations around the table quieted and all eyes turned to Isaac and Jael.

Isaac's eyes narrowed and his brow furrowed, "I remember God said, 'Do not stretch out your hand against the boy, and do nothing to harm him; for now, I know that you fear God since you have not withheld your son, your only son from me.' God spoke thus to my father, but to me, he did not speak."

Now even Esau and Jacob were listening closely. They knew how this story brought pain to their father Isaac.

Jael said, "God spoke of sacrifice. He spoke of the cost of serving Him. He spoke of the cost of sin which must be paid for the unrighteousness we bear. He spoke of taking that cost from us because of His love for us. He spoke of trusting Him and obeying Him not out of fear or obligation, but because we love Him and we would sacrifice all else that we love for Him.

Because He spoke, you can know that His word will stand forever and His promises will never be broken. Because He spoke, you, Isaac, may know that He loves you and wants you to walk with Him in the life He has called you to and the service He has set before you."

Only the light flapping of the linen canopy over the table could be heard. The eyes and ears of the night waited for Isaac's response.

Isaac settled back on his seat and remembered the joy he found in the sacrifice he first made at Beersheba. He thought back to comfort and peace his father Abraham had found. He said, "I shall carefully consider your words. Tell me, Jael, how has the Most High spoken to you?"

Pleasant conversations resumed. Food was tasted and the fine wine sipped.

Jael laughed, "God set before me a priest who praised God in all that he saw, heard or did. I saw in the eyes of this priest and heard from his lips passionate words lived in a life dedicated to the God he worshipped. I saw that what he had burned like coals within him and I desired the same in my life."

Rebekah laughed, "I remember you sitting wide-eyed listening to Zimri-Ruel as he sat with elder Dov, your father, Hod, and my father, Bethuel. How much my father wanted all of Nahor to worship God and be led by Zimri-Ruel."

Jael returned to feast before him. He was particularly fond of the game.

Abiel asked, "When Zimri-Ruel left the flocks, what was he looking for? It could not have been obedience to God for he was not obedient to his masters?"

Deborah said, "Husband, please let the man eat!"

Jael swallowed his food, took a sip of his wine and said, "What you say is true, obedience to a slave is not something he offers, it is obligated for his very survival. No, it was his desire to know God. He recognized there must be a God, a creator, and in the order of our world, he surmised God, like a workman, cares for the work of his hands. God intervenes in nature because He cares, so he sought out one who had heard the voice of God."

Lemuel spoke, "Please forgive my interruption, but was his desire merely knowledge of God or was there a need within him he sought to bring to God?"

Jael looked intently on Lemuel, "Do we not all have needs and desires that drive us? Zimri-Ruel was an orphan. An orphan whose name was unknown and a slave to a people who showed him no love. His questions haunted him: 'Who is this God? and Who am I.' He found the answers to these questions were connected. God knew him, He knew all about Him. God told him, 'I attended your birth, I know your father and your father's fathers to the end of generations. I know your mother and your mother's mothers to the end of generations.' But God did not tell him his birth name or the names of his parents. God told him the name He had reserved for him, his true name and his true identity in God. While God calls many to obedience, obedience to God came naturally for Zimri-Ruel. God had another issue for him."

Jael paused to take another bite of Isaac's favorite stew.

Jacob said to Esau, "Did you hear brother, obedience came naturally."

Esau replied, "What would you know of it? Why earn what you can steal!"

"Enough Esau and you too Jacob!" Isaac scolded.

Jael set down his cup and said, "For some obedience comes naturally and for some it is difficult. Truly we must obey God, but obedience must come from the heart. Obedience is a sweet aroma to our God when it is a loving response to His call. Obedience is much like worship. When we sacrifice to our God is it the blood of our sacrifice that God desires? I tell you the blood is but sign to us of the price of sin which must be paid; that price is death. But the price is not paid by the innocent lamb, no, that too is a reminder. Is not the innocent lamb God's own? God pays the price. So, when we make a sacrifice to God He looks to our heart. Is it broken by sin? Does it seek cleansing forgiveness? Does our heart yearn for fellowship with our Maker and lover of our soul? So it is with obedience; better an obedience which comes late and is from the heart than one which comes from habit and without thought for God."

Isaac asked, "You said God had other issues with him."

Jael replied, "Yes. God said there was one thing he lacked. Love. He did not love other men. He did not love those who enslaved him; and as much as he wanted to love God, his love would fall short. The challenge was this: how can you love God if you do not love those He loves? Zimri-Ruel did something unusual, he learned to love others. He sought to love all men; he learned to love even men with evil intent. I watched him learn this when Amorites soldiers drove us from our village. I watched him struggle to love the Assyrian soldier who slew his only son."

Jacob asked, "How can a man love someone he hates?"

Jael replied, "Only by denying himself."

The conversation paused, the food tasted and the wine drunk, but the minds were engaged.

Deborah had been sitting and listening as her papa was described by Jael. She began to sob and after wiping tears from her eyes said. "I miss Papa so much. O how he did love! He was so loving to everyone; his thoughts for others were almost an embarrassment. But I shall never forget how he loved me. No matter how much he loved others, I always felt he could not have loved me more. But he would always say God's love is better."

Rebekah turned the conversation to happy memories in Nahor. The cool evening breeze rose and brought refreshment to everyone at the table. The smell of the sweet waters of Beersheba added to the aroma of spices and flowers. In the growing merriment of the evening, the lilt of happy voices kept harmony with the leaping torch flames. The great tent itself shook it flaps inhaling deep breaths of the fresh night air.

Lemuel thought, 'Is my obedience merely habit? I must carefully consider what my grandfather has sent me.'

Isaac, too, was deep in thought, 'How will nations that come from me, remember me? I must build on the foundations of my father, Abraham. They must know that they are people of promise, God's people according to God's promise! They must know this truth in their hearts; but what is it like to be God's people?'

Esau and Jacob exchanged ugly stares and went about finishing their dinner.

Chapter Twenty-Two

By faith Abraham, when he was tested, offered up Isaac, and he who had received the promises was offering up his only begotten son; it was he to whom it was said, "In Isaac, your descendants shall be called." He considered that God is able to raise people even from the dead from which he also received him back as a type.

Hebrews 11: 17-19

Some months later, after Abiel had returned with his mother, Abaigael, in the privacy of their own tent, Abiel and Deborah continued the argument they heard once again in the tent of Isaac and Rebekah.

Abiel began, "What Isaac says is true, Rebekah is far too hard on Esau. She must have patience with him and love him. He will learn; he will grow into a righteous man. Time. Time and prayers and he will be a man of God's calling."

Deborah replied, "Time, you say? Time and patience and he will learn? Husband, Esau is a grown man, well past forty years. He is married. Married not once, but twice.

"And who has he married? I'll tell you! He has married idol worshipping daughters of the Canaanites. Do not their idols pollute this household?"

Abiel fumed, "You know my mother and father are Canaanite! Do I pollute this household as well? And my father did not worship the Most High until the hair on his head was gray. Did not your own father say God loves all men? Are you the one to say God has abandoned Esau?"

"Do not put words in my mouth!" Deborah shouted. "This is not about you or our father. It is about Esau, a man who has never changed. As a child, he was a brute and bully. As a young man, he brought dishonor to his father's house, selling his birthright for a bowl of red stew. Has anyone forgotten this dishonor? No! To this very day, he is called, Edom! Did he listen when Isaac and Rebekah told him to have no dealings with the people of Gerar? No! He enjoyed their table, curried their favor and married two of their women! God's patience can end with any man, though we do not know when. But we all know bad seed will not produce a good crop."

"And Jacob is good seed?" Abiel scoffed. "Is there any opportunity he will not use to take from his brother? Does Jacob's obedience come from the love for his father? Does he not position himself against his brother?"

Deborah argued, "Jacob is conscientious; he learns the business of the house. Esau never seeks to learn. Where is he? Not with you or Lemuel, he is off hunting or with his idol worshipping wives."

Abiel looked at Deborah crossly, "Yes, Jacob sits in the tents of the camp. But is it not because he desires the easier life and sees the opportunity to discredit Esau? I will agree Esau is impetuous and must grow, but Jacob is a sly usurper. Now, I will have no more of this conversation. I am off to bed."

Deborah replied sharply, "Go to bed. I will remain here."

Deborah blew out the candle and settled down on the rug outside their bedchamber. Hurt and upset she lay down. As she closed her eyes, she recalled God's prophecy before the birth of the twins, a prophecy she never shared with Abiel or anyone else. Did Rebekah share it with Isaac, she wondered? Then she began to sob. She prayed God to forgive her cruel judgment and give her the strength to love two flawed men, sons of a master and mistress she deeply loved.

The next morning, Abaigael came to Deborah and said softly, "Beloved daughter, I could not help hearing words between you and my son last night. Two people who love each other as you do should not take the quarrels of others to their bed. I prayed it is well between you and take comfort knowing that the Most High God has gifted you as one who loves."

Deborah hugged her mother-in-law and weeping said, "It is just as you say. We fought as Isaac and Rebekah and I did not join my husband. In my foolish pride, I lay weeping outside our bedchamber. This morning it all seems so foolish."

"Does Abiel find it foolish as well?"

Deborah shook her head yes and said, "He came out this morning and hugged me tightly. He kissed me and said how much he loves me and counts our lost night as a waste of God's precious gift to us."

"Then all is now well."

"All is well."

Abaigael looked at Deborah as if puzzled and then said, "I was upset at what I heard and struggled to go to sleep. But then I had the strangest of dreams. I think I am to share this dream with you, the daughter of my dear friend Zimri-Ruel."

Looking once more at Deborah's questioning eyes, she began, "I dreamed I was walking on a road, I had been walking a very long time. I was tired, near exhaustion. I was following a man. He was dressed in white, the brightest of white. I could only glance to see he was still in front of me; his robes were too bright to gaze upon."

"An angel of the Lord?" Asked Deborah.

"I did not know. But he stopped and turned around and I recognized his face. I recognized his warm and gentle smile. I knew that face! And when he spoke, I knew his voice. It was the face and voice of King Melchizedek! He looked at me just as he did that day he blessed me on the road outside of Salem when I was on the donkey being led by my husband Jared. The day he prophesied that I would have a son and his name would be Abiel. I am sure it was King Melchizedek, priest of the Most High God."

"What did he say? You heard his voice, what did he say?"

"He said, 'Daughter Abaigael, do you grow tired in the walk? Do not fear, your walk here will soon end. We shall still walk together in another realm. Your feet shall never grow weary, and your heart will be renewed. Others you cherish walk there ahead of you, Jared, Zimri-Ruel, Zadok, and Obed. Many more whom you love. But I ask you to take a few more steps. Come to the mountain top and look. See what lies ahead. See the blessing the Most High God will give to all nations.'"

"Mother Abaigael, did you see the blessing he spoke of?"

Abaigael's eyes looked beyond Deborah. Eyes that were radiant with light and power. "I walked to the top of the hill and I saw a man riding on the back of a donkey. A small donkey, only yet a colt. And there were people along the road on which he traveled and they threw their cloaks and palm branches on the road before him and they shouted and sang joyfully."

"Who was he? Where was he going? You must tell me, why were they rejoicing?"

Abaigael looked down at Deborah and said, "I do not know his name. He passed from my sight as one afar off walking into the morning fog. Only king Melchizedek remained and he said, 'This is the true son of the promise. The one by whom all nations will be blessed. He goes to fulfill the promise of God to father Abraham and to Isaac. He travels to the altar where he will lay himself out upon the wood, like Isaac, it is the will of his father and the will of God that he does this. Like Isaac, he will be raised up again in life, but his body will be broken and his blood shed as an atonement for sin. He gives himself as a gift, a sacrifice for the sins of all men. His blood is the perfect atonement given once and for all time. He is the perfect gift of God, and God's own king whose reign shall never end.'"

Abaigael became silent her eyes still affixed to the images in her mind.

Deborah said, "Abaigael, you are a prophet of the Most High, what does this mean?"

Smiling, Abaigael closed her eyes and said, "This was not like any prophecy I received from the Lord. There was no command given to me. No word of repentance to be passed on. No, I think this dream was given as a blessing and a reward. I will soon sleep and as your father said, 'simply go for a walk with the Most High.' I share this with you, Deborah, as the daughter of a disciple of King Melchizedek to find strength, trusting in our God and walk faithfully with Him loving God and loving all whom He loves."

Deborah reached out to Abaigael and hugged her once more. The two women joined in their embrace, wept.

Not long after this, Abaigael, a prophet of the Most High God died peacefully and was buried at Beersheba. Deborah and Abiel mourned her passing and rejoiced in the memory of her life.

Chapter Twenty-Three

See, the smell of my son is like the smell of a field which the Lord has blessed.

Genesis 27: 27b

As Isaac grew old his vision began to fail him. When he became blind, fearing death, he called Esau and said, "I am old and do not know how much longer I will live. Please, take your bow, go out into the field and hunt game for me. Make my favorite stew and bring it to me so that my soul may bless you before I die."

"I go immediately, father," Esau replied, and he left.

Rebekah overheard the conversation and called Jacob and told him what she heard. "Jacob, do as I say. Bring me two choice kids from the flock. I will prepare the stew just as your father likes it and you shall take it to him and receive your father's blessing."

Jacob hesitated. It was one thing to prey upon his brother's weakness and take the inheritance which Esau had despised with such dishonor, but to deceive his father? But, it is his mother who tells him to do this, Isaac's one wife and his 'eyes' towards his sons.

Jacob replied, "I know my father's sight is gone, but surely he will touch me and know it is not Esau because I am not hairy as he is. Then he will find me a deceiver in his sight and curse me rather than bless me."

Rebekah remembered the prophecy and with determination growing within her heart, said, "Your curse be upon me, my son, go and get the kids as I have told you."

When Jacob returned with the young goats, Rebekah made the stew. While it cooked and simmered, she took some of Esau's finest clothes which were kept in their tent and told Jacob to put them on. She tied the skins of the goats on his hands and around his neck, she gave the stew to Jacob and sent him into Isaac.

Jacob entered his father's bedchamber and said, "Here I am father."

Isaac replied, "Who are you, my son?"

"I am Esau, your firstborn. I have done just as you told me; I have brought your favorite game stew. Eat it that I may receive your blessing."

"How is it you have done it so quickly?"

"Because the Lord, your God, has caused it to happen to me."

Isaac said, "Please come close so that I may feel you, my son, so that I may know that you really are my son Esau."

Jacob cautiously stepped near and let Isaac touch him.

Isaac said, "The voice is the voice of Jacob but the hands are the hands of Esau."

Isaac asked definitively, "Are you really my son Esau?"

"I am."

"Bring your stew to me and I will eat of my son's game."

After Isaac ate of the game and drank of the wine Jacob brought him, he asked, "Please come close and kiss me, my son."

Jacob came close, leaned over Isaac and kissed him.

Isaac smelled Esau's clothes and blessing him said, "See, the smell of my son is like the smell of a field which the Lord has blessed; now may God give you of the dew of heaven and of the fatness of the earth, and an abundance of grain and new wine; may peoples serve you, and nations bow down to you; be master of your brothers and may your mother's sons bow down to you. Cursed be those who curse you and blessed be those who bless you."

No sooner had Jacob left his father's tent than Esau returned with a wild mountain goat. He immediately set about stewing the meat and adding the spices and vegetables he knew his father enjoyed. Esau was happy, the dishonor of selling his birthright could be forgotten for he would receive soon his father's blessing. His blessing meant honor would be restored and his father's pride in him made known. When the stew was perfectly prepared, he took it to him.

"Let my father sit up and eat his son's game, that you may bless me."

Isaac said, "Who are you?"

"I am your son, your firstborn, Esau."

Isaac trembled violently in anger, "Who was he then that hunted game and brought it to me, and gave it to me to eat before you came? Who was it I blessed? Yes, for he shall be blessed."

When Esau heard him, he cried out in bitter agony, "Bless me, father, bless me also!"

"Your brother came deceitfully and has taken away your blessing."

Then Esau screamed, "Is he not rightly called Jacob, for he has supplanted me twice. First, he took away my birthright and now he has taken away my blessing!"

Then wailing, Esau pleaded, "Have you not reserved a blessing for me?"

Isaac knew that a father's blessing to his son was like God's blessing to a favored person. A blessing carried with it a covenant, an agreement to stand behind the blessing just as God stands behind His promises. As Isaac remembered this, and all the counsel of Rebekah, it occurred to him that somehow, this was God's will.

Now composed, Isaac said, "I have made him your master and all his relatives I have given him as servants, and with grain and new wine I have sustained him. Now as for you, what can I do my son?"

"Do you have only one blessing, my father? Bless me, bless me also, please, my father."

Saying this, Esau began to weep.

In love for Esau Isaac gave a blessing of a consequence but also with eventual release. He faced Esau with sorrowful blind eyes. "Behold, away from the fertility of the earth shall be your dwelling. And away from the dew of heaven from above. And by your sword, you shall live, and your brother you shall serve; but it shall come about when you become restless, that you shall break his yoke from your neck."

As Esau left his father's tent, his tears and sorrow turned to hatred and resolve for revenge. He promised himself but his words were spoken aloud, "The days of mourning my father are near; then I will kill my brother, Jacob."

Esau's words were overheard and reported to Rebekah. She sent for Jacob and told him, "Your brother Esau is consoling himself by planning to kill you. Now listen to me, go to Haran, to my brother Laban. Stay with him some days until your brother's anger calms and he forgets what you have done to him. I will send for you from there. Why should I be bereaved of both of my sons in one day, for surely if Esau slays you, he too, will be slain."

While Jacob was still preparing to leave, Rebekah spoke to Isaac, "I am tired of living because of the Canaanite wives of Esau. If Jacob takes a wife from the Canaanites of this land, what good will life be to me?"

"Jacob would flee his brother? Is Esau's anger so bitter that he would slay his own brother?"

"He has said as much."

"My wife, do you believe it to be God's will that in Isaac God's promises of blessings to all people made Abraham will be fulfilled?"

"It is just as it was prophesized while they were yet in my womb."

Isaac nodded, "Yes, what you say is true. Send for Jacob. I shall send him away to your people to find a wife who will not pollute his house with idols."

Jacob fearfully entered his father's tent, overtaken by guilt said simply, "My father, it is your son Jacob."

Jacob lifted his face towards him, blessed him and said,"You shall not take a wife from the Canaanites. Go to Paddan-Aram, to the house of Bethuel, your mother's father; and from there take yourself a wife from the daughters of Laban, your mother's brother. And may God Almighty bless you and make you fruitful and multiply you that you may become a company of peoples. May he also give you the blessing of Abraham, to you and your descendants with you; that you may possess the land of your sojournings, which God gave to Abraham."

After Jacob left with his father's blessing, Esau realized how much the daughters of Canaan displeased his father, so he went to his uncle Ishmael and married a third wife, Mahalath, the daughter of Ishmael.

Returning to Isaac and finding no praise for his actions or new wife, Esau asked his father for his inheritance, one-third of all that Isaac owned. Such a request to a living father was the greatest of insults. This request meant, 'You are dead to me.' Isaac did not address the dishonor of this request but gave Esau what he asked. Esau gathered up his wives and his inheritance and moved his house east, away from Beersheba and set his tents between Mamre and Hebron.

Because Isaac loved both his sons, when Esau determined to leave, Isaac called Abiel and said, "My son Esau will depart with his inheritance. I ask that Lemuel go with him to serve him and advise him as you have so faithfully served and advised me. And have Jachin follow my son Jacob and see he returns to his mother and me safely."

The following day Abiel returned to Isaac, "Surely, master Isaac, Lemuel will serve master Esau, but he asks this of you. Lemuel is pledged to marry Yagon, daughter of your servant, Jachin. They ask to marry before her father Jachin departs."

Isaac smiled, "God blesses my house with love in a hard time of anger. Surely, permit Jachin to give his daughter in marriage to Lemuel before they depart my house. Let their marriage bring some joy to Rebekah and Deborah."

Jachin gave his daughter in marriage to Lemuel and watched her depart Beersheba with the house of Esau. Jachin's heart was heavy watching her depart. He was happy with her marriage to Lemuel, a good and righteous man who would surely comfort her and love her but Jachin felt alone and alone he set off after Jacob.

Jacob was a man of the tents, he had spent little time in the fields or with the flocks. He had spent almost no time alone. His first days of walking were made swift with fear and determination to put distance between himself and his raging brother. But gradually his anxiety decreased and he became aware of the country through which he passed. When he reached the hill country new vistas opened before him. The land was rich with pastures, fields, and forests. Rivers meandered around the hills green with vineyards and olive groves, creeping silently towards the majestic great sea which enticed their waters and which it patiently swallowed with the setting sun. Small villages and walled cities could be seen in every direction. Such a large land and beautiful, he thought. And people, so many people. All those people living life with family and tribe, but he was alone. Would he ever see his family again? Was the birthright and blessing he stole worth the cost? Would he ever hug his mother again, or be received with pride by his father? Would his brother ever forgive him? Would God forgive him? All the words of righteousness he had ever heard spoken came back to him as accusing witnesses at his trial. The verdict was known to all.

One night, Jacob stopped and lay down under the stars, so he chose a stone to prop under his head. The bright canopy of stars in the vast night sky helped drain the remaining worries and anxieties that followed him from Beersheba. He soon fell asleep and began to dream. Jacob dreamed a ladder was set on the earth with its top reaching to heaven; the angels of God were ascending and descending the ladder. The Lord stood above it and said, "I am the Lord, the God of your father Abraham, and the God of Isaac; the land on which you lie, I will give it to you and to your descendants, Your descendants shall be like the dust of the earth, and shall spread out to the west and to the east and to the north and to the south; and in you and in your descendants shall all the families of the earth be blessed, And I am with you and will keep you wherever you go and will bring you back to this land; for I will not leave you until I have done what I have promised you."

When Jacob awoke he said, "Surely, the Lord is in this place and I did not know it. How awesome is this place! This is none other than the house of God, and this is the gate of heaven."

Early the next morning, when Jacob arose, he took the stone that he had put under his head and set it up as a pillar and poured oil on it. He called the place, Bethel, 'House of God,' though it had been known as Luz.

Jacob made a vow to God saying, "If God will be with me and will keep me on this journey that I take and will give me food to eat and clothes to wear, and I return to my father's house in safety, then the Lord will be my God. And this stone, which I have set up as a pillar, will be God's house; and of all that You give me I will surely give You a tenth."

Chapter Twenty-Four

Then Jacob went on his journey and came to the land of the sons of the east.

Genesis 29: 1

Jacob continued his lonely walk north along the caravan road. He crossed the great river Euphrates at Carchemish and followed the road east away from the mountains. The plains of Nahor opened before him with green grass under a bright blue sky; a great city appeared on the horizon. The walls of the city were just coming into view when he came upon a well where he saw three flocks of sheep gathered beside it.

As he approached the well, Jacob said to the shepherds, "My brothers, where are you from?"

"Haran," came the cautious reply.

Jacob asked, "Do you know Laban, a son of Nahor?"

The older one answered, "We know him."

"Is it well with him?"

The old shepherd replied, "It is well, look, his daughter Rachel, is coming with the sheep."

Seeing Rachel coming, Jacob turned again to the well and

said, "It's only midday, too early to gather all of the livestock. Water the sheep and take them to pasture."

Emboldened by his senior, a young shepherd replied, "We cannot until all of the flocks are gathered then they roll the stone from the mouth of the well and we water the sheep."

As he was speaking, Rachel arrived shepherding her father's sheep. When Jacob saw Rachel, he went to the well, rolled away the stone and watered her flock. While Rachel stood wondering about this stranger, Jacob came, kissed her and weeping with joy at finding his relative, said, "I am a relative, son of Rebekah, your father's sister."

Surprised and perplexed, Rachel ran home and told her father what just happened.

When Laban heard the news, he ran to the well to meet Jacob. Laban greeted his nephew warmly, embracing him and kissing him. "Come to my house, I want to hear everything,"

As he led Jacob home, Laban listened patiently to his story and then said, "Surely, you are my bone and my flesh. Stay with us."

Laban had two daughters, Leah, whose name meant *weary*, was the oldest. She was a quiet young woman with no sparkle of life in her eyes, indeed Jacob found them weak. He found it difficult even to look at Leah; her eyes disturbed him, they always looked away.

She would turn her head so one eye would look at him when he spoke but the other looked off to the side in apparent disinterest. If the eyes are the window to the soul, the eyes of Leah shut out any sight of a woman of remarkable strength, strength to persevere, a strength of character and strength to see other people as they are.

Leah could not work in the fields. Her father Laban, knew she could not perceive the distance of objects. She would close one eye while milking goats and working near the home. She was not permitted to tend the cooking pots. But Laban knew Leah heard everything that was said, nothing needed to be repeated. She was an obedient daughter and silent. Laban recognized Leah's strength and devotion. He loved her deeply.

Rachel whose name meant *ewe*, was the younger. She was beautiful in figure and face and full of life and energy. Her eyes sparkled as she spoke. They revealed a happy and adventurous spirit, full of mischief and fun. Rachel had to be reminded of everything Laban said, not because she was intentionally disobedient, but she just didn't always listen. Her thoughts and plans for adventure, her love for the outdoors and flocks and awareness of the beauty of the world around her closed her ears to the mundane instructions of the daily routine. Everybody liked Rachel, especially the other shepherds, even when she didn't follow the established rules.

Jacob had stayed with Laban for a month when Laban said, "Because you are my relative, should you, therefore, serve me for nothing? Tell me, what shall your wages be?"

Jacob loved Rachel so he said, "I will serve you seven years for your younger daughter, Rachel."

Laban looked thoughtfully at the love-struck Jacob and said, "It is better that I give her to you than some other man; stay with me."

Jacob agreed to live in the house of Laban and shepherded his flocks for seven years on the promise of Rachel to be his wife.

The following day Jachin arrived in Haran and was led to the house of Laban.

With both of his sons gone, Isaac lay in his bed waiting to die. Isaac did not die. Rebekah came to him and said, "Husband, you may be blind but you are not dying. Get up from your bed and sit with me when the shepherds return. I have game in your favorite dish at our table."

Isaac heard the words of his wife and sat up straight. "Sit beside me, Rebekah, and I will get up."

Rebekah sat beside Isaac and he caressed her. "If only I could see your flowing red hair and sparkling green eyes one more time. And your smile. The smile I saw the night we wed. Remember when we first saw each other in the tent, and when you first removed your robe? I never wanted to take my eyes from you. How strong was our love! How many times have I lifted you above me and let your red hair encircle our heads, blanketing us as one?"

Rebekah laughed, "Husband, may your memory always be better than your sight! My hair is as white as yours and I fear you will never again sweep me off my feet. But it is good to sit beside my husband."

"Better to lay beside me, my love!"

"Only if you promise to get up!"

That evening Isaac and Rebekah sat together and heard the reports of the shepherds. Soon everyone in the house of Isaac heard how the master and mistress again sat together, hand in hand, their affection as warm as in their youth.

As Isaac enjoyed his game stew, he said, "You were right to send Jacob for the blessing, I was blind to Esau's weakness of the flesh."

Rebekah answered, "It is as the God of Abraham told me while our sons were yet in my womb. 'The older shall serve the younger.'"

"Yes, and I have blessed Jacob to be master of his brothers, for this is the will of God. When I had eyes to see Esau's disobedience, his disregard for his inheritance and his marriage of not one but two idol worshipping Canaanites, I was blind to God's word to my wife. Are we not one? Yet I chose another way, against you, not your way or God's way."

Then laughing lightly, he continued, "And now that I am blind to my sons, I see the will of God and His promise to come through Jacob. We must both pray together for Jacob to become a righteous man and walk with God. We must pray, too, for Esau to repent of his ways and become a nation blessed by the Most High."

Rebekah asked soberly, "And what do you say of Esau's marriage to Mahalath, the daughter of Ishmael?"

Isaac sighed, "Esau saw his brother go off to marry your niece. He sought my favor by marrying my niece."

Then with a snort he asked, "What man needs three wives?"

After a pause, Isaac said, "Did I provide no instruction to my sons? Is this the work of the son of promise to Abraham? Is this the legacy of a father of two nations and of a people by whom all nations will be blessed?"

A tear welled up in Rebekah's eye. She reached across and squeezed Isaac's hand. "You are a good man; did you not trust God to keep His promise to you just as He kept his promises to father Abraham? Did you not trust God and bless Jacob, even as I sent him to deceive you? And did you not show your sons and all of the people of our house that a man should walk with one wife, as one flesh, as God intended when He gave Eve to Adam in the garden."

Isaac said, "I see clearly that my life would have been hard indeed without a wife beside me, to walk with me as one."

Then Isaac's dull blue eyes brightened, "The well, I must make my oath to you at the well just as Bethuel made his oath to your mother."

Rebekah laughed, Eliezer found me at my father's well, and we marched around father Abraham's well twice the night we married. It was by the well we married and you made your oath to me. I trust your oath, husband, I always have and always will."

Isaac moved his tents from Beersheba to the Oaks of Mamre, near Hebron. He found comfort in being in the favorite camp of his father Abraham, near the tombs of his parents at the cave of Machpelah. There were no more quarrels between Isaac and Rebekah. They spent much of their time with Abiel and Deborah as friends rather than as master and servant. They were united in the loneliness parents face when their children set off to make their own lives. There remained in them, buried deep in their hearts, a place of emptiness despite the business of the day. Isaac remembered the conflicts he had with Abraham over Ishmael and Keturah. *How foolish I was. Oh, how warm was his welcome when I returned from wandering the Negev! I pray that the God of Abraham sends my sons home safely; I long to embrace them once more. Soon, Lord, send them home soon.*

Jacob returned in the evening to find Jachin waiting for him. "Master Jacob, I bring you news from your father Isaac and your mother. They ask you choose your bride and return quickly. Mistress Rebekah assures you it is safe; your brother Esau has taken his inheritance and set off. He has allied himself in marriage with your uncle Ishmael and has determined to take his herds and follow the mountain south from the salt sea, across the Arabah, near Oboth. I am to see you and your wife safely to Beersheba."

Jacob stared at Jachin. "Return quickly? With my wife? No, I cannot obey, I have pledged my service to my uncle Laban."

Jachin mumbled, "Master, Jacob, I do not understand..."

"I have chosen his daughter, Rachel. I love her. I have pledged to serve him seven years to marry her. You see, I must stay and serve my uncle, then I will return."

"What man makes his nephew, the son of his own sister, serve seven years to marry his daughter? It is a father's duty to give his daughter to a good man; to a man who will love, honor and protect his daughter. This is not a good thing. Where is the honor?"

"He did not set the price, I offered to serve him and he accepted."

"A father who loves his daughter sends gifts to her husband and seeks God's blessings on them that they prosper, just as I have done when I gave my daughter to Lemuel. No master, Jacob, I will stay and serve you. You cannot put trust in a father-in-law who puts his daughter's betrothed into service."

"First take word to my father and mother and then you may return if it is my father's will."

Some weeks after Jachin departed for Beersheba, Laban told his kinsman, all of them sons of his uncles, of his good fortune in finding a husband for his younger daughter, Rachel, so blinded by love that he was willing to work seven years to have her as his wife. The man, his own nephew, Jacob owned the birthright of their wealthy cousin, Isaac.

"What good fortune cousin," one said, "To keep your daughter, gain a servant, and marry her to a man with a great birthright!"

"You should be more concerned with your older daughter, Leah," another said, "She grows old and no one in Haran has come forward to marry her. Who will care for her in her old age?"

Laban considered their words. *I must find a husband for Leah as well.*

Jacob's love for Rachel grew and his desire for her made the work easy. His thoughts were only on his future happiness. He lived in Laban's house and was treated with respect by his father-in-law. One evening as Laban and Jacob sat at his table, Jacob told Laban about the dream he had and the pillar he erected at Bethel. "I dreamed the heavens opened up and I saw a ladder reaching from earth to heaven with the very angels of God going up and down between heaven and earth, and then the Most High God who called your sister, Rebekah, to marry Isaac, the God of Abraham and Isaac, this same God and maker of all things, spoke to me. He made the promise to me that he made to my fathers, Abraham and Isaac. A rich promise of all the lands from the Euphrates to the Great sea, a promise of a nation and a blessing to all peoples. I put up a pillar at the place and named it Bethel. Truly, the God of Abraham and Isaac lives and speaks and pours out his blessings. I shall never forget and never doubt that the God of Abraham and Isaac is El Bethel, the one God and my God."

Laban looked thoughtfully at Jacob, "I have heard of the

promises of the Most High to Abraham and your father Isaac. And truly He did call Rebekah from my father's house. I have heard of the wealth and blessing he has brought them. Such a promise to you would be truly a good thing."

Jacob looked at the household idols kept prominently in Laban's house and asked, "Tell me, master Laban, do the sons of Nahor still worship the Most High? I have heard stories from my mother and her nurse Deborah, of sacrifices and worship to God. And songs, songs of worship sung in praise."

Laban fought for words to reply, "There was a time... You see we still remember the Most High God, truly He is God... but ah, we no longer have a priest to lead us in sacrifices and praise to the Most High God. Does not God love us even if we do not sacrifice bulls and sheep? Yet, there are some among us who still worship, a few from the hill country people, Dabar El'Elyon it was called; some of them still make sacrifices and worship."

A year passed before Jachin returned to Haran, having visited his daughter and Lemuel in the service of Esau after giving news of Jacob's service to Laban to Isaac and Rebekah. Jacob rejoiced to see Jachin, "Welcome Jachin, faithful servant of my father and protector of his household! What news?"

Jachin replied, "Master Jacob, I have delivered your message to your father Isaac and mother Rebekah. They encourage you to return when you can, they hope and pray it will be soon. They pray the God of Abraham and Isaac shield you and return you to the land of the promise."

"They are well?"

"They are well. Your father has left his bedchamber and has resumed his place beside mistress Rebekah at the door of the tent where they hear the shepherds' stories and consult with Abiel. He has pitched his tent under the Oak of Mamre as did his father Abraham before him."

Smiling broadly Jacob exclaimed, "My father lives! Praise God Most High! And my mother is well. Good news indeed!"

Jacob's face turned serious, "And my brother Esau? How does he fare?"

"Your brother is building a city for his sons, his daughters and his people in the land south of the Salt Sea and to the east of the Arabah river. He has named his city Bozrah, 'Sheepfold.' I have been there; I visited my daughter and son-in-law Lemuel. Lemuel still serves your brother as his steward and chief servant. He has established trade at Tamar and with the caravans to and from the Egyptian mines. I do not think Esau will return to Canaan, and certainly not to the house of Isaac."

"And your daughter, Yagon, is she well?"

Jachin smiled. "Yes master, she is well. She and Lemuel are well matched. I pray they enjoy the love of master Isaac and mistress Rebekah, and the heart of Abiel and Deborah."

Jacob smiled, "My love for Rachel makes the work easy, and as I live in Laban's house I grow to know her better each day."

Then clasping Jachin's shoulders he said, "I will speak to Laban and find a place for you among the servants. And we should make a sacrifice of praise to the God of Abraham and Isaac for your good report and safe return. I am told that the house of Laban has not made a sacrifice of atonement or thanksgiving since my grandfather Bethuel went to his father's tomb, but there are yet some from Deborah's people who still worship the Most High. We shall worship with people of Deborah, the people of Dabar El'Elyon."

Jacob took Jachin to meet Ranon, 'Joyful,' and his wife, Mincah, 'Gift,' grandchildren to Tivzi and Rouvin, shepherd friends of Zimri-Ruel from the high hills above Khalab. They brought two sheep, without blemish by the shepherd's eye and offered them as a sacrifice of praise to the Most High God, the God of Abraham and Isaac, the God who spoke to him at Bethel. Ranon joined them in their sacrifice of praise and sang the songs of Zimri-Ruel, taught to them by their parents. Ranon told Jacob and Jachin of others who still worshipped God. He explained how one son of Dabar El'Elyon was a traveler who shared with worshippers throughout the plains of Nahor and Mesopotamia, to Damascus, Canaan and the great deserts, stories of encouragement and trust in the Most High. He urged all men to love God with all of their heart and all of their soul and to love all whom God loves. This man continues the work of their priest, Zimri-Ruel. A learned man named Jael ben Hod. Perhaps he said, Jael will visit again and you will hear from him such wonderful stories.

Amazed, Jacob said, "I know the man."

Jacob found strength in the company of his new friends, worshipers of the God Most High.

Chapter Twenty-Five

*So Jacob served seven years for Rachel and they seemed to him
a few days because of his love for her.*

Genesis 29: 20

Seven years to the day of his dedicated service for
Rachel, Jacob sought out Laban and with
determination built upon those years of expectation
confronted him boldly with his rehearsed demand, "My time is
completed. Give me my wife that I may go into her."

Laban lifted his eyes to the earnest man before him and
smiled. "Why Jacob, son-in-law, of course I shall give you my
daughter for your wife." Laban stood up and put an arm
around Jacob's shoulder and said, "And for such good service
I shall give your wife a maid, Zilpah, 'Frailty' to serve her!"

Surprised by Laban's ready compliance, Jacob's stiff back
and determined grimace relaxed. A smile formed on his
relieved face.

Laban still smiling stepped back and looking directly into
Jacob's eyes said, "But first let me prepare a wedding feast."

Jacob was irritated when Laban insisted on a great feast
and all of his kinsman and relatives from Haran and all across

the plains of Nahor. Once again Laban smiled broadly, "Patience, my son. After seven years what are few more days?"

The house of Laban was filled with excitement as the preparations were made and the guests began to arrive. Jacob of was toasted and congratulated by all of Laban's kinsman as they gathered. "Such an honor, Jacob, to become son-in-law to such a noble man as Laban!"

The day of the feast arrived and it was indeed every bit as grand as Laban had promised. Musicians and dancers entertained the eyes and the ears. Wonderful delicacies enticed the nose and pleased the tongue. Every guest insisted on sharing a toast with Jacob. The wine was very good indeed! When Jacob arose and asked to be excused to go to his bride, Laban would smile, "Not so, my son, stay a bit longer. Patience is always rewarded. Here is more wine. This night is for celebration! You earned it! And I must indeed celebrate the industrious new son who joins my family. The night is yet young. Your wife will be even more happy to see you!"

After the last guest stumbled off, well into the night, Jacob was led to his wife. No candle was lit in the tent. Jacob's head was spinning and he could barely keep his feet beneath him as he stumbled into bed and fell into the warm arms of his wife. Wordlessly he loved her and then fell into a deep wine induced sleep.

When Jacob arose in the morning he saw the sweetly perfumed woman lying beside him was Leah and not Rachel. He screamed as if in agony. Leah sat up in the bed clutching the blanket in front of her. Her face was distorted by pain, one eye focused on Jacob the other staring off to the side with a tear falling from it.

Jacob's stomach sickened and his anguish turned to rage. Without a single word or so much as a glance to Leah, he quickly dressed and rushed to find Laban who he found sitting comfortably in his receiving room. Jacob screamed, "What is this you have done to me? Was it not for Rachel that I served you? Why have you deceived me?"

Laban sat enjoying his breakfast, slowly finishing the food in his mouth. Finally, without even looking up at Jacob he calmly said, "It is not the practice of our people to marry off the younger before the firstborn."

"Rachel! Only Rachel do I desire for my wife!"

Still studying his meal before him Laban said, "I have heard how you have deceived your brother and you have deceived your father. But this cruelty, Jacob, I did not foresee. You know if Leah is sent back to me she is ruined forever. No honorable man marries a bride returned to her father. What is the fate a woman without a husband? She will have no sons to care for her. There is a better way."

Jacob's anger became confused and mixed with guilt. Pain. Pain mixed with rage kept him silent.

Laban casually lifted his face to Jacob. His smile now gone, he said, "Complete the week of the wedding feast, and I will give you the other daughter."

Again Jacob screamed, "Rachel. You will give me Rachel!"

Laban smiled again and said quietly, "Yes, of course, Rachel. For the service you give me of another seven years, I will give Rachel also."

Jacob stared at Laban.

Once again, Laban's face became stern, "In one week you shall have Rachel as your wife. But in return you must give me another seven years of service."

Jacob was still silent.

Laban smiled again. "Where would you go? We are family. Stay. Work. It is all for us."

Jacob trembling with internal rage, turned and walked out.

Jacob completed the week of wedding feast for Leah and then took Rachel as his wife. Rachel and her maid, Bilhah 'Bashful,' joined her sister, Leah, and Zilpah in the house of Jacob. Jacob loved Rachel more than Leah and he began his service to Laban for seven more long, hard and unhappy years. Leah and Rachel fought. Each despised the other, so Jacob kept them in separate tents along with their maids.

Despite not loving Leah, it was she who bore Jacob his first son. She named him Reuben, 'Look, A son,' Leah proclaimed, "Because the Lord has seen my affliction, surely now my husband will love me."

Still, Jacob loved Rachel and not Leah. Leah bore Jacob a second son who she named Simeon, 'Hearing,' because, she said, "The Lord has heard that I am unloved. Therefore, He has given me this son also."

Then Leah bore Jacob a third son. She named him Levi, 'Attachment,' saying, "Now, this time my husband will become attached to me because I have borne him three sons."

Jacob's affection did not change. Leah conceived a fourth time and bore Jacob another son she named Judah, 'Praise.' And then she stopped bearing children.

Jacob doted on Rachel. He gave her his time and attention. Whatever she desired he gave her. What Rachel did not have was a child. She despised the infrequent visits that Jacob made to the tent of her sister Leah. Her jealousy of Leah could not be assuaged. One night in their bed Rachel screamed at Jacob in frustration and fear, "Give me children, or else I will die!"

Jacob very angrily replied, "Am I in the place of God, who has withheld from you the fruit of the womb?"

Rachel leered at her husband and then said, "You will give me children! I will not be second wife to Leah. You must give me my child! Bilhah, go into her that she might bear. I will take her child on my knees, as my own, that through her, I too, will have children. Take her as a wife also. I must have a son!"

To please his wife, Jacob took Bilhah as his third wife. When he did this, Jachin approached him and said, "Master Jacob, I am but your servant, but also a friend. I have lived a long life and seen many things. Forgive, me, but what you do is not wise. Did not father Abraham take Sarah's maid, Hagar as his wife? And did not Hagar's son, Ishmael bring only strife and jealousy to Sarah. She found no joy taking Ishmael on her knees and had both Hagar and Ishmael sent away only to be saved by the Most High who heard Hagar's cries? Master, do not make the mistakes of your fathers. Do not sin where they sinned."

Jacob scowled and then answered, "You rightly say you are my servant, not my master. I will do as I see right to bring happiness to my wife Rachel. You are become an old man, perhaps too old to serve me as a trained man."

"I serve you at the request of your father, Isaac, whom I served at the request of father Abraham before him. I have served you faithfully and with honor."

Jacob replied, "Yes, you have met your duty; you have served me faithfully. I release you from your service to me on account of my father."

Isaac's words pierced him like no arrow could. Jachin stood tall before Jacob, his face calm but his heart shattered, he bowed and left. Jacob was immediately overcome by guilt but foolish pride kept him silent. Jachin packed his few belongings, slung his bow over his shoulder and left the house of Jacob. To his great regret, Jacob feared he would never again hunt game or listen to the stories of his boyhood mentor and never again be offered the wisdom of his friend Jachin.

Bilhah conceived and bore Jacob a son. She obediently gave the boy to Rachel, who placed him on her knees and said, "God has vindicated me, and has indeed heard my voice and given me a son." She named him Dan, 'Justice.' Bilhah lovingly nursed Dan.

Bilhah became pregnant a second time and bore Jacob another son. Again, she took the infant boy to Rachel who placed him across her knees and proclaimed, "Many times I have wrestled with my sister. I have wrestled and I have prevailed!" Rachel named the boy Naphtali, 'Wrestling' and handed him back to Bilhah.

Leah saw what her sister, Rachel, had done and resented the mocking by her younger sister. Leah gave her maid Zilpah to Jacob as well, that Zilpah might bear more sons for Leah. Again, foolishly or selfishly, Jacob took Zilpah as his wife. She bore him two sons, the first Leah named Gad, 'Fortune' for the good fortune he brought; the second she named Asher, 'Happy,' as she said: "Happy am I for women shall call me happy." Zilpah prayed in her heart that Asher would find more happiness than his natural mother.

The jealousies and fighting within the house of Jacob, between his wives and their sons brought no happiness to Jacob. Jacob ceased going to the tent of Leah and slept only in the tent of Rachel.

Leah taught her eldest son, Reuben, to identify important plants, useful leaves, roots, and fruits. One day, during wheat harvest, Reuben brought home to Leah rare mandrakes. The mandrake was sought both as an aphrodisiac and as a fertility aid. When Rachel saw Reuben give the mandrakes to Leah she asked, "Please give me some of your son's mandrakes."

Leah said, "Is it a small matter for you to take my husband? Would you also take my son's mandrakes?"

Rachel said, "Jacob can sleep with you tonight in return for the mandrakes."

When Jacob returned from the fields that night, Leah went out to meet him and said, "You must sleep with me tonight, for I have hired you with my son's mandrakes."

Jacob did not question her, he had no desire to hear of the squabbles between his wives. He longed for the counsel of his friend Jachin, but he had no one to confide in. He had no one he could trust. He slept with Leah.

Leah was once again pregnant. She delivered Jacob her fifth son, exclaiming, "God has given me my wages," she named him Issachar, 'Reward.'

Once again Leah was able to draw Jacob from his favorite, Rachel, and she again conceived and delivered her sixth son saying, "God has endowed me with a good gift; now my husband will dwell with me because I have borne him six sons." She named him Zebulun, 'Dwelling.'

When Jacob's second seven years of service was nearing an end, Leah bore Jacob her last child, a daughter she named Dinah, 'Avenged.'

Rachel alone among Jacob's four wives bore no children. Her life was all bitterness and strife. Finally, she prayed to God in her despair and God in His mercy answered her. She conceived and bore a son. Finding some joy at last, she said, "God has taken away my reproach, may the Lord give me another son." So, she named him Joseph, 'May God give the increase.' Rachel did not have another son in Haran.

After Joseph was born, the time of service required of Jacob was completed. Jacob went to his father-in-law and said, "It is time I leave for my own country and make my own home. Give me my wives and my children for whom I have served you and let me depart, for you know the service I have rendered you."

Laban replied, "Stay with me, please. Don't go. I have seen that the Lord has blessed me on your account."

Laban paused and then said, "Name your wages and I will give it."

Jacob quickly answered, "You yourself know how I have served you, how your sheep and cattle have fared with me. You had little before I came and it has increased to a multitude, and the Lord has blessed you wherever I turned. But when shall I provide for my own household also?"

Laban asked again, "What shall I give you?"

Finally, Jacob could negotiate. He looked at his father-in-law with the same stern face Jacob saw fourteen years earlier. Directly he replied, "You need to give me nothing, just agree to one thing."

Laban nodded, "Name the one thing you require."

Jacob's voice let Laban know there was no room for negotiation. "Let me go through the flocks. I will take every speckled and spotted sheep, every black lamb, and every speckled or spotted goat. In this way, you will know I am honest. If you find any sheep or goat in my flock that is not speckled or spotted, you may consider it stolen and take it away. It is yours."

Laban sighed in relief and quickly responded, "Good, let it be according to your word."

Chapter Twenty-Six

The last enemy to be destroyed is death.

1 Corinthians 15: 26

Rebekah's death was a shock to everyone in the house of Isaac. She was always healthy even as she and Isaac aged. Everyone worried about Isaac's health, but Rebekah? Isaac awoke to find the wife he loved with all of his heart dead beside him. Shock and pain gripped him. What would he do without her? He was only half himself. He relied on her in every aspect of his life. How could God do this to him? Why did He take his helpmate? Truly they were one soul, even when they argued and fought in the past, the battles were really internal struggles from within each of their souls, just one voicing one side and the other voicing the other side. In all things, they were one. His grief could not be consoled. So, Isaac mourned.

Isaac laid Rebekah in the cave of Machpelah, in the field of Ephron, facing Mamre; the field which Abraham bought for a tomb for Sarah. The very cave where Abraham was laid next to Sarah. The cave of Machpelah was the resting place of the three people Isaac loved above all others. He would guard and protect it with all of his vast resources and would never give it up as it was his most precious possession.

Deborah, more than anyone else, shared Isaac's grief. She had devoted her life to her mistress and friend. And now she was gone. What would she do? Who was she without Rebekah as her mistress?

She painfully realized she received as much support and love from Rebekah as she provided to her beloved mistress. Were two women ever as close? They had a bond of trust and love which was never broken, never even sorely tested. There was no custom to acknowledge Deborah's mourning. She was not a wife, mother or sister to the dead. She was not family to Rebekah; her mourning was hers alone. Her grief could never be solaced like the grief of Isaac or even Esau and Jacob. She was but a friend of the dead woman, or less, a servant to a dead mistress.

It fell to Abiel to console his wife and his grieving master. Yet, he found there were no words that can console grief. There were no answers to the questions of hurting souls. Abiel could only sit and listen patiently in true compassion. He gave them his time. He was there. He let them mourn, and he mourned with them. The only help Abiel could offer besides his understanding, was encouragement and reminders to these people he truly loved, to eat, sleep, and meet the most basic requirements of life; to live through their pain one day at a time.

"You must eat," he would say and sitting with them he would begin, "Remember when..." After the hours passed and the shadows gave way to darkness he could be heard saying, "You must sleep, God will be gracious. Trust Him; there is healing in His love."

With true love and compassion, he watched them learn to deal with the pain and reality of loss and slowly both Isaac and Deborah grew stronger. But the suppressed pain and grief in his own heart stayed with him, a private silent pain.

Isaac would meditate outside the cave of Machpelah and

remember how his family buried there had guided his life. He knew all three loved him. He knew all three struggled in life. They struggled with God, learning how to trust Him, and trust God they did. He remembered how they changed as their trust grew, finally, he remembered that they were called by God and all three had heard the voice of God, and the promises He made to them.

Then Isaac remembered that God spoke to him as well. God made the same promise to him that He made to these three, remarkable and precious people. They trusted God. They believed the promises of God and lived as they believed. Isaac resolved to live by faith, trusting in the promises of God.

Isaac's mourning changed into determination, a determination to live as Rebekah had lived; to live as Sarah had lived, but most of all to live as his father, Abraham, had lived. He sat in front of his tent, listening for the footsteps of the shepherds returning from the fields, his dead blue eyes staring straight ahead. Patiently, Isaac heard their reports and discussed their recommendations. He sat with Abiel, and the tradesman, servants and trained men as they made the daily decisions of life for a great and wealthy house. Isaac's heart warmed. He was kind, and patient in all of his dealings.

Some weeks after Rebekah died, Isaac asked Abiel, "Abiel, my dear friend, forgive me for being slow to ask, but how is Deborah? Surely, she has mourned Rebekah. They are, were, as sisters. I should have been there to console Deborah, she has such a tender heart. Truly she is in pain."

Abiel said, "As you say, she mourns for her mistress. They have loved each other since youth. I try to console her as best I can. Deep in her soul, she knows God will comfort her, but yet she mourns."

"And here, I take so much of your time, time that could be spent consoling your wife. Forgive me, I have been selfish."

"May it never be said! No, master Isaac, you must mourn. You must be consoled. Who else is there to sit by your side? Do not apologize to me. You are the master I love; do we not share our joys and griefs? Has not the God of Abraham drawn us close all these many years?"

"Would Deborah see me? Could I sit beside her as she mourns?"

"She would find comfort sitting with you and mourning with you the one whom you both love."

Isaac went to Deborah, not as the master to his servant, not as a friend to a friend, but as one closer. He hugged her as a brother hugs a sister he loves. "Nediva Deborah, forgive me for not sitting beside you. I know you are in pain, and I ... But I talk too much, please, let me sit with you. I am here because you mourn one you love, one who has touched your heart forever just as she has touched mine. Are you not the sister I love?"

Deborah smiled weakly, tears in her eyes. She squeezed Isaacs' hands and said only, "Thank you."

Esau did not come to bury his mother. Perhaps he never believed she loved him. Esau did not comprehend the unconditional love Isaac shared with Rebekah. He did not know a man could be one with his wife. Esau did not understand that people in love still fight; he did not understand the responsibilities that accompany love, for Esau did love his mother and his father but could not face the vulnerability love demands.

Word of Rebekah's death was slow to reach Jacob. He was bound in service to Laban and consumed with the jealousies of his wives. But Jacob mourned his mother in his heart.

Slowly, life found a new normal in the house of Isaac. Quiet laughter could be heard in the camp. Children played their silly games and sang the joyful, carefree songs of childhood. Rebekah was indeed loved by all, but she was now gone. She was gone the way all men and women will go. She would be remembered fondly. Had any shepherd had a champion such as she? Their future was still secure, Isaac's house still had need of them and Nediva Deborah was still here, still kindhearted and warm. And Abiel kept everything in order.

Once Deborah could smile again she told Abiel she wanted to thank the house of Jacob for all of their kindness. As a tribute to Rebekah, she decided to visit the shepherds in the field and deliver figs and cakes as she had with her mistress many years ago before Esau and Jacob were born. The anticipation of reviving this old tradition brought back the warm laughter in Deborah's voice. Joy filled Abiel's heart as he listened to Deborah happily recount memories of Rebekah and her shepherd competitions.

As they made their way down a rocky section of the path, Deborah stumbled on a stone and dropped her basket of figs and cakes. Abiel, bent over and without a word picked up the basket. As he did, several of the figs rolled out onto the ground and made their way under a small rock. Without a thought, he reached under the rock for the figs. Surprise and pain flashed across his face. He quickly pulled out his hand only to reveal a long black serpent with its jaws clamped across it. Only when its body was half way off the ground did the snake release its fangs and quickly slide off under another large rock.

Deborah and Abiel stared at each other. They knew of this kind of snake, a black desert cobra. Its bite meant certain death. Abiel and Deborah hugged each other tightly, then turned and made their way silently back to their tent.

Abiel's legs weakened as they walked. His fingers became paralyzed, his hands and feet went numb. His head ached and his vision began to blur. Abiel laid down on his bed and quietly asked Deborah to hold him. Even in his pain his words were slow and clear and betrayed any fear. Deborah was sobbing, "It is all my fault! Why did I bring you along on this foolish errand? I am so clumsy! It is my fault. I must not lose you Abiel. What will we do?"

Abiel shook his head, "No, Deborah, you must not blame yourself! You were right go to the shepherds. You were right to want to thank them. It is not your fault. I will not hear of it any further!"

Deborah looked up at Abiel, wiped the tears from her eyes and said, "We shall seek the Lord. We shall make sacrifices and pray!"

Deborah shouted out for help. One of trained men heard her cry and upon hearing what happened he reported the news to Isaac. Isaac was led to Abiel and hearing Deborah's cries and Abiel's struggled breathing, he tore his robes. "Prepare an offering for the Most High God! We shall call out to the God of Abraham that He might spare the life of His servant Abiel."

As Isaac had ordered, the sacrifice was made. The men of Isaac's household paced slowly outside of Abiel's tent. The women gathered near the well and talked quietly among themselves. Inside Abiel's tent, Abiel laid with his head in Deborah's lap. His breathing became labored. Deborah wiped the sweat from his forehead and gently rocked him like a baby. She caressed his hair and softly sang love songs. Deborah was unaware of Isaac's continued presence. She had lost all sense of time and place. For Deborah, there was only the present, there was only her beloved Abiel lying beside her his head cradled in her arms.

As a tear fell from Deborah's eyes onto his forehead, Abiel opened his eyes and smiled at Deborah, Weakly, he voiced, "You will go on my love. There are still others that need the power of your love. Our master has called for His servant. Has He not blessed my life with your love?"

Abiel's voice fell silent. His breathing ceased and his eyes lost their glow. Deborah cried in anguish. "No. Lord! Do not take my Abiel! Please God."

And then there was only the sounds of Deborah crying.

All that was normal in the house of Isaac was gone. Not a year had passed since the death of Rebekah, and now Abiel, the rock and pillar of the household servants and staff had died. Isaac worried if Deborah could endure the pain of loss upon loss, so he wasted no time opening his heart to her, consoling her in mourning. Isaac too mourned his friend. He too felt the pain, but somehow, something deep within his heart gave him strength and he comforted his beloved new sister, Deborah.

As Deborah wept on his shoulder, Isaac said, "I have sent for your son, Lemuel. He will come soon, he is a loving son and a good man, much like his father whom he loves. But Deborah, know this: whether he comes or not comes, you are my family. You will always have a place here. My strongest desire is for you stay in this house, a house you helped build, a family you served and loved. Truly my house and my people will always love and support you."

Deborah hugged Isaac and tried to smile through her weeping eyes.

Isaac buried Abiel in field of Machpelah, near the cave with the tombs of all those he loved. First, the shepherds came. Their wives wailing in mourning for Abiel. "We grieve and mourn with you, Nediva Deborah," their spokesman said. "You do not mourn alone. Please know, kind lady, you shall never want. It is said the master has sent for Lemuel, a good son, and a good man. We ask, dear lady, that when Lemuel comes you still make your home with us. Never leaves us. Is this not your home? Are we not one people? We will comfort you. Our wives and our children shall provide for you to the end of your days. We know you grieve, stay here where you are loved."

Deborah smiled at the man and hugged him. Wiping away her tears she smiled broadly and not saying a word hugged each of them. They too were weeping. They too said nothing.

A similar scene played out as the household servants came and tradesmen came and the weavers came and the cheese and milk workers came and the trained men came. They all made the request and the same promises. "You are our beloved Nediva Deborah. Please stay with us, we will care for you as long as you live."

Deborah knew she did not grieve alone. She knew she was neither abandoned nor forgotten and God was working through this pain. The love she had shown others returned to her one hundredfold.

Chapter Twenty-Seven

Blessed are those who mourn, for they shall be comforted.
Matthew 5: 4

When the messenger from Isaac arrived at the house of Esau, the servant immediately took him to see his master. When the messenger was announced Esau stood and asked, "Is all well with my father Isaac?"

"Lord Esau, your father is well and tells his first-born son he longs for his return."

"So, my father sends a servant to beg the son he has wronged to return to him like a run a way slave."

The servant replied, "No my Lord. Though your father prays for your safe return to him, that is not why he has sent me. Your father wishes that you release Lemuel who he has sent with you. For Abiel, Lemuel's father has died and Lemuel is to come with me to comfort his mother, Deborah, and care for her."

Esau sat down. "Abiel dead? Abiel was a good man, and always fair towards me. Yes, I will release Lemuel. It is a son's duty to care for his widowed mother. Deborah's kindness should not go unpaid."

Turning to his servant he said, "Tell Lemuel I need to see him. Say nothing more to him. Go."

When Lemuel was shown into the room, Esau said, "You have always been a faithful servant and true in your counsel to me. My father Isaac has asked you to return to his house that you may be a comfort to your mother in the death of your father, Abiel. You are released from your service to me. Go comfort your mother, Deborah."

Lemuel's jaw dropped and confusion contorted his face, "My father is dead? How so? He was always a healthy man."

The messenger answered, "A viper. He was bitten by a desert cobra and though everyone in the house of Isaac prayed and fasted, Abiel died. He was deeply mourned. He lies in the field of Machpelah near the cave of the tombs of father Abraham, Sarah and Rebekah."

Esau walked to Lemuel, hugged him and kissed his cheek. "Gather your family and go in peace."

"My lord Esau, may your servant Jachin return with us? He is now very old and finds comfort with his daughter and grandchildren."

"Yes," Esau replied. Take the old warrior with you."

Lemuel bowed and asked Esau, "My lord is most gracious. Does my lord have a message for master Isaac?"

Esau sighed and looked down with closed eyes. "No. I send no message to my father. Now go, your mother has need of your comfort."

Lemuel told Yagon, his wife, the news that they would return to the Oaks of Mamre, to the house of Isaac and take in his mother, Deborah. Yagon nodded and said, "Husband, it is a good thing that you do. It is a good thing that Deborah sees her grandchildren."

As they were busy packing all of their belongings for the journey to Hebron, ten-year-old Nediva asked "Where are we going? Why must we leave?"

Yagon patiently replied. "We are going to the house of Isaac, father of Master Esau. It is where your grandmother

Deborah lives."

"The one you called, 'Nediva,' just as I am named?"

"Yes. Your name is an honor to your grandmother and a prayer that you too, would grow up with a great and kind heart. She is now alone and she will live in our house."

Nediva thought and then said, "Why is she alone? Does not grandfather Abiel care for her?"

As they were talking, Jachin came in to help carry out bundles to the pack camels. Seeing the tear in Yagon's eye he softly told Nediva, "Grandfather Abiel has died. A snake, you remember to be careful of snakes? Well, a snake bit him and he has died. Now your father must care for his mother. Do you understand?"

Nediva's eyes and forehead wrinkled in concentration. "Why was God angry with grandfather Abiel? Why did He punish him? Was he bad?"

Jachin kneeled in front of Nediva and placed his hands on her shoulders, "God did not punish grandfather Abiel. Your grandfather was a good and righteous man. God loved your grandfather! He still does."

"Then why did God let him die?"

Jachin said, "All men die, both good and bad. Death is a bad thing, yes for certain it is very bad. So just as death is a bad thing that awaits all men, bad things happen to the righteous and the unrighteous. God does not spare anyone from death, but to the righteous he sends His promises and blessings. Even our righteousness is a blessing and a gift from the Most High."

"What promises, grandpa? What promises and blessings?"

"The most wonderful promises! He promises to love us and to make us His own. He promises to gather us to Him and walk with Him, forever!"

"And blessings, grandpa, what blessings?"

Jachin smiled at Nediva, "Blessings like you, Nediva! Blessings that carry us through pain and suffering and mourning. With blessings we can look at the bad things and remember the love and joy in our life. God does not reward righteousness with long life, though He may grant it, no, He rewards righteousness with blessings which can overpower pain. With God's blessing grandma Deborah and your papa will remember the love and the joy they shared with grandpa Abiel and they will find a healing sweetness even in mourning."

"Papa is mourning too?"

"Yes Nediva. You must be a blessing to your papa. And when you meet your grandma Deborah, you can tell her that you have come to love her. You can give her the love that she needs now that grandpa Abiel is no longer with her. Do you think you can do that, Nediva?"

"Yes grandpa, I will love grandma Deborah. And papa. And mama, and you too! Then Nediva asked, Grandpa Jachin, did you like grandpa Abiel?"

Jachin remembered the journey from Haran to Canaan nearly a lifetime earlier, "We had each other's back." And then with a smile he said, "Yes, I liked him very much."

Nediva smiled, "I am glad. I think I would like him too."

Hugging her he said, "You are rightly named, Kind Hearted!"

After warmly greeting his mother, Deborah, Lemuel went to see Isaac who was sitting at his open tent.

As he approached, Isaac said, "Is that you, Lemuel ben Abiel? I am told you had come. You are most welcome, most welcome indeed! Come. Come sit by me and tell me everything. Tell me of my son, Esau. I have time to listen. And you, Lemuel, you are well? Children; tell me of children, Sit here beside me. And who is that with you? I hear another's footsteps, much like an old friend's but slower..."

"Master Isaac, it is me, Jachin, one of your trained men, I travel with my daughter and son-in-law."

"Jachin! Of course! One of my trained men indeed. You humble yourself, Jachin. You were the leader of my trained men and my teacher in the bow, the hunt, and arts of war. Sit here beside another old man, like yourself."

Lemuel and Jachin sat beside Isaac. A servant brought a bowl of wine and a basket of fresh fruit. "Master Isaac," Lemuel began, "Your son Esau is well. He prospers and has settled his house in a city of his own. He builds houses of brick and stone in the hill country south of the salt sea and across the Arabah. His sheep and cattle fill the land they call Edom. It is a land of red earth and the name by which Esau is known in that country. He no longer considers the name Edom a slander, it has become a name of independence to him."

Isaac replied, "His wives are from Gerar, they never were ones for living in tents. So, my son builds his city. He prospers? Tell me more."

Lemuel said, "Esau builds his city near the caravan road from the Egyptian mines. He has learned the way of trading. He builds a city for trading, letting others come to him rather than driving his herds and flocks to other towns and cities."

"My son gains wisdom, I am glad. But with its walls, a city brings risk. It is a place where wealth can be found for the taking and evil builds its nest."

Jachin answered, "It is as you say, Master Isaac, a city can bring both risk and reward. Esau has located his city well. His position in the hills is highly defensible, with good views of any approaching. And he has built defensive redoubts above each of his pastures and folds. I have trained his men to watch and warn. His marriage to Mahalath, daughter of Ishmael, has made him welcome with the Ishmaelites, your relatives. Together, they have become a strong people."

Isaac laughed, "And hearing your approach, I thought here comes an old man! But you are still the warrior at heart."

Jachin replied, "Truly, Master Isaac, I am indeed a tired old warrior, but I can advise from my house and still ride a donkey to the redoubts. Was I just to sit by and allow the safety of my daughter and grandchildren to be risked by inexperienced and brash Ishmaelites? Or should I allow the son of my master to be misled and put in danger? No, I did my duty to your kin and my kin."

Isaac smiled and said, "Your faithfulness and honor is unchallenged, and I am glad to have you sit beside me once more."

Lemuel spoke, "Master Isaac, when word came that my father died and my mother sent for me, Master Esau released me, all of us, from our obligation to serve him on your behalf and I…"

Isaac interrupted, "You shall remain in the house of Isaac. Look after your mother, Deborah, but stay with us. Deborah is much loved by all of the people and by me. I have lost the wife I love. My sons have left me; do not take my Nediva Deborah, she has become the heart of my house."

And then turning his blind eyes to Jachin, "Your home is always with us my faithful friend. Please, sit by me in my tent, if your family will share you with me. And game, yes game! We shall eat game together!"

Jachin smiled, "I am honored, master. And yes, I shall bring game!"

The smile left Isaac's face making his dull eyes even more disturbing. He turned to Lemuel, "Esau did not come to bury his mother."

Lemuel answered, "No master. He mourns her, but he was not ready to face you. He knows he dishonored you; he dishonored himself. He will not come until he can come in honor and you can have pride in him as a son."

Isaac sighed, "He must know he has my love and that is worth much more than pride. And his brother, does Esau still desire the blood of his brother Jacob?"

"He hears his brother has reaped what he has sown in hard service to his father-in-law and uncle, Laban. Though he does not speak of it, I believe much of his bitterness is passed. Esau has a large house of his own with all of the issues that require his attention. His three wives bicker among them and he longs for peace in his house."

Isaac nodded and then said, "Perhaps the God Abraham is still working His will in my son. Tell me, Lemuel, does Esau walk with the Most High God?"

Lemuel thought for a few moments and said, "Esau walks as the sons of Ishmael. He does not doubt that the Most High is God, he just ignores Him. He does not follow after the gods of Canaan, and he does not stop his wives and servants from their idol worship, he just follows no god."

Isaac closed his eyes and said, "What you say is a hard thing. I remember my brother Ishmael; he was always waiting and listening for the voice of God. He did not worship and he never heard God. I think seeking God is more than listening for a voice or a vision. The Most High God speaks in many ways, but we must seek His face."

After a few moments of silence, Isaac said, "Go to your mother, comfort her. And your wife and your children and love them. You are never too old to show love."

When Lemuel returned to Deborah she was going through Abiel's things. "Oh, Lemuel, good; you are back. You must take these robes and sandals; they are still as new. And this belt and look at this, I forgot your father had this. A jeweled knife, a gift from Keshet no doubt. Do you remember what Keshet called your father? I'm sorry, I'm sure you don't. He called your father 'his shadow.' Your father followed him everywhere and learned all the ways of trading from Keshet. He was a wonderful man, Keshet, and righteous. Do you know he made a statue in his garden of a little boy following an old man, 'me and my shadow,' he called it."

Deborah handed the scabbarded knife to Lemuel, turned away and began to sob. Lemuel came close and put his arm around his mother. Deborah grasped tightly to his arm and through her sobs said, "So many have passed. It seems my life is only memories."

Lemuel's hug passed through Deborah's heart and touch her soul. Gathering her strength, she continued, "Isaac is so kind, indeed as tender as any brother, but I have no one to serve and nothing to do."

The sweet smile of a loving mother came to her face, "But now you are here and your tender wife and my grandchildren, I can begin living again."

"Mama, you will live in our house. You have served others so many years; let us serve you."

"To me, to serve is to live," Deborah replied.

"Please let those who love you serve you now. Would you deny your family the joy of serving you? Should not you be loved as well as loving others? You should take a lesson from my father-in-law, Jachin; he seeks the joy of family every day."

Then a thought came to Lemuel, "Mother, there is something else I would like to share with you. Do you remember when Jael ben Hod came with news of grandfather Jared's death?"

"Yes, Abaigael sent him to fetch your father. We were at Beersheba."

"Well, Jael gave me something. A scroll. A chronical he wrote; the words and teachings of your father, Zimri-Ruel. I would like to read it to you, mama, I think you would find comfort and joy hearing the story of your beloved father, your papa."

That evening, in the tent of Lemuel, three generations sat and listened as Lemuel read the faith journey of Zimri-Ruel. Even Jachin insisted on sitting in. "I'm family too," he said as sat next to Nediva and placed little Hephzibah, the baby, on his lap. Everyone listened attentively.

Little Nediva remarked first, "Great Grandpa was a slave? He was an orphan and they made him a slave?"

Her younger brother, Jared, asked, "What does he mean when he says he has no genealogy?"

Deborah smiled and answered, "Great-grandpa never knew his parents. He had no family until he married great grandma, Leah."

"I'm confused," Jared continued. "First, he said he had no name, but people called him names, and then he had a new name, a better name?"

Deborah explained, "When great-grandpa met king Melchizedek, he learned the name God had reserved for him, 'Zimri-Ruel,' which means 'my praise, friend of God.' God gave him that name because he gave Great Grandpa a marvelous gift of singing songs to God. The Most High God was his truest friend."

Lemuel continued to read. When he came to the account of Melchizedek explaining to Zimri-Ruel the blessings to come to all men through father Abraham, the night before he received Abram's tithe following the rescue of Lot, Deborah's face became serious. "Read that section again, Lemuel," she asked.

After Lemuel read a second time the prophecy of King Melchizedek, a prophecy that a new nation will come through Abraham's descendants, and a tribe of priests, instructed by God in atoning sacrifices for the people, but only for a time, until one descendant, one man would lay down his life a sacrifice to atone for all the sins man; one time and forever. Deborah's eyes brightened, "Yes, and remember too, Abaigael's dream! Just before she died. King Melchizedek came to her in a dream and showed her a man on a young donkey going to lay himself down as an atoning sacrifice. He called this man the true son of the promise. He said he would lay himself on the wood just as Isaac was, and he would be raised up, like Isaac. But he would be raised after his body was broken and his blood was shed. He would be raised from death to life. This is the promise of God."

Deborah paused, everyone sat silently, watching; her face brightened and her eyes glowed. "And with all of our sins atoned for, we too can rise from death and walk with the Most High God! That is what papa meant! An atonement for all time means now as well as the future! Our hope is true! There is nothing to separate us from walking with God just as Adam and Eve walked with Him in the garden. Oh, what a blessing! How happy Abaigael was and papa too...when death came, they went to walk with God."

Then Deborah nearly shouted, "We must sing! Sing praises to God! Lemuel, read us some of the praise songs papa would sing. No wonder papa could not stop singing praises to God!

Chapter Twenty-Eight

Then the Lord said to Jacob, "Return to the land of your fathers and to your relatives and I will be with you.
Genesis 31: 3

Once Laban agreed to Jacob's terms to stay and work for him, Jacob moved his wives and sons out of the house of Laban, out of the city of Haran. Jacob determined to lives in tents outside of the city wall, separated from the evil and idol worshippers of Haran. Then Jacob went through the flocks and separated all of the black, spotted or striped sheep and goats which were now his property. There could be little argument as to ownership but even so, Jacob kept his flocks widely separated from Laban's.

He left his flocks in the care of his sons three days journey from the flocks of Laban. Rueben, at nineteen was the oldest. He was put in charge but Simeon questioned Reuben's leadership, always arguing for a different, easier way, his own. Whenever Reuben went to meet with Jacob, Simeon tried to stir the other brothers against Reuben, but only Levi would agree with his hot-tempered brother. Reuben patiently reminded his brothers what they had been taught by Jacob and would allow no untried care with the family flocks.

On one visit to Jacob at mating time, Reuben watched as Jacob cut away bark leaving white stripes in rods of poplar, almond and plane tree branches.

Reuben, watching his father asked, "Father, what are these striped rods you leave in the troughs of the strongest sheep?"

Jacob smiled, then looked up and said, "Have your brothers gather more branches of almond, poplar, and plane, and carve them to show white stripes. Place them in the troughs before the strongest sheep and goats and watch what the God of Abraham can do!"

Reuben and his brothers did as Jacob said and placed the striped rods in front of the strongest sheep but left the weaker sheep and goats to nature. Simeon was skeptical but obeyed without questioning him. When the ewes lambed, more black, spotted and striped lambs and goats were born and they became Jacob's and the fewer white sheep and goats became Laban's. Jacob's flocks prospered and grew. Jacob faithfully tended Laban's flocks, seeing they had good pasture and water but they did not increase as much as his own flocks.

As Jacob's prosperity grew, he hired servants for his family. His friends, Ranon and Mincah, grandchildren of shepherds from Dabar El'Elyon, helped him recruit families of those who still worshipped and sacrificed to the Most High God. Jacob remembered father Abraham's and Isaac's steadfast refusal to bring idol worshippers into his household and his requirement that all of the men who served him must be circumcised in accordance with God's promise to Abraham. Ranon told the men of Dabar El'Elyon that circumcision was the sign of the Most High God's promise to be their God and for them to be His people. After conferring, the men of Dabar El'Elyon exclaimed, "We are followers of the Most High God, the God of Abraham and Isaac. Cut away and join us in covenant with the Most High God!"

As Jacob's wealth grew he added more skilled servants and bought many camels and donkeys for his household. There were soon few worshippers of El'Elyon in all the plains of Nahor who were not aligned with the house of Jacob.

Leah was happy to be away from Haran and her relatives. She set about establishing the house of Jacob, seeing that the servants understood what was expected of them and the growing city of tents harmoniously worked as one. Rachel missed the city. She missed the attention she received for her charm and beauty, but she enjoyed Jacob's growing status and having more servants.

While Ranon knew to bring all reports, problems and concerns regarding the shepherds, tradesman and merchants to Jacob, Mincah brought all questions and problems encountered by the household's women servants only to Leah. Mincah would hear from Rachel only concerns of service to herself, Jacob and Joseph.

Laban's sons, younger brothers to Leah and Rachel, would visit the flocks in the fields and made note that the flocks of Jacob increased much more than the flocks of their father. Laban's sons were jealous of Jacob and his larger flocks. They grumbled among themselves, "Jacob is cheating us! He is stealing what is our father's! He steals our inheritance!"

"Yes, he grows rich at our expense."

"He is only a servant, yet he hires man servants to do his work and women servants to tend our spoiled sisters."

"Brothers, let it be agreed among us, we shall take back all that is rightfully ours."

"Agreed, but we must convince our father before we act."

Jacob had little regard for the animosity of his brothers-in-law, and visits to his house by his in-laws became infrequent. One day Laban appeared unexpected. Jacob welcomed Laban and insisted he stay and sit with his family for the evening meal. Laban shouted, "No, I will not stay. But hear Jacob what I have to say against you."

Jacob jerked back in surprise and was about to speak.

Not waiting for Jacob's response, Laban said, "After all I have done for you, given you my daughters and servants for my daughters, and provided for you to have flocks of your own, now I learn you have deceived me! You have taken most of my flock! You reserve the strong and leave me the weak. My sons will have nothing and my name will be lost."

Angered, Jacob replied, "Father in law, you asked me to stay; you set the terms. If you had asked for the black, spotted or striped I would have taken the white. I have served you faithfully all of these years. How many times have you changed my terms of service? My prosperity comes from God not from you and not by deceit."

Laban pointed his finger at Jacob's face, "I will not be deceived! I will have what is rightfully mine!" Then he turned and walked off.

The next day while Jacob was in the field tending Laban's sheep, he stopped during the heat of the day to rest under the shade of a terebinth tree. He closed his eyes and dozed off. As he slept, the Lord again came to him in a vision and said, "Return to the land of your fathers and to your relatives, and I will be with you."

Immediately, Jacob awoke and sent one of his servants for Leah and Rachel to join him in the fields. When they arrived he told them, "Your father no longer trusts me nor is he willing to honor the agreement we made. He is jealous of our wealth. You know how hard I worked to serve him. You know how he cheated me and changed my wages. But God did not allow him to hurt me! I stayed because he asked and he agreed to the terms. I see now God has taken away his livestock and given them to me."

Leah answered, "Yes, husband, what you say is true."

Rachel stared in confusion.

Jacob paused, closed his eyes and said, "At the mating time I had a dream. I dreamt that all of the goats that were mating were striped, speckled or mottled. Then the angel of

God said to me in the dream, 'Jacob, do you see that all of the goats which are mating are striped, speckled or mottled? For I have seen all that Laban has been doing to you. I am the God of Bethel, where you made a pillar, anointed it and made a vow to Me. Now leave this land and return to the land of your birth.'"

Leah and Rachel looked at each other, and in a rare moment of unity agreed.

"Do we still have any portion or inheritance in our father's house?" Rachel asked.

"And are we not treated as foreigners?" Leah said, "He has sold us and spent our purchase price. Surely, all of the wealth which God has taken away from him belongs to us and our children."

Rachel nodded to Leah and turned to Jacob, "Now, husband, do whatever God has said to you."

Jacob, Leah, and Rachel went home and Jacob told Ranon, "Pack all my household, everything. Pack it on the camels and donkeys, we leave today!"

Seeing the surprise on Ranon'a face, Jacob said, "The servants are all welcome to come with us. I will make their wages, or they may stay and seek service in the house of Laban."

Ranon bowed and was about to leave, then he stopped, looked Jacob in the face and said, "I will do as you command, but I can say now that all of your servants will go where you go. We find service to the house of Jacob much better than remaining in Haran with Laban and his sons."

Warmed by Ranon's voice of support speaking for all of his servants, Jacob smiled and said, "Thank you, Ranon. Thank you and all of the people of Dabar El'Elyon. I have learned to value the counsel of those who serve me, of those who worship the Most High God."

Jacob and his sons went out to the fields and began driving their flocks south. He left Ranon in charge of moving the household. Laban and his sons were sheering their flocks and did not know Jacob was leaving, but before they left, Rachel, returned to Haran, went into her father's house and stole his household idols.

Three days passed before Laban was told Jacob had left. By then, Jacob had already crossed the Euphrates and was moving south towards the hill country of Gilead. Laban sent for his sons and his kinsmen. His sons arrived first and enraged, advised their father, "Jacob, the deceiver, has stolen what is ours. Gather our kinsman and pursue him! We will take back what is ours!"

Laban tried to reason with them, "Surely Jacob will fight for what he has. Would you slay your sisters' husband, the son of my sister?"

"Pursue him and recover what he has taken by deceit! Let him live if you must, he came here alone and with nothing, let him leave alone and with nothing!"

When Laban's kinsmen arrived and heard of Laban's plan to pursue Jacob they argued, "Follow after him in peace and inquire of him and we may accompany you."

Laban's sons shouted at them, "He has taken our flocks by deceit. Come with us and we will recover what is ours!"

Laban's kinsman ignored Laban's sons and calmly asked Laban, "Is not Jacob our kinsman as well? Is he not a son of Isaac and a son of promise to father Abraham, who was a brother of Nahor and Haran? Is not the God of Abraham and the God of Nahor with him? Is not his mother your own sister? You may follow after him and inquire of him and we will join you."

Their caution troubled Laban but he wanted their presence as a strong show of force when he caught up with Jacob. Laban nodded and answered, "All that you say is true. Come with me and we will follow him and let him return what is mine."

The kinsman cautiously reminded Laban, "Did you not make an agreement with him on your flocks? Has he not served you faithfully twenty years? How can you say he has stolen from you? And take heed, for Isaac is as a prince in his land with great wealth and power and Jacob is his heir."

In desperation Laban huffed, "There is the matter of my household gods. They were stolen. And he has deceived me. Come with me and we will inquire of him."

The kinsman conferred among themselves and then told Laban, "We will come and hear what Jacob has to say."

It took another seven days before Laban, his sons and his kinsman caught up with Jacob in Gilead, southeast of the sea of Chinnereth (Galilee). The night before Laban overtook Jacob, he had a dream unlike he had ever had before. This dream unnerved Laban. He knew it was God who came to him in and said, "Be careful that you do not speak to Jacob either good or bad." Laban could not get this dream out of his mind.

Jacob had camped in Gilead with tents for each of his wives, sons, and servants. His flocks were all about him, so when Laban arrived with a large number of armed men, Jacob had no choice but to hear what his father-in-law had to say.

Laban slowly rode forward on his donkey. Stopping in front of Jacob he said, without dismounting, "What have you done by deceiving me and carrying away my daughters like captives taken by the sword?"

Only the animals could be heard snorting as the sun burned overhead. Laban straightened his back in the saddle, "Why did you run secretly and deceive me? Why didn't you tell me you were leaving? I might have sent you away with joy and celebration and song! You did not allow me to kiss my grandsons and my daughters! What you have done is foolish."

Laban turned and pointed to his sons, each with a weapon in his hand and the large entourage of kinsman, "It is in my power to do you harm, but the God of your father spoke to me last night, saying, 'Be careful not to speak good or bad to Jacob.' And now you have left because you longed for your father's house. But why have you stolen my gods?"

Jacob fearing Laban's kinsman, replied softly, "I was afraid. I was afraid you would take your daughters away from me by force."

Jacob paused. He looked confused and then said loudly for the kinsman to hear, "But I have taken nothing; in the presence of our kinsman, point out what is yours among my belongings. The one with whom you find your gods will not live."

Laban searched Jacob's tent. He searched Leah's tent and the tents of the wife maids, Bilhah and Zilpah, and the tents of the servants and he found nothing. His anger increased with each unsuccessful search. When he went in to search Rachel's tent she did not rise in the presence of her father as it was the custom to do. She was seated on a camel's saddle in her tent, the very saddle where she hid her father's idols.

"Do not be angry with me, father, I cannot stand because it is my time of the month."

Laban impatiently searched Rachel's tent while she sat. He found nothing. Having come up empty in his search, in his silence he was rudely confronted by Jacob, "What have I done wrong? What is my sin that you have chased me like a criminal? You have searched all my tents and belongings. What have you found? Set it before our kinsman. Let them see what you say I have taken! Let them judge between you and me!"

Laban was silent. The kinsman, watching also said nothing.

Jacob's indignation grew, "These twenty years I have been with you; your ewes and your female goats have not miscarried, nor have I eaten the rams of your flocks. That which was killed by beasts, I did not bring to you, I bore the loss myself. You held me accountable for any sheep stolen by day or stolen by night. And so, I worked, by day consumed by the heat, by night the frost and my sleep fled from my eyes. These twenty years I have been in your house; I served you fourteen years for your two daughters, and six years for your flock, and you have changed my wages ten times."

Jacob looked at Laban's sons and his kinsman and

shouted, "If the God of Abraham, and the fear of Isaac, had not been for me, surely now you would have sent me away empty-handed. God has seen my affliction and toil of my hands, so He rendered judgment last night."

Laban downcast, answered quietly with sincerity, "The daughters are my daughters, and the children are my children, and the flocks are my flocks, and all that you see is mine. But what can I do this day to these, my daughters or to the children they have borne?"

Laban paused and looking into Jacob's eyes said, "So now come, let us make a covenant, you and I and let it be a witness between you and me."

Laban's sons screamed, "But father, our inheritance!"

Laban turned to his sons and angrily replied, "Put away your swords, you have no skill as trained men. I know what is mine and what is not. I will determine your inheritance!"

The young men meekly put away their weapons. Laban's kinsman watched with grim faces.

Laban turned back to Jacob and waited.

Jacob studied Laban's face, nodded and then took up a long stone, set it up as a pillar and said to his kinsman, "Gather stones."

They gathered stones and piled them together and called the heap of stones, Galeed, 'the heap of witness,' and the pillar, Mitzpah, 'watchtower.' They said, "These stones are a witness between you and me this day, may the Lord watch between you and me when we are absent one from the other."

Laban's voice strengthened as he loudly affirmed, "See this pile of stones is a witness and the pillar is a witness that I will not pass by this heap to do you harm and you will not pass by this heap and this pillar to do me harm and if you mistreat my daughters, or if you take wives besides my daughters, although no one sees to tell me, God is witness between you and me."

Jacob replied, "The God of Abraham and the God of

Nahor, the God of their father, judge between us." So Jacob swore by the fear of his father, Isaac.

Then Jacob called out to his kinsman, "Come lets us offer a sacrifice to God on the mountain!" After sacrificing to God Most High, Jacob invited his kinsman to a meal. They ate the meal and spent the night on the mountain. Early in the morning, Laban arose, kissed his daughters and grandsons and blessed them.

To Rachel he said, "My beautiful Rachel, I will miss your smiles and your charm. Take your beauty and charm as an adornment for your husband Jacob."

"I love my husband and will always seek to honor him."

Laban came to Leah and said, "Have I not always loved you, my daughter? Your beauty lies within. A beauty of wisdom and heart. Take your strength, wisdom and strong heart as an obedient wife to Jacob and mother to your children."

Leah looked at her father, "I honor and serve Jacob, father, but do not call what you did to me or my husband, love."

Leah's words struck at Laban's heart. Saying nothing in reply he mounted his donkey, signaled to his sons and kinsman and he returned to Haran on the plains of Nahor.

Jacob loaded his tents and belongings on his camels and moved his flocks south. On the way, Jacob went back to make certain they were no longer being followed. As he rode alone a man approached him. The face of the man was unlike any he had ever seen. The face was both beautiful and terrifying. It was bright and brought light in its presence. Jacob threw himself prone on the ground for he recognized that an angel of God met him. The angel looked down upon Jacob and said, "This is God's place."

Chapter Twenty-Nine

Awake, and rise to my defense! Contend for me, my God and Lord.

Psalm 35: 23

Jacob continued south through Gilead following the caravan road east of the Jordan, as he neared the Salt Sea, the road ran in a valley between two mountain ranges. He was approaching Edom, the land settled by his brother Esau. Twenty years had passed since Jacob fled from his brother's anger, now he was approaching his lands. How would Esau, receive him? He could not go back to Haran and surely Esau would learn of his presence. Jacob longed for the advice and preparations of his old guardian and mentor, Jachin. How foolish he had been to send him off.

Jacob sent for Ranon, chief of all of his servants and a man who trusted in God. When Ranon came with the chief of the shepherds, the chief of the oxen, and the chief of the camels, Jacob said, "Go ahead of us as we travel and take a message to my brother, Esau. Tell him, 'These are the words of your servant, Jacob. I have sojourned with Laban from when I left our father, Isaac, until now. I have oxen and donkeys and flocks, and male and female servants; and I have sent to tell my lord that I may find favor in your sight.'"

Ranon found Esau in his well-fortified city, bustling with trade. They were led past penned animals, through the busy market and into the quieter precincts. Esau's house was in the center of the city, and the messengers thought, *Surely, this is a palace!* Esau received the messengers while he was seated in his shaded courtyard being fanned by a servant while several leaders of his trained men stood beside him. His hair was oiled but still black as coal, his beard trimmed and perfumed. He sat and listened with dignity as the king of his city. When Ranon and the other messengers spoke the words of Jacob, Esau stared at the men in disbelief.

After a long pause Esau put down his golden goblet of wine and began to laugh. At first, it was a light chuckle and then his face brightened and he spoke out merrily, "My brother, Jacob, comes! This is good news, good news indeed!"

Esau rose from his seat, his white linen robe swaying in the breeze of the fans, he turned to the head of his trained men, "Gather four hundred of our men. We go to meet my brother!"

To Ranon, he said directly, as one accustomed to giving orders, "Go back to my brother and tell him I will come to meet him."

Ranon and the other servants stood confused and then retreated from Esau's house. They could not understand what they witnessed but returned directly to Jacob.

Jacob waited impatiently for Ranon and the others to return. His mind ran through the possibilities. How would he defend his family? Could he defend his family? Surely his brother's temper had cooled. Was he not now a wealthy lord in his land? *The Lord God has protected me to this day, He would take my family from me now. He would not remove His shield from me, would He?*

When Jacob saw them return, immediately he asked, "What word?"

"Your brother is coming to meet you with four hundred of his men."

Jacob was gripped with fear. He asked Ranon, "When you spoke to my brother, what was his temper?"

Ranon said, "He was surprised to hear of you, but he became happy. He said it was good news. And then gave the order to gather four hundred men to come with him to meet you."

Jacob asked, "Was he happy to see me again as a brother, or happy for a chance at vengeance?"

Ranon looked at the others who went with him. They all shrugged. Ranon answered, "Truly, my lord, I do not know."

Jacob was deeply troubled. He Told Ranon to divide the people, the camels, the herds and the flocks into two companies. And told his servants and his sons that if Esau came and attacked one company the other should escape.

As his camp set about preparations, that night, Jacob went out of the camp alone and stayed under the heavens. He fervently prayed, "O God of my father Abraham, and God of my father Isaac, O Lord, who said to me, 'Return to your people and to your relatives, and I will prosper you,' I am unworthy of all the lovingkindness and all of the faithfulness which you have shown to Your servant; for I had only my staff when I crossed the Jordan, and now I have become two companies. Deliver me, I pray, from the hand of my brother, from the hand of Esau; for I fear him, lest he comes and attacks me and the mothers with the children. For You did say, 'I will surely prosper you, and make your descendants as the sand of the sea, which cannot be numbered for multitude.'"

In the morning, his resolve, if not his faith, restored, Jacob selected from what he had in his company, a present for his brother: two hundred female goats and twenty male goats, two hundred ewes and twenty rams, thirty milking camels, forty cows, ten bulls, twenty female donkeys and ten male donkeys. Jacob delivered the droves to the head shepherd. He told the shepherds to herd the livestock ahead of us but put a space between each drove of animals.

Finally, he told Ranon to go in front of the livestock, "When my brother Esau meets you and asks you, 'To who do you belong, and where are you going, and to who do these animals belong?' Then you shall say, 'These belong to your servant Jacob; it is a present sent to my lord Esau, and Jacob follows behind us."

Jacob instructed each shepherd leading each drove of livestock to repeat the same message. One by one the droves of livestock slowly crossed the Jabbok River and traveled south. After the livestock gift to Esau forded, the remaining herds and people carefully crossed over. Finally, Jacob led his wives and children across the river and set up their tents. Jacob returned to the other shore and spent the night alone under the star filled sky.

That night while Jacob was alone halfway between asleep and awake, a man appeared from nowhere and said, "Get up!"

Jacob arose warily and the man sprang at him shouting and grabbing. He attempted to throw Jacob to the ground. Jacob fought back and struggled against the stranger. Jacob struggled and sweated, grabbing and pulling the man. Back and forth they went, wrestling all night with neither man taking the advantage. The man wrestled with him until daybreak. Jacob was gasping for breath, exhausted but still refused to be subdued. When the man saw that he had not prevailed against Jacob, he touched the socket of Jacob's thigh, and his thighbone was dislocated. The man said, "Let me go for the dawn is breaking."

Jacob replied through gasps for air, "I will not let you go. I will never let you free unless you bless me."

The man said calmly, not in the least fatigued, "What is your name?"

"My name... my name... my name is Jacob."

"Your name shall no longer be called Jacob, but Israel, 'God Contended,' for you have striven with God and with men and have prevailed."

Jacob laid on his back in pain and struggling to recover, still gasping said, "Please tell me your name."

Still calm, the man said, "Why is it you asked my name?"

After a moment of silence, the man blessed him there. "Hear, Israel, in you comes the promise of God to Abraham and to Isaac, a promise of blessings to my people."

Jacob named the place Peniel, 'The face of God,' for he said, "I have seen God face to face, yet my life has been preserved."

Jacob had no time to ponder the meaning of his strange encounter. He limped his way across the river, holding his thigh and looking up he saw his brother Esau fast approaching with his four hundred men. He divided his wives and children into three groups. He put Bilhah, Zilpah and their children in the front, and then Leah and her children and last Rachel and Joseph. Then Jacob limped out in front as Esau arrived, fell to his knees and bowed seven times to his brother. Esau dismounted, ran to Jacob and embraced him with a warm hug. Esau kissed Jacob, laid his head across Jacob's neck and both brothers wept.

After a long embrace, Esau wiped the tears from his eyes and looked at the three groups of women and children standing behind Jacob.He asked, "Who are these, brother?"

Jacob was also crying and after wiping away his tears replied with a smile, "The children who, God has graciously given your servant."

Zilpah and Bilhah approached with their children and silently bowed before Esau. Then Leah and her children came forward and bowed before him and lastly, Rachel and Joseph came forward and bowed before Esau. Jacob's sons watched in amazement as their father humbled himself before their uncle.

Esau asked, "What do you mean by all of this company which I have met, sheep, goats, cattle, donkeys and camels, company upon company?"

"To find favor in the sight of my lord."

"I have plenty brother, keep what you have for yourself."

"No, please, if now I have found favor in your sight, then accept my present from my hand. For I have seen your face, which is like seeing the face of God and you have accepted me. Please accept my blessing that is brought to you, because God has dealt graciously with me, and because I have enough."

"As you wish, brother. Let us journey on our way. I will go ahead of you."

Jacob answered, "My lord knows that the children are frail and that the nursing flock and herds are a care to me. If they are driven hard for one day, all the flocks will die. Let my lord pass on ahead of his servant, and I will lead on slowly at the pace of the livestock and the pace of the children until I come to my lord."

Esau said, "Let me leave you some of my people who are with me."

"What need is there? Let me find favor in the sight of my lord."

Esau nodded, "As you wish, brother, It is good that you have returned."

Esau signaled to his men and they silently turned around and drove the livestock Jacob had gifted Esau south on the caravan road.

After Esau and his men were lost in the dust on the southern horizon, Jacob turned his flocks west and followed the Jabbock river a few miles downstream to an area of good pasture for his flocks. He built a house and pens for his livestock and stayed there, east of the Jordan river while his herds and flocks rested and recovered from the long, rushed journey from Haran.

While the house of Jacob rested beside the river Jabbock, Jacob had time to reflect on all that happened to him since he fled from his brother. For twenty years God had been blessing him and preparing him. God gave him wealth and prosperity.

God gave him many strong sons and faithful servants, not idol worshipping hirelings. But now God was speaking to him again, the same God who appeared to him at Bethel twenty years earlier has spoken to him again in his warning to leave Haran and through a strange man who wrestled with him through the night. And God had given him a new name. He was no longer Jacob, 'The Trickster,' but Israel, for he has striven with God. And God heard his prayer! Did not Esau receive him as a loving brother?

Rachel and Leah listened to Jacob as he recounted the events the night before Esau arrived. Rachel warmly smiled and said, "Surely God has delivered us, but shall we stay here? There is no city, where shall we trade?"

Leah listened and said, "Husband surely the God of Abraham and the God of Isaac is the God of El' Bethel and the God of Jacob. He has a new name for you, and to me, you are now Israel. And surely Israel is the promise made to your fathers, Abraham and Isaac. But the man you wrestled, you believe he was God? Can a man contend with God and prevail?"

Jacob looked at Leah differently and said, "The man told me, 'Your name shall be Israel, for you have striven with God and prevailed.' He was no ordinary man. Do I not have a limp in my thigh where he touched me? With this limp, I will never forget. That is why I named the place Peniel, 'The face of God.' I looked him in the face. Who else could it be? And after my prayer?"

When Ranon came to find Jacob and report on the household, he found him sitting at the opening of his tent. The wisdom of Leah's words lingered in Jacob's mind. 'Can a man wrestle with God and prevail?' Jacob told Ranon about all that had happened to him, He told him of his prayer and he told him how he wrestled all night with the man who would not give a name but blessed him and gave him a new name. He then added, "Can a man wrestle with God and live?"

Ranon sat beside Jacob and thought for a few moments.

"Master, you have fine, strong sons. Did you ever wrestle with them as young boys?"

Jacob laughed, "Not like I wrestled with Esau! But yes, gently so as not to hurt them."

Ranon smiled, "Of course. But you never forced yourself on them. You let them wrestle to their ability. I think you let them prevail against you. You want strong and confident sons. And so it is with our father God. He wants to strengthen you and strengthen your trust in Him."

Jacob nodded, "What you say is true. And I do know I can trust Him."

Then Ranon added, "Master Jacob, you say you prayed, prayed fervently before Esau came. Is not a fervent prayer wrestling with God? Do not the struggles of life, our worries and concerns fight within our very soul? When we pray to God Most High we are wrestling and He permits us to prevail."

Jacob looked into Ranon's eyes and warmly replied, "It is just as you say, Ranon, I must remember to wrestle with God all the more. I shall wrestle through my prayers!"

Jacob named the place he camped Succoth, 'Booths,' for there he built the booths for his livestock. After his flocks and herds were strong again, he crossed the Jordan river into the hill country of Canaan and came to the city of Shechem. The land around Shechem was good for pasture, located between Mount Ebal to the north and Mount Gerizim to the south. He bought the land where he pitched his tent from the sons of Hamor, Shechem's father for one hundred pieces of silver. Jacob erected an altar and called it El' Elohe-Israel, 'A Mighty God is the God of Israel' and Jacob worshipped the Lord God.

Chapter Thirty

"Honor your father and mother" (this is the first commandment with a promise), "that it may go well with you and that you may live long in the land." Fathers, do not provoke your children to anger but bring them up in the discipline of the Lord.

Ephesians 6: 2-4

Jacob prospered in Shechem and his flocks and herds multiplied. Like Abraham and Isaac before him, Jacob chose to live in his tents outside the city walls. He maintained good relations with Hamor, king of Shechem and his sons. He traded with them honestly and brought new wealth to the city. Jacob would not attend their feasts or permit the idols of their gods to be brought into his household. Jacob would not bring an idol worshipper into his service. But God is good! The sons and daughters of Dabar El'Elyon who served him in Haran prospered and grew, and their children served the house of Jacob faithfully. Jacob rewarded his servants with flocks and herds of their own which were traded with those of Jacob. Jacob grew in the favor of the Lord.

One day, after returning from a sacrifice of worship to the

God of Abraham and Isaac, Jacob went into his tent showing a troubled face. Rachel, seeing her husband did not reflect his normal joy of praise following his worship, said, "Husband, something troubles you. It pains me to see the husband who loves me, with such sadness in his eyes. Tell me, Jacob, for I would comfort you."

Jacob looked at Rachel, then went to her and hugged her. "Truly, Rachel, God has blessed us. He gives us safe pasture for our flocks, fair trades for our goods, wealth and honor. He has given me strong sons and a fine daughter. And I make sacrifices to please him. He has caused my brother to receive me well and we have reconciled. But my heart weighs heavy within me for I have sinned and not repented; I have not given my father and mother the honor I owe them. I have wronged my father and I must bring him peace before he joins Abraham in his tomb."

Rachel said, "Husband, go to your father. Give him the honor you desire. What prevents us? We shall all go. The God of Abraham and Isaac will surely bless you and them. Does He not pour out His love and blessings upon you and on us? How can it be other? All is well here, let us go to your father's house!"

Jacob listened to Rachel and told Ranon to prepare for the journey south to Hebron and the Oaks of Mamre. All of his wives and children would go with him to pay honor to Isaac. Ranon, Mincah and the household servants would serve them on the journey. The Shepherds and field servants would stay and care for the herds and flocks. It would not be a long journey but Jacob determined his house would live in their own tents and be served by his household servants.

As Jacob and his family approached the tents of his father, Isaac, he was gripped with fear and apprehension. It was not only his brother, Esau, he had deceived but his father as well. He knew that God had changed the heart of his brother towards him, would he not touch the heart of his father as well?

Jacob slowly led his family into Isaac's camp. He could see his father sitting at the entrance of his tent. Jacob motioned for his family and household to stop. He dismounted his donkey and walked slowly towards his father. Isaac's sightless, clouded blue eyes stared ahead betraying no emotion.

Isaac flung himself prone on the ground in front of his father and nearly wailed, "Father, I have sinned against you and against the God of Abraham and Isaac. I have stolen the blessing you intended for my brother Esau. I have deceived you from the day I was born until the day I fled. God has dealt with me according to my sins, now, father, I lie prone before you, deal with me as you will."

Before Jacob had finished his plea, Isaac was on his feet walking towards him with open arms. "Jacob, my son, it is you! Jacob get up out of the dust, embrace your father! How I have prayed for this day! And your mother prayed as well. Come embrace me! And there are others I hear."

Jacob stood up, dusted himself off and ran to Isaac. Hugging him tightly he said through his tears, "Yes father, my wives and your grandchildren, eleven strong sons and a fine daughter!"

Isaac waved an arm, "Come, all of you, I want to embrace each of you and know you. Come!

Jacob, bring them forward and tell me their names."

As was his habit, Jacob brought forward his family in groups by his wives. First, he brought Zilpah and her sons. "This is Zilpah, handmaid to Leah and my sons by her, Asher and Gad, whom Leah has taken across her knees as her sons."

Jacob then brought forward Bilhah, "This is Bilhah, handmaid to my Rachel, and my sons by her, Naphtali and Dan, whom my Rachel has taken across her knees as her sons."

Next came Leah, "This is my wife Leah, and my children by her, Reuben, my first born, Simeon, Levi, Judah, Issachar, and Zebulun. And my daughter, Dinah."

Finally, Jacob brought Rachel, "And this is my Rachel, whom I love as you loved Rebekah. And our son, Joseph."

Isaac listened closely to Jacob. When Jacob finished, he called each of them before him and hugging them correctly saying their names. He asked each of them to greet him as father Isaac and to repeat their names telling them he wished to recognize their voices. After each introduction, he gave each a blessing in the name of God. When he came to Dinah he knelt down in front of her and said, "Mother Rebekah would have greeted you with her special love and devotion! One fine daughter among so many brothers! I pray that you bring love and unity to them and grow into as strong a woman as my Rebekah."

"I will try, father Isaac," she replied meekly.

Isaac clasped her shoulders and said, "I know you will."

Isaac stood up and shouted, "Lemuel! Lemuel!"

"Here I am," he replied.

"A feast! See that there is a feast for my family! A feast for my son who has been lost to me for many years has returned! He has returned with the blessings of God! He has returned as the father of his house!"

Lemuel replied, "It will be just as you desire, master Isaac."

Jacob said to Lemuel, "It is a blessing of the Most High that I find my old friend well! Here are Ranon and Mincah, they lead my household. They too, like your mother, Deborah, are children of Dabar El' Elyon and follow the One True God."

Lemuel said, "It is indeed a blessing to see you again, master Jacob. My mother will rejoice to see you again."

Jacob's eyes brightened, "Deborah is here!"

Then Isaac said, "Yes, Deborah will share in my joy but come, my son, we have much to discuss. Lemuel will see to your family's comfort. They will be provided refreshment and rest. Come and sit with me awhile."

As they walked, Isaac held fast to Jacob's arm. "I was told you had returned from Haran and that you received your brother Esau before pitching your tent near Shechem. Be careful of Hamor and his people, they are Canaanites and idol worshippers."

"Yes, father, I dwell outside the walls in my tents and will permit no idol worshippers in my household. Just as you taught me and as did father Abraham before you."

"Good, very good. And your brother, Esau, he is well?"

"He prospers greatly. He has built a city, and his land is called, 'Edom,' in which he takes great pride."

"He received you well, that is good. I pray he will return to me one day. I would receive him well."

"Father, we pass your tent, shall I show you the way?"

"No, my son, we walk to the cave of Machpelah, to the tomb of Abraham, Sarah and now Rebekah. You shall see where your mother lies and where you shall soon lay my bones."

"Surely, not soon!"

Jacob paused and then said, "How I regret not telling mother one more time I love her and to tell her God has dealt with me for my transgressions. I would have had her know that God has blessed me and I seek to walk with Him. Her favor towards me has been rewarded."

Isaac tightened his grip on Jacob's arm and said, "She knew you loved her. She knew God would bless you. It was my stubbornness to favor your brother. God told her before you were born 'The older would serve the younger. The stronger would serve the weaker.' She trusted God."

"God spoke to her?"

"Abaigael, a prophet of the Most High, gave her the word from God while you were yet in her womb. She did not share it with you, she chose to trust God who can make all things work to His good will."

They made their way to the end of the field and walked under the shade of the oak trees. The wind in the leaves whispered 'peace,' as they made their way towards the rocky mountain wall. The canopy of cool shade brought silence to both father and son. When they arrived at the entrance to the tomb. Jacob began to weep. As his eyes began to give up their tears, he fell to his knees and his weeping grew into sobs and crying. Isaac stood beside him gently patting him on the back. Softly Isaac told Jacob, "When I sit at the entrance of my tent I face this tomb. It comforts me to know Rebekah waits here for me. I will meet her here and walk with her in the company of God just as He walked with Adam and Eve, just as He intended for all men in the garden."

As the sun set, Jacob, Rachel, Leah and the children were led to the tent of Isaac. Ranon and Mincah were directing Bilhah and Zilpah in setting out the table alongside Lemuel and Isaac's servants. Isaac was seated alongside an elderly woman.

Rachel asked Jacob, "Who is she? I thought Isaac took no other wife or concubine."

Jacob stared at the woman and was about to speak when Isaac said, "Jacob, introduce your family to Deborah."

Jacob smiled broadly and greeted Deborah who rose to hug him. "Nediva Deborah! God has blessed me to see you once again! Truly you keep the love of God and my mother, Rebekah, alive in the house of Isaac!"

Deborah held Jacob tight and said, "My heart rejoices that my eyes can see the son of God's promise! And your family! So many sons and such a strong daughter! Rebekah would love her and your sons, just as she loved you."

Jacob smiled warmly at Deborah.

Isaac said, "My good friend Jachin cannot join us this evening. He lies in his bed, I fear he will not again arise from it. I will miss sitting beside him at the entrance to my tent and hearing his stories. But the God of my father Abraham has blessed him and he finds comfort with his family, he always has a grandson or granddaughter in his lap to bring a smile to his face and laughter across his lips."

Jacob laughed, "He is the most tender of warriors! I must

see him, for I have wronged him as well."

Isaac paused in reflection and then said, "I ramble on. Please, sit, sit! You must eat. You have had a long journey. Jacob, tell me everything! You say God has dealt with your trespasses and yet you are now a man of wealth, head of a great house. Tell me, my son, how has God dealt with you?"

Jacob recounted his story. He told of his dream and the altar he built at Bethel. He told of his service to Laban and how God provided him flocks and great wealth and warned him to leave Haran. He told of his prayer before meeting Esau and how he wrestled with God. As he told his stories, Deborah and even Lemuel joined Isaac in questioning him.

Rachel tried to ask Jacob quietly, "Is it honorable for servants to sit at the master's table and to question the master's son and guest?"

Before Jacob could answer, Isaac, whose hearing improved as his sight declined heard his daughter-in-law and replied, "Who is master, but God? Are we not all but servants of Him?"

Zilpah and Bilhah both cast their eyes to the ground, so not to betray the hurt at Rachel's challenge and the surprise at Isaac's response. They continued to serve and listen in silence, their presence of no consequence to Jacob and Rachel. Only Leah watched them go about their duties, but she kept her thoughts to herself.

Isaac continued, "Deborah was nurse and servant to Rebekah since childhood, but also her friend. She loved Rebekah as a sister. I love Deborah as my sister. She has served, now let her be served. Her husband, Abiel, served me and their son Lemuel as well. Now we all serve one another and walk together with the God of Abraham. Yet I would pray that one day I have the gift God has given to Deborah."

Leah asked, "What gift is that, Father Isaac?"

Isaac replied, "Love. She knows how to love. Love God and love whom God loves. We all need such love. Love requires great strength."

Twelve-year-old Dinah asked meekly, "Father, Isaac, I don't understand much about love. I love my father and mother, and they love me and my brothers. How does love require strength?"

Isaac smiled at Dinah, "God gives us mothers and fathers to teach us love. He gives fathers and mothers children to teach them love as well. Without the love between parent and child, we could never understand that love is costly. Because we love our children we are willing to pay the price of love. But it becomes harder with other people. Love requires strength because love must be given even to people who we do not like or who we think do not deserve our love. Love puts others before ourselves. It must be so because God loves us and we do not deserve His love."

Then turning to Deborah, Isaac said, "Sister, you are never too old to love. Do you think you could teach this daughter and her brothers to love? And with all these boys, do you think you can make her strong like Rebekah?"

Jacob spoke, "Father, Deborah has earned her rest, let her..."

Deborah smiled and said, "If Rachel and Leah, Zilpah and Bilhah, could accept the service of an older sister, I would find great joy in serving them."

Lemuel added, "Master Jacob, surely you, of all men, know my mother lives to serve. To her, it is all joy. When have you or I been able to change her mind? There can be no argument!"

Jacob laughed, "What you say is true! No one ever questioned the word of Nediva Deborah except perhaps my mother Rebekah, but then they agreed in every way."

Turning to Rachel and then to Leah, Jacob asked, "Can we not accept the service of my mother's nurse and wise servant, Deborah?"

Rachel and Leah looked at each other. Leah said, "I am not one to turn down the help of another."

Rachel said, "Yes, I will accept her service."

"Good! It is done then," Jacob said smiling at Deborah and he continued to enjoy his meal.

Bilhah and Zilpah were silent and continued to serve at the table.

That night Jachin died. When Jacob arose then next morning, he did not find Isaac at the entrance to his tent. A servant led Jacob to the tent of Jachin where Isaac was grieving with Lemuel and his wife Yagon. She was surrounded by little children crying, "Grandpa! Why can't we see Grandpa? What is wrong with Grandpa?"

"Grandpa missed your grandma and has gone to visit her. He is well and so is she. He is well..." Yagon's tears and sobs told another story.

Jacob was wounded in his soul. Jachin had passed before he could even try to make things right with him. Such a good man. A mentor; such a faithful servant and friend. Jacob's last words to him were not only ungrateful but cruel.

Isaac heard the sigh of Jacob's as he entered the tent and said, "It is good to grieve my son, but also remember Jachin with joy. A man blessed by God, not with wealth or riches, but a man who found happiness in life even after the passing of his wife whom he loved. See how he is mourned! He loved and was loved."

Jacob sobbed, "Yet another person I loved and wronged has been gathered to his people before I could set right the wrongs I did him."

Isaac grasped Jacob's arm. "God makes no promises to preserve those we wrong to the day we repent. No, the lesson my son is to repent soon for no man knows when our God will call someone to walk with Him."

Jacob had no words for Yagon or her children, he just kept repeating, "I'm sorry, so sorry. A good and righteous man; I'm sorry..."

Jacob and Isaac helped Lemuel bury Jachin under the oaks of Mamre near the cave of Machpelah. The whole household of Isaac wept. It was known that Jachin was called away a contented man, the happiest man in the house of Isaac. His infant granddaughter was asleep in his lap at the very end. Jachin kept the covenant of circumcision he made when he entered into the service of Abraham. He had only cut away what he did not need. His was a circumcision of the heart. He was a man who sought God, believed God, trusted God and loved God. Jachin the Hittite, was a great warrior who was drawn to the God who brought victory to his followers. And this was the victory of Jachin, a fearless warrior who never had to let fly his arrow towards an enemy or swing his sword in battle, who but once killed another man loved by God, and then only in protection of Rebekah on her way to Canaan. This was a victory worthy of a warrior for God.

After the burial of Jachin, Jacob determined to return to his flocks at Shechem. As preparations began to move his household, Isaac sent Lemuel to bring Jacob to him, alone. When Jacob arrived, he found his father sitting at the entrance of his tent facing the tomb of Machpelah. "Jacob, my son, sit beside me a while before you depart."

Jacob sat down and said, "I am here, father."

Isaac kept staring ahead. "How much more I see now that the God of Abraham has blinded me from distractions! You must learn, my son, where to look if you are to see the blessings of God. Our God looks at the hearts of men. He looks for justice for the wronged and mercy for the sinner. He looks for obedience to His will and trust in His promises. He looks for love in our hearts, for Him and for others."

Jacob replied, "Yes father, there is wisdom in these words."

Isaac continued, "A man must look at Himself as God sees him. He must look honestly and see his transgressions. For God will not hold a man faultless whose sin is not atoned for. Do you see your sin, Jacob?"

Jacob was hurt. "Father, that is why I came, I have sinned against you. I have repented and God has dealt with my sin."

Isaac said, "Yes, my son, I know. The sin I speak of is the sin of your fathers which you have seen and know and follow in yourself. These are hard sins to put right."

Jacob lifted his eyes and looked across to the tomb of Abraham and Sarah. Finally, he said, "You speak of Hagar and Ishmael."

Isaac looked straight ahead, "You sin against Bilhah and Zilpah. They bear your children yet you do not accord them as wives. You sin against Leah, your first wife, you do not love her or honor her, you place her second to Rachel. You sin against your sons and daughters by favoring only Rachel and Joseph, setting them in order of favor. Is this loving them? You say you love Rachel. It is good that you love her. You say you walk as one as I walked with Rebekah. This cannot be, for you and Rachel do not walk as one for five cannot walk as one man and wife. As surely as bitterness fell on Hagar and Ishmael when they were sent off and on the sons of Keturah who were sent off, so too, will there be strife in your house and among your sons."

Jacob looked down at the ground and sighed. "There is strife in my house. I do not know how to bring peace between my wives. What now, can I do?"

"You can love all of them. You can listen to them. You must know their hearts, their needs and their desires. You must give to them. Give of yourself! Pray to God who can work His will and bring good from our sin. Good can come, but there will be much pain."

Jacob sighed, "I love all my sons, and I try to love my wives, but Rachel stays in my heart."

Isaac said, "Look to Deborah. Learn from her to love others. She has strength in her love. Trust El' Elyon and Jacob, keep your house from idols!"

"I will learn from your words, father."

As Jacob began to stand up, Isaac added, "Make no covenants with Canaanite kings. God has promised this land to your descendants and mine, to our people. Who are you to sell the birthright promise of God Almighty?"

"I shall not despise my birthright; goodbye father."

As Jacob walked off Isaac shouted, "Stay outside the walls, permit no idols in your house. Go with my blessing and with God."

Chapter Thirty-One

Now Dinah the daughter of Leah, whom she had borne to Jacob,
went out to visit the daughters of the land.

Genesis 34: 1

Jacob kept his camp outside the walls of Shechem. The busy city was a curious attraction to Dinah. Unlike her brothers who made occasional visits for trading with Jacob or Ranon, Dinah's knowledge of the city was limited to her imagination. Every day she saw people coming and going from Shechem. So many people! Why did they come? Where do they go? What is in this city she must never enter? Other young women enter and leave, why are they permitted but she is not?

When Dinah asked Deborah about the city, Deborah said, "Yes, from here Shechem appears bright and inviting, but you must understand that the Canaanites are known for their idol worship and young women can be at risk during festivals which include the most detestable ritualistic sex. It is not the place for a young woman learning to walk with the Most High God."

Dinah said, "How long will I be treated as a child? I am a

woman of fourteen! It cannot be so bad, I see other young women my age coming and going."

Deborah replied, "They are Canaanite women from the city. Their families are there. You do not know how they live or whether they suffer."

Dinah thought to herself, *Certainly, they appear happy to me.* "Deborah," she asked, "Have you ever visited a city?"

Deborah responded, "Yes, but my safety was assured, I was escorted. I visited Damascus many years ago when grandma Rebekah came from Haran. And father Isaac once took us to the cities of Egypt."

"What was it like? Please tell me. I can only guess."

Deborah found herself joyfully recounting her experiences in the markets of Damascus, Thebes, and Itj-tawy. She described the wonders of the markets, the sights, and smells, the strange things and strange people. She could not hide the fascination that remained ingrained in her memory.

Dinah said, "It is not fair my brothers can go into Shechem but I cannot. Will you take me there?"

Deborah's face turned serious, "It is not my place to question a father's will for his daughter. If it is his will that you go with him to Shechem, he will take you."

Thoughts of Shechem would not leave her mind. She was told she must not enter the city but surely, she could talk to the young women she sees coming and going. They looked happy and respectable to her. What harm could come from asking them what lies inside?

One day while Jacob and his sons were in the fields and Ranon and Mincah were busy, Dinah saw three young women laughing and talking as they walked towards Shechem. Not even stopping for a head scarf, Dinah rushed out to join them. As she approached she cheerfully asked, "Are you going to Shechem?"

The tallest of the three answered, "Of course, the market is open and you must get there early for the best fruit."

"Are there many things to choose from in the market?"

Dinah asked.

One of the other girls answered, "What a silly question! Of course, there are many things in the market. Haven't you been to the market? You live so near."

Dinah blushed at her ignorance, "My fathers, brothers, and servants enter the city, I stay here in our camp. Can you tell me about the market?"

The tall one said impatiently, "Tell you? No, but come along with us and see for yourself. There is nothing to be frightened of, come and look for yourself."

Dinah found herself walking to Shechem with her three new friends. She felt a twinge of guilt as they passed through the gates but it soon passed as the busy market appeared before her. She stopped and gazed at the scene in front of her. So many booths! So many people! So many strange things and strange smells! She looked all around her and then noticed her three new friends had kept walking and were lost in the crowd around the fruit and vegetable vendors. She could follow them she thought, or just wander around and gaze at what lay before her.

Dinah slowly wandered aimlessly through the market. She had no baskets, no servants attended her, she wore no headscarf. She was the only person in Shechem with no schedule, no agenda, and no plan. As she shuffled about the market, a young man approached her, "Woman, you look about the people in the market, have you lost your friends?"

Dinah turned and saw a smiling and handsome young man richly attired in fine robes. "No, my lord, I am just looking at your market. It is a wonderful market indeed. So many choices, and nice things."

The young man answered, "Are you new to our city? I do not recall seeing you before. I am Shechem son of Hamor, King of Shechem."

Dinah bowed, "My lord, I am Dinah, daughter of Jacob. I live in the camp outside the city wall."

Shechem replied, "I know of your father, he purchased the

field from my father and brothers. I know of your brothers as well, but I did not know they had such a beautiful sister. You must be tired and warm walking in this sun with your head uncovered; come with me; rest and have refreshment. Come, it is not far."

Dinah looked at him with her soft brown eyes and sheepishly answered, "Would that be all right, I am alone and..."

Shechem smiled, "Of course it is all right! You will be safe with me, am I not a prince of the city? Come along."

Dinah blushed which made her only more attractive, and she followed Shechem to his house. They passed through a gate which opened into an airy courtyard behind high walls, surrounded by apartments. The high walls and awnings kept all but the center fountain well shaded and cool. The peace and tranquility inside were in sharp contrast to the noisy market not far outside. As they entered, Shechem led Dinah to a well-shaded private alcove. They were met by a servant as they walked across the garden courtyard.

The servant bowed to Shechem, "Welcome home master, is there anything..."

Shechem did not wait for him to finish, "Hud, bring us a bowl of wine and fresh fruit, that we may refresh ourselves."

When Hud returned with the wine and fruit Shechem said, "Now leave us and see that I am not disturbed."

As Hud left, Shechem poured a cup of wine for Dinah. Seeing the uneasiness in her eyes, he said softly, "Please forgive me, Dinah, but Hud is rather thick as a servant and I find it unfortunate that I must be very direct with him."

Then motioning with the cup in his hand he continued, "Is this not an excellent garden? Where better to refresh yourself. A beautiful woman like yourself should not long bear the heat and dust of the market. Now that we know one another, you shall always be welcome here."

Dinah smiled weakly. "It is a beautiful garden. But I must not stay, I will be missed."

Shechem smiled, "Of course, I shall not detain you. Rest but a few moments and taste the wine. The fruit will certainly lift your spirits."

Dinah tasted a few grapes and sipped on her wine.

Shechem asked, "I have never lived in a tent, can it be as comfortable as this house? With no garden how does one find cool refreshment?"

As Dinah began to answer, Shechem moved to sit beside her say, "Please let me sit here, I find the sun is in my eyes."

Shechem settled next to Dinah and said, "I find this wine very good, not at all sweet and not towards vinegar."

After another sip, he said, "You really are beautiful you know, please don't object to me saying you are an attractive woman. I could drink your eyes as surely as I drink this cup!"

Shechem leaned over and embraced her.

"No Shechem, please don't!"

"Shechem stop, please stop!"

Dinah began to cry, "Stop! Stop! No! Shechem No!"

Shechem did not stop.

Dinah's wails could be heard over the sound of her clothes being torn from her. Time stood still as Shechem forced himself on her. It seemed the violence would never end as she sobbed, moaned and begged him to stop.

When Shechem finally let her up, she gathered her clothes and threw her robe around her disheveled self, the tears running down her eyes were encircled by her tangled black hair. She ran from him sobbing. Shechem fumbled with his own clothing and called to her, "Dinah, wait, do not go! I am sorry! I did not mean to hurt you. You're different than all of the other women in the city. You're beautiful to me, and sweet. Stay with me. Marry me! I can make you a princess!"

She ran out of the courtyard to the locked gate. She pulled on the handle in frustration before falling to the ground in front of it, wailing and crying. "What have I done? I have brought dishonor on my father's house. I have disobeyed and dishonored him. He shall surely put me out! I am at my end! I am shamed forever! Just let me die!"

Shechem followed her to the gate trying to console her, "Stay with me, I will never hurt you, I love you. Stay. We can be happy. It will be good between us. Cry no more. Stay!"

When Dinah did not return to her mother's tent, Leah sent a servant to find her. The servant was told that Dinah was seen walking with other young women into the city. When Leah heard this news, Deborah, who was with her said, "I shall go into the market and bring her home. Do not fret, your husband Isaac will be home soon. You must wait for him."

Deborah walked to Shechem and went into the market as it was closing for the day. Only a few shopkeepers remained to clear their stalls. None remembered a stranger, a young woman shopping at their booth. "We see so many women shopping, but I remember no new customer," one said.

In desperation, Deborah began to shout out, "Dinah! Dinah, daughter of Jacob! Answer me, Dinah!"

Her voice rang through the market and echoed off of the silent stone walls. "Dinah, Dinah bath Jacob! Answer me, Dinah!"

In prince Shechem's quiet courtyard, Dinah heard Deborah calling. "It is our nurse, Deborah! I must speak to her. Please! Let me speak to her! You must let me tell her I am safe. Surely, my mother has missed me."

Shechem asked, "Will you stay with me? Give me your word you will stay and I will send for her now."

"I will stay. Please let me speak to her. Her name is Deborah, send for her at once!"

Shechem sent his servant and he brought Deborah to the courtyard.

Dinah flung herself before her and wrapped her arms around Deborah's feet. She began to cry, "I am so sorry, so sorry, tell mama I am sorry, I have brought dishonor on myself and on our family. I have slept with Prince Shechem and now I must stay with him. Tell mama I am sorry."

Deborah kneeled down and took hold of Dinah's

arms."Tell me, what has happened."

"I went to talk with some other women on their way to Shechem, I only wanted to ask them about the market, but they brought me along. I went to the market and a man, a prince of the city, enticed me. He brought me to his house and lay with me. I have brought dishonor on my father's house, I have disobeyed him and dishonored him. But Prince Shechem has asked I stay with him and marry him."

Deborah drew Dinah close and hugged her. "Only your father can give you in marriage. You cannot be carried off, even by a prince!"

Deborah held Dinah's shoulders tight, looked into her eyes and said. "You are a daughter of the Most High. He will surely save you. Does not your father love you? And your brothers and everyone in the house of Jacob? I go to your mother and father and I will return to you and I will stay with you. Now go and wash, brush your hair and ask Shechem to provide you clean clothes. Wait for my return, I go to speak with your mother Leah and your father, Jacob."

Leah tore her clothes when she heard what happened. Jacob was greatly distressed when he heard the news. All of his sons were still in the fields. He told Leah to say nothing to anyone until he determined what to do. Seeing the pain in Leah's face, Jacob embraced his wife with true warmth and said, "With the help of God we shall get through this. My Dinah, our poor Dinah, she must be comforted. The shame shall not be hers to bear."

Shechem went to his father, Hamor, and said, "Father, do for me one thing, get Dinah, daughter of Jacob to be my wife. She only, do I love, I can love no other woman. She knows of my love, I have told her and asked her to marry me, but after I lay with her in my love she sent her maid back to her father's tent. Speak to Jacob for me, father, I meant no harm to her. Truly, I love her and want her as my wife."

Hamor looked at his son in shock, "You lay with the daughter of Jacob? A man blessed by his god who keeps his people separate? This is not a good thing! He is a strong and wealthy man! We depend on his flocks and herds. No this is not a good thing, my son."

"I never meant to harm her, I love her! I could not restrain my love. Go to Jacob, he will respect you. You are the King of Shechem."

Hamor loved his son and he respected Jacob. What had happened could not be undone. He thought to himself, *Is not marriage the best solution? He loves the girl, she shall become a respected wife and princess, there can be no dishonor in that. And will not a marriage between the house of Jacob and Shechem bring prosperity to the city?*

Hamor took Shechem to see Jacob. As Hamor and Shechem were going into Jacob's tent, his sons arrived from the fields. Seeing them, Reuben asked "Why are Hamor and his son in our house? Our father only deals with them at the gate of the city."

Leah told them what had happened to Dinah. Immediately they went into their father's tent where Simeon angrily confronted Hamor, "You come here after your son has disgraced this house?"

"Silence!" Jacob shouted.

Hamor spoke to Jacob, "My son loves your daughter, his soul is grieved, he wishes her no harm or dishonor. He loves her and asks that she be given to him in marriage."

Hamor could see the uncertainty in Jacob's face. He continued, "Intermarry with us. Give your daughters to us in marriage and take our daughters in marriage for yourselves. Live with us and the land will be open before you. Live here and trade in the land, acquire property, fields for crops as well as pasture."

Shechem nervously spoke, "If I find favor in your sight, please give me Dinah as my wife, then I will give whatever you say to me. Ask me whatever bridal payment and gift you seek and I will provide it, only give me Dinah in marriage."

Simeon shouted, "Father, No!"

Jacob stared down Simeon and answered Hamor, "Let me consider what you ask and a fair bridal payment. I will have an answer for you tomorrow."

Hamor bowed to Jacob, Shechem followed his father's lead, and they went back to the city.

Jacob's sons left Jacob's tent and went where they could be alone. Reuben said, "Shouting at our father will do nothing, Simeon."

Simeon still angry, replied, "Shechem has raped our sister! Are we to do nothing?"

Levi spoke up, "We must have justice!"

Reuben said calmly, "This is about Dinah, our sister. What should be done for her? What will become of her? This is what our father considers."

Simeon replied, "Would you have our sister the wife of an idol worshipping rapist? It shall never be!"

Levi then said, "Brothers, does not our father require all the men in our house, even our servants to be circumcised. Should not he require Shechem's circumcision in addition to the price of the bride?"

Reuben nodded, "This is true brother, why do you... "

Simeon interrupted, "He must require every man in the city to be circumcised before our sister be permitted to live in the city."

Reuben answered, "That will be a difficult thing for the men of Shechem."

"Let Hamor and Shechem persuade the men of the city. It is they who seek this marriage."

After pausing Simeon continued, "They will be in pain for many days!"

Reuben nodded, "It is the least they should do!"

As the brothers left, Simeon said to Levi, "Please stay brother, I would have a word with you."

Hamor and Shechem returned as agreed. Jacob and his sons met them in Jacob's tent and answered them, "I have considered your proposal and..."

Simeon interrupted, "We cannot give our sister to one who is uncircumcised, for that would be a further disgrace to us. Only on this condition will we consent to you: if you become like us, in that every male of your people be circumcised. Then, we will give our daughters to you in marriage and we will take your daughters in marriage for ourselves and we will live with you and become one people. But if you will not be circumcised, Dinah will stay with us and we shall leave Shechem."

Jacob was surprised by the words of Simeon, his son. He found wisdom in them but did not know they were meant to deceive.

Hamor and was also pleased to find a solution, especially one which cost no money. Shechem thought only of his desire for Dinah. He immediately complied. Now they needed to convince the men of Shechem.

Hamor with Shechem hiding the pain of his circumcision, went to the gate of the city and spoke with the leading men.

Hamor explained, "Jacob and his sons are our friends. They live outside our city wall and trade with us. They bring wealth to Shechem. There is enough land for them and for us. Let us take their daughters in marriage and give our daughters in marriage to them. I have asked that we become one people, Jacob and his sons have agreed to this but they have one condition. They will consent only if every male among us becomes circumcised as is their custom."

The men answered, "Is this necessary? Why should we do this now? We have their trade already."

Shechem was more respected than his father. He knew the men of the city and he was well liked. He spoke up, "Brothers of Shechem, listen to me. Will not their flocks and herds, their property and all of their animals be ours? I have already consented, and I stand before you this day. Let them live among us. The pain will soon be forgotten and the gain will be ours."

The men Shechem agreed and all went out of the gate of the city and were circumcised. Every male was circumcised and returned to his house to recover. Two days later, while the men were all in their houses still in pain, Simeon and Levi, sons of Leah and brothers to Dinah, arose early and made their way into the city. The guard at the gate did not come from his post for the pain kept him sitting in agony. Simeon drew his sword and slew the man where he sat and they walked into Shechem. The city was quiet and the streets empty. Simeon and Levi entered the house of Hamor and killed him in his bed. Levi struck down every male servant in the house. They calmly walked to the house of Shechem and after slaying the servants entered Shechem's bedroom. Levi dragged Dinah from the bed and Simeon put Shechem to the sword without a word.

Dinah screamed, and Simeon commanded her, "Quiet! Gather your things and wait for us at the gate."

Dinah was sobbing, but managed to nod her head, yes.

Simeon and Levi broke up and went house by house, killing every male in Shechem. When Reuben and his brothers saw Simeon and Levi covered in blood with the weapons red to the hilt, walking towards them with Dinah, they challenged them, "What word, brothers?"

"We have brought our sister home. We take her to our mother's tent."

Reuben asked, "And Shechem?"

Levi answered, every man in Shechem has paid for the injustice shown our sister!"

With that the younger brothers ran to the city crying, "Shechem is ours!"

They entered the city and wildly looted everything they could find. They carried off every object of value. They took the flocks and the herds. They took the donkeys and camels. They took the crops, the food and all that belonged to the merchants. They captured all of the city's wealth and took every woman and child captive as a slave.

Reuben followed after them screaming. "No harm to the women and children. You must not harm the women and children!"

When Jacob saw his sons returning with the loot, the flocks and herds and the captives, he said to Simeon and Levi, "What you have done is an evil thing! Surely you have brought trouble upon me and my house. You have made me loathsome among the nations of the land. Surely the Canaanites, the Perizzites, and their allies will come against us and attack us. We are too few in number to stand against them. I shall be destroyed and all of my house!"

Simeon and Levi turned from watching their brothers gather the spoil. Looking into Jacob's face they said, "Should he treat our sister as a harlot?"

Deborah stood silently beneath the shade of a great oak tree watching the women and children of Shechem slowly march by. Deborah watched and she wept.

Chapter Thirty-two

Not because of your righteousness or for the uprightness of your heart are you going to possess their land, but because of the wickedness of these nations the LORD your God is driving them out from before you, and that He may confirm the word that the LORD swore to your fathers, to Abraham, to Isaac, and to Jacob.

Deuteronomy 9:5

Deborah went to see Isaac and with anger and sorrow she said, "You must show mercy to the women and children of Shechem. Are they an enemy to be punished? How many times has the Most High forgiven you? How many times has He waited for you to repent? How has justice been served? More victims will not bring justice to Dinah! Is this the faith you have learned from your father Abraham?"

Isaac listened and let Deborah finish. "All that you say is true. There is neither justice or honor in the acts of my sons. My sons. I can hardly believe they are my flesh. But as you say, their sins are on my head. I have sent Lemuel to the widows and orphans of Shechem. If they have family or somewhere to go they will be permitted to leave. If they have nowhere else, they can stay as servants free to stay or free to go. Only if they stay they shall give up their idols and their sons shall be circumcised according to the covenant the Most High has made with my father Abraham. It is already done. But it is good you come to me and hold me accountable."

That night, the God of Abraham and Isaac, the God who came to Jacob at Bethel, came to Jacob once more, "Go to Bethel and make an altar to God who appeared to you when you fled from your brother, Esau."

When Jacob awoke he remembered how God had rescued him when he fled Esau. He remembered the covenant God made with him. Would God rescue him now that he must flee once more? Bethel was only fifteen miles south of Shechem, was that far enough? If he was to build an altar and sacrifice to the God who saves, he must be clean. His house must be clean. So, Jacob gave orders to his house, "Put away the foreign gods which are among you and purify yourselves, change your garments and let us go up to Bethel. I will make an altar there to God, who answered me in the day of my distress, and has been with me wherever I have gone."

So, the sons of Jacob and all of the servants of his household gave to Jacob all the foreign gods they had, even from the loot of Shechem. Rachel came forward and gave Jacob the household gods she had stolen from her father, Laban's, house. Jacob closed his eyes in pain to the evidence of Rachel's years of unrepentant sin. He could not look upon her as she placed them in the pile at Jacob's feet. When all of the idols, the talismans and reminders or foreign gods, even the charms and rings taken from his people's ears were collected, Jacob hid them forever under an oak tree near Shechem.

Only after all of the unclean idols, talismans and foreign gods were removed from his household, did Jacob lead his people to Bethel. As they journeyed, a great terror came upon the cities and villages near Shechem and none dared pursue the sons of Jacob. Jacob and all of his house reached Bethel in the land of Canaan but the Canaanites called the place Luz.

Jacob went to the place where he had set up his pillar those many years ago and built an altar. Again, he called the place El-Bethel, 'The God of the House of God.' This was the place God revealed Himself to him when he fled his brother. Jacob made sacrifices on the altar for himself and his house and he worshipped God with heart and soul. The horror of what he saw in Shechem sickened him. His daughter had been raped and justice was required, but to kill every male of Shechem, to loot everything of value and to take the women and children as slaves? There was no justice in that. And all of the idols found in his own household, were the actions of his sons any less detestable than the practices of the Canaanites? His sin and the sin of his house buried him under a mountain of guilt.

Deborah loved Dinah and comforted her day by day and she loved Jacob but his pain was different. Dinah could be comforted, she brought no shame to her father's house. She was loved. She would suffer but she would heal. But Jacob withdrew and would not be comforted.

Deborah knew both the old Jacob, the trickster-deceiver, who bought Esau's birthright for a bowl of lentil stew and stole his brother's blessing. She now knew the new Jacob, Israel, who contended with God, and now believed God and trusted in His promises. She saw the pain of guilt which brought him to the depths of despair.

"My lord, Jacob, I have known you from the day you came forth from Rebekah's womb. I have watched you grow into a man, into a great man and head of a great household. I have seen how the Most High God, the God of Abraham and Isaac has called to you and changed your heart. Trust Him. He has saved you and He will bring salvation to your house for He is a keeper of His promises. His will be done!"

Jacob answered, "Where is God's will in the slaying of so many men? Shechem was certainly guilty, but so many others?"

Deborah nodded and then replied, "Truly, Shechem was an evil city and truly Dinah was wronged. Has not the Almighty God, promised this land to Abraham, Isaac, and Jacob? And so it shall be! Has it not been said that the land will not belong to the Canaanites? Indeed, there has been great injustice, but you have shown mercy to the widow and the orphan. Has not Abaigael prophesied to the cities of Canaan that they shall fall by the sword but any Canaanite that turns from idols and returns to the Most High God will surely live? Are there not Canaanites from Shechem now living among us in peace? Their sons now circumcised under the promise of the Most High? It is true our God is a God of second and third chances, but God's patience can run its course with any man or any city."

Jacob answered, "Let God punish those he chooses! My sons were no less evil. And the gods and idols I found among my people!"

Deborah replied, "It is as you say. You must teach your sons. They must learn as you did from your fathers, Abraham and Isaac before you. They must listen for the calling and the voice of the Lord. But you must lead them. You must show them. You must love them and you must intercede for them with the Most High."

Jacob pondered Deborah's words. As one who opened his repentant heart to God, Israel prayed earnestly trusting in the mercy he had discovered:

"Cleanse me O God for I am a sinner.
Cleanse my house of all evil.
Sweep away every idol from my household
And every evil from my heart.
I have become loathsome to the sight
of all around me.
Do not all the nations of the land hate me?
Cleanse my soul for I am a son of sinners
And my sin blinds my eyes to your righteousness.
I follow in the sins of my fathers

and their fathers before them.
Their transgressions have become my transgressions
And the transgressions of my sons are as mine.
Cast afar my guilt and shame.
Who can atone for the sins of many generations?
Who can bring salvation to my house?
Your voice O Lord has called out to me;
Your strong arm has lifted me up;
Your shield has protected me.
Can You not remold my heart?
Can You not breathe life into my soul?
I place my heart before You.
I yield my soul to Your will.
I listen for Your commands
Teach me as you taught my fathers,
Abraham and Isaac.
Shout or whisper and I shall hear.
For I desire to trust in You alone.
For I desire to obey.
For I desire to love You O, my God and my Savior."

It was at Bethel that Deborah died. She had not been ill. Like Rebekah before her, she passed quietly in her sleep. All of Jacob's wives mourned Deborah as did Dinah, and his sons and all of his household. Jacob had no words at her loss, only tears and weeping. Jacob buried Deborah under the forest canopy below the pillar and altar at Bethel. She was laid under the cover of a great oak tree, it was named Allon-Bacuth, 'the Oak of Weeping.'

Epilogue

Deborah did not live to see Rachel die giving birth to Benjamin, or watch Jacob suffer through the lie of Joseph's death. She did not live to see Joseph's salvation of Israel in Egypt, which prefigured the salvation of all who believe in Jesus.

It is written. "There is no fear in love, but perfect love casts out fear, for fear has to do with punishment..." The Apostle John could have written, "but perfect love casts out sin, for if we love God with all of our heart and all of our soul and all of our mind and all of our strength, if we love God *perfectly* we can be one in Him and one with all He loves, and there can be no sin in perfect love. O to love as we are loved by our Creator and Savior who loves us perfectly, who loved us to the point of sending His son to die for us! This is the eternal hope of our salvation. This is the crown that awaits us.

Deborah might ask us this day: What is obedience without love? Where is hope without love? Is there faith without love?

Saint Paul teaches us in Corinthians, "Now there abide these three: faith, hope, and love. But the greatest of these is love."

While mourning the death of Deborah, God appeared once more to Jacob and said to him: "No longer shall your name be called Jacob, but Israel shall be your name."

And God said to him, "I am God Almighty: be fruitful and multiply. A nation and a company of nations shall come from you, and kings shall come from your own body. The land that I gave to Abraham and Isaac I will give to you, and I will give the land to your offspring after you."

Jacob, that is Israel, died in Egypt, in the land where his son Joseph, by the salvation of God Almighty, was second only to Pharaoh. Before he died, he called all of his sons, "Gather yourselves together, that I may tell you what shall happen to you in days to come."

"Assemble and listen, sons of Jacob,
listen to Israel, your father.
Reuben, you are my firstborn, my might,
and the first fruits of my strength,
Preeminent in dignity and preeminent in power.
Unstable as water, you shall not have preeminence,
Because you went to your father's bed;
Then you defiled it – he went up to my couch!
Simeon and Levi are brothers;
Weapons of violence are their swords.
Let my soul come not into their council;
O my glory, be not joined to their company.
For in anger they killed men,
and in their willfulness they hamstrung oxen.
Cursed be their anger, for it is fierce,
And their wrath, for it is cruel!
I will divide them in Jacob
And scatter them in Israel.
Judah, your brothers shall praise you;
Your hands shall be on the neck of your enemies;
Your father's sons shall bow down before you.
Judah is a lion's cub;

From the prey, my son, you have gone up.
He stooped down, he crouched as a lion
And as a lioness; who dares to rouse him?
The scepter shall not depart from Judah,
Nor the ruler's staff from between his feet,
until tribute comes to him;
and to him shall be the obedience of the peoples.
Binding his foal to the vine,
He has washed his garments in wine
And his vesture in the blood of grapes.
And his teeth whiter than milk.
Zebulon shall dwell at the shore of the sea,
He shall become a haven for ships,
And his brother shall be at Sidon.
Issachar is a strong donkey,
Crouching between the sheepfolds.
He saw that a resting place was good,
And that the land was pleasant,
So he bowed his shoulder to the bear,
And became a servant at forced labor.
Dan shall judge his people
As one of the tribes of Israel.
Dan shall be a serpent in the way,
A viper by the path that bites the horse's heels,
So that his rider falls backward.
I wait for your salvation, O LORD.
Raiders shall raid Gad, but he shall raid at their heels.
Asher's food shall be rich,
And he shall yield royal delicacies.
Naphtali is a doe let loose
That bears beautiful fawns.
Joseph is a fruitful bough by a spring;
His branches run over the wall.
The archers bitterly attacked him.
Shot at him, and harassed him severely,
Yet his bow remained unmoved;

His arms were made agile by the hands
of the Mighty One of Jacob
(from there is the Shepherd, the Stone of Israel),
By the God of your father who will help you
With blessings of the deep, that crouches beneath,
Blessings of the breast and of the womb.
The blessings of your father
Are mighty beyond the blessings of my parents,
Up to the bounties of the everlasting hills.
May they be one on the head of Joseph,
And on the brow of him who was set apart
from his brothers.
Benjamin is a ravenous wolf,
In the morning devouring the prey
And at evening dividing the spoil."

After he blessed them, he said to them, "I am to be gathered to my people; bury me with my fathers in the cave that is in the field of Ephron the Hittite, in the cave that is in the field of Machpelah, to the east of Mamre, in the land of Canaan, which Abraham bought from Ephron the Hittite to possess as a burying place. There they buried Isaac and Rebekah his wife and there I buried Leah – the field and the cave that is in it were bought from the Hittites."

When Jacob finished commanding his sons, he drew up his feet into the bed and breathed his last and was gathered to his people.

The Hall of Faith

Hebrews Chapter 11
(excerpts from the English Standard Version Bible)

Now faith is the assurance of things hoped for, the conviction of things not seen. For by it the people of old received their commendation. By faith we understand that the universe was created by the word of God, so that what is seen was not made of things that are visible…

By faith Abraham obeyed when he was called to go out to a place that he was to receive as an inheritance. And he went out not knowing where he was going. By faith he went to live in the land of promise, as in a foreign land, living in tents with Isaac and Jacob, heirs with him of the same promise. For he was looking forward to the city that has foundations, whose designer and builder is God.

By faith Sarah herself received power to conceive, even when she was past the age, since she considered him faithful who had promised. Therefore from one man, and him as dead, were born descendants as the innumerable grains of sand by the seashore…

By faith Abraham, when he was tested, offered up Isaac, and he who had received the promises was in the act of offering up his only son, of whom it was said, "Through Isaac your offspring shall be named."

He considered that God was able to raise him from the dead, from which figuratively speaking, he did receive him back. By faith Isaac invoked future blessings on Jacob and Esau. By faith Jacob, when dying, blessed each of the sons of the sons of Joseph, bowing in worship over the head of his staff...

And what more shall I say? For time would fail me to tell of Gideon, Barak, Samson, Jephthah, of David and Samuel and the prophets—who through faith conquered kingdoms, enforced justice, obtained promises, stopped the mouths of lions, quenched the power of fire, escaped the edge of the sword, were made strong out of weakness, became mighty in war, put foreign armies to flight. Women received back their dead by resurrection. Some were tortured, refusing to accept release, so that they might rise again to a better life. Others suffered mocking and flogging, and even chains and imprisonment.

They were stoned, they were sawn in two, they were killed with the sword. They went about in the skins of sheep and goats, destitute, afflicted, mistreated—of whom the world was not worthy—wandering about in deserts and mountains, and in dens and caves of the earth.

And all these, though commended through their faith, did not receive what was promised, since God has provided something better for us, that apart from us they should not be made perfect.

THEREFORE, since we are surrounded by so great a cloud of witnesses, let us also lay aside every weight, and sin which clings so closely, and let us run with endurance the race that is set before us, looking to Jesus, the founder and perfecter of faith, who for the joy that was set before him endured the cross, despising the shame and is seated at the right hand of the throne of God.

Also by David Martyn

The Praise Singer:
A Disciple of Melchizedek

The story of God's revelation to a simple shepherd; a new testament story lived in old testament times.

An orphaned and nameless slave called only Jael, meaning "mountain goat," is left to tend the village flocks. He sees the revelation of God all around him.

His journey takes him to Salem where King Melchizedek disciples him and confides that God has one thing against him. Jael faces personal tragedy and doubt in his new flock, but through it all, his encounter with God in Melchizedek's garden is his solid foundation of faith.

Jael's journey, like ours, is a lifelong struggle to keep his promise to God, to first love God and then love all men.

About the Author

David Martyn lives in Gig Harbor, Washington with his wife Karen. Retired from a career in the Maritime Industry he can keep watch over the ships passing to and from Tacoma and the Vashon Island Ferry. He still loves the sea, ships and the men and women who sail them. David believes God reveals Himself and sets us on a journey of discovery that brings us by the revelation of God's Word, to the very heart of God. His love of Scripture, which burns in our hearts, as expressed by the disciples on the road to Emmaus, has been strengthened by years of home Bible Study groups which brought insight on Bible passages and confirmation of God working in the lives of His people. Pouring over Scripture put flesh on the bones and blood in the veins of the men and women of the Bible. Real people who struggled with sin and doubt. Men who failed God time and again, yet by the grace of God were victorious and today wear the victor's crown. It is David's hope that his stories awaken the seed of revelation God planted in the reader's heart, provides a fresh love for the fathers of our faith and brings hope to a new generation.

Made in the USA
Lexington, KY
19 November 2018